## "The only way I'm sleeping in your bed is if you're there with me."

Jake's voice caressed her, soothing and tempting her all at once. She looked away and tried desperately to concentrate on something else.

"Go to sleep in your own bed, Annie," he said at last, his expression gentle. "I'll be fine out here."

"At this stage of my pregnancy, I don't generally sleep very well. You might as well take the bed," she insisted.

"I'd rather be closer to the door."

"So you expect trouble?"

"No, not at all." He grinned slowly. "It's a guy thing, that's all. I'd rather be the protector than the protectee. Male ego and all that."

His smile, so purely masculine, tore past her defenses. Everything feminine in her awakened. Aware of the danger, she braced herself to resist his temptation.

"Annie," he whispered and reached for her hand....

# Christmas Witness
## Aimée Thurlo

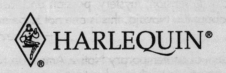

# HARLEQUIN®

TORONTO • NEW YORK • LONDON
AMSTERDAM • PARIS • SYDNEY • HAMBURG
STOCKHOLM • ATHENS • TOKYO • MILAN • MADRID
PRAGUE • WARSAW • BUDAPEST • AUCKLAND

To Annelise Robey and Angela Catalano—
No author could have a better team behind her.

ISBN 0-373-22544-X

CHRISTMAS WITNESS

Copyright © 1999 by Aimée Thurlo

All rights reserved. Except for use in any review, the reproduction or
utilization of this work in whole or in part in any form by any electronic,
mechanical or other means, now known or hereafter invented, including
xerography, photocopying and recording, or in any information storage
or retrieval system, is forbidden without the written permission of the
publisher, Harlequin Enterprises Limited, 225 Duncan Mill Road,
Don Mills, Ontario, Canada M3B 3K9.

All characters in this book have no existence outside the imagination of
the author and have no relation whatsoever to anyone bearing the same
name or names. They are not even distantly inspired by any individual
known or unknown to the author, and all incidents are pure invention.

This edition published by arrangement with Harlequin Books S.A.

® and TM are trademarks of the publisher. Trademarks indicated with
® are registered in the United States Patent and Trademark Office, the
Canadian Trade Marks Office and in other countries.

Visit us at www.romance.net

Printed in U.S.A.

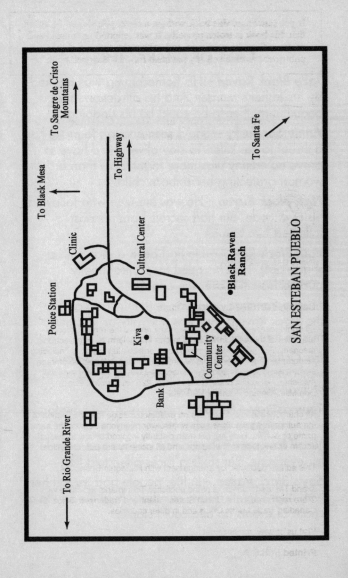

To Sangre de Cristo Mountains

To Black Mesa

To Highway

To Santa Fe

To Rio Grande River

Clinic

Police Station

Cultural Center

Kiva

Black Raven Ranch

Bank

Community Center

SAN ESTEBAN PUEBLO

# CAST OF CHARACTERS

**Jake Black Raven** — His homecoming was marked by his father's murder. And his attraction to a beautiful mother-to-be could be his undoing....

**Annie Sandusky** — She'd seen enough to make her a threat to the killer. To stay alive, she'd have to prove no enemy was more formidable than a woman protecting her unborn child.

**Nick Black Raven** — He was the twin who followed his own code. But had secrets from his past followed him home?

**Paul Black Raven** — He had been a man with a shady past. Had his need for control finally pushed his killer over the edge?

**Martin Sanchez** — He was determined to protect the Black Ravens. But was it loyalty or another motive that kept him with the family?

**Iris Ortiz** — She claimed everything she'd done was out of love. But how dangerous could a woman scorned really be?

**Thomas Ray** — He liked taking risks. But how far would he go to get what he wanted?

**Virgil Lowman** — The banker always had a smile for everyone. But smiling faces often told lies.

**Saya Black Raven** — In life, people had trusted her with their secrets. Now, her diary held the key to a chain of events no one could stop....

## ABOUT THE AUTHOR

Aimée Thurlo is a nationally bestselling author. She's written forty novels and is published in at least twenty countries worldwide. She has been nominated for the Reviewers' Choice Award and the Career Achievement Award by *Romantic Times Magazine*.

She also cowrites the Ella Clah mystery series, which debuted with a starred review in *Publishers Weekly*, and has received quotes from Diana Gabaldon, Carolyn G. Hart, Tess Gerritsen and Tony Hillerman.

Aimée was born in Havana, Cuba, and lives with her husband of twenty-eight years in Corrales, New Mexico. Her husband, David, was raised on the Navajo Indian Reservation.

## Books by Aimée Thurlo

HARLEQUIN INTRIGUE

| | |
|---|---|
| 109—EXPIRATION DATE | 377—CISCO'S WOMAN |
| 131—BLACK MESA | 427—HER DESTINY* |
| 141—SUITABLE FOR FRAMING | 441—HER HERO* |
| 162—STRANGERS WHO LINGER | 457—HER SHADOW* |
| 175—NIGHT WIND | 506—REDHAWK'S HEART** |
| 200—BREACH OF FAITH | 510—REDHAWK'S RETURN** |
| 217—SHADOW OF THE WOLF | 544—CHRISTMAS WITNESS |
| 246—SPIRIT WARRIOR | |
| 275—TIMEWALKER | *Four Winds |
| 304—BEARING GIFTS | **The Brothers of Rock Ridge |
| 337—FATAL CHARM | |

# Chapter One

Annie Sandusky listened to the lively guitar of "A Cowboy Christmas" on the radio as she worked on her latest wood chip carving. She'd promised to deliver the piece and another she hadn't even started to a Santa Fe gallery by December twenty-second and today was already the twelfth. Her folk art carvings had been steadily gaining in popularity throughout the southwest and with Christmas approaching the demand for her work had more than doubled.

Leaning back in her chair, she studied the twenty-six-inch-high carving of an angel guarding a man tilling the soil. The lines on the man's face attested to his struggle as the angel looked on, his protector from harm. The entire scene was depicted in a piece of arched basswood designed to remind the viewer of a stained-glass window.

This piece was turning out to be one of her best. The joys and sorrows of living were etched in the expressions of both figures, giving them a lifelike quality that transcended the medium.

Annie shifted in her wide wooden chair, adjusting the small pillow that helped support her lower back. Normally she would have hated a chair as hard as this one, but being eight and a half months' pregnant had changed almost everything in her life. At least from the chair she didn't have to struggle to get back on her feet as she did when she sank down onto the sofa.

Annie placed one hand over her swollen stomach as the baby kicked. "Easy there, kid," she whispered, rising from the chair.

As her thoughts shifted to the tiny life within her, worries began to crowd her mind again. Concerns for the future seemed to take up a lot of her time lately. She couldn't help but worry about giving birth alone, with no one there to offer support, let alone how she'd manage to take care of an infant all by herself. She had no one to count on except Paul Black Raven, the older Pueblo man who'd become her art patron, allowing her to work for him in exchange for living on his property rent-free.

Feeling tired, Annie stepped away from the low carving table and stretched her back. As she walked around the long, narrow room of the former bunkhouse, her gaze drifted to the photo of her and Bobby, taken just last year. Her hands started shaking and tears came unbidden to her eyes as memories overwhelmed her.

Bobby had been her constant companion and her most dependable ally in the church-sponsored children's home where they'd both been raised. The closeness between them had never diminished even after they'd grown up and gone after their own dreams—she, to college and to try to establish herself as a serious artist, Bobby to the army.

Finally, shortly after her twenty-seventh birthday, they'd married. But in the end, Bobby's wild streak had taken the ultimate toll on their short life as husband and wife. His motorcycle accident and death, after weeks of hospitalization and surgery, had left her emotionally and financially devastated.

Then, at what seemed to be the worst possible moment, she'd learned she was carrying his baby. The news had terrified her, but as the months passed, she'd come to see the child within her as Bobby's final gift. Now, in his absence, the child was just that much more precious to her.

Hearing a vehicle coming up the lane, Annie parted the white muslin curtains at the window and glanced out. It was Ralph Ortega's old Ford pickup. He was heading toward the main house, driving much faster than he should have been down the graveled track. She glanced at her watch. Ralph was late, and that explained it. He was to play Santa and the children would be arriving in another half hour or so.

Paul Black Raven's annual Christmas party, held here at the ranch, which snugged the eastern border of the pueblo, was a twenty-five-year tradition enjoyed by everyone in the community. Usually held on the night of the Feast Day of Our Lady of Guadalupe, the party marked the beginning of the Christmas season for many New Mexicans.

Looking toward the main house, Annie noted that the Christmas lights still hadn't been turned on. Knowing Paul would need help with them, she changed from her work clothes into an emerald-green velvet dress and tied back her light brown hair with a gold and green ribbon. Wrapping her coat around her, she stepped outside and started down the lane.

Annie slowly picked her way along the road, careful to keep her balance crossing the icy spots. Her gaze shifted to the main house, hoping to see the Christmas lights blink on now that Ralph was there to help Paul. A hundred yards or so away, the house remained a gloomy outline.

Poor Paul. He was probably going crazy by now, switching plugs and adding extension cords to keep from overloading a circuit and throwing the electrical breakers. She owed him so much she didn't like to see anything upset him, not even party arrangements. That's why she'd taken time from her own work to help him get ready. Her benefactor was in his early sixties and, with his wife deceased and his twin sons having left home years ago to make their way, Paul Black Raven was very much alone. Despite the company of the ranch foreman and the few horsemen from the pueblo who came daily to help with the work, Annie suspected that Paul Black Raven was a very lonely man.

Stepping through the low gate of the courtyard, she walked up to the front porch and felt a flush of pride as she viewed the decorations she'd set out earlier today. Garlands adorned with bright red ribbons framed the massive wooden entrance doors, each holding a large pine bough wreath. The scent of piñon filled her nostrils.

Annie was looking forward to this party. She had helped pick out the gifts for the children, decorated most of the tree, and prepared refreshments that were safely in the kitchen on trays. All she had to do was set them out on the dining room table.

Annie knocked as she opened the door, then stepped inside onto the worn brick floor. Houses were rarely locked on the pueblo. Such security simply wasn't needed. Even so, she knew that Paul had started to lock the place up whenever he was going to be away. He'd noticed signs such as partially opened drawers and items out of place, that suggested someone had been disturbing his privacy, so he'd had locks put on the doors. He'd laughed, however, when she'd suggested a burglar alarm. Those were for Anglo homes, he'd joked.

As she looked around she noted that the curtains were drawn, and it was darker inside than out. She could barely see into the next room. Myriad shiny glass Christmas ornaments, a few obviously locally handcrafted, captured the brightness of the flames dancing in the beehive-shaped fireplace and revealed the presence of the tree. But none of the hundreds of bulbs on the string of lights was aglow. Obviously Paul's problem with the wiring was a major one or he would at least have had the tree lights on by now.

She moved past the living room and into the darkened hallway carefully, not wanting to trip over any unseen obstacle. "Paul? Ralph? Where are you?"

Suddenly she heard the thud of footsteps on the wooden stairs. A familiar-looking shape in a red-and-white suit was in a hurry, taking the steps two at a time. He came down so fast that, before she could jump back, the Santa Claus-clad figure collided with her, knocking her completely off her feet. She landed on her behind, the brick floor hard and cold. "Ralph, what on earth—"

Instead of helping her back up and apologizing, the man whirled and waved a large, bloody knife, forcing her to scramble back in panic to avoid the swinging blade. Then, spinning around, "Santa" ran out the door without saying a word.

This was no stunt or practical joke. Her heart at her throat, Annie struggled to her feet, and called Paul's name. The eerie silence and darkness around her made her blood turn to ice. More afraid than she'd ever been in her life, she made her way upstairs as fast as she could.

Annie stepped into the first room to her right, Paul's bedroom. The door was wide open. Bright moonlight filtering through the curtains cast sinister shadows on the wall. The small safe was open and empty. She looked around frantically.

"Paul?" It was impossible to mistake the sickening odor of blood. She reached for the wall switch and clicked it back and forth. The power was off here, too.

Fear left a bitter taste in her mouth. In the silence she could hear rapid, shallow breathing somewhere in front of her. Then she heard a man's agonized moan. "Paul?" she called again, terror gripping her.

Reluctantly she inched forward, toward a large figure lying on the carpet beside the dresser. In the semi-darkness she could barely see his face, but instinct and logic told her it had to be Paul even before she dropped to her knees beside him.

As her eyes adjusted to the darkness, and she could make him out more clearly, horror filled her. His features were distorted with pain and his chest was covered with a dark stain. When he reached out to her, blood flowed from the wounds on his hands and arms.

Her heart breaking, she gently wrapped her hand around his. "What happened? Why did Ralph do this to you?"

"Not…" He dragged in a shuddering breath. "No time…listen." He struggled to speak. "My boys…" He tried to reach for a photo on the dresser, but couldn't manage it.

Annie brought it down for him and followed his gaze as he looked at the high school photo of Jake, with his hard features, and Nick with his easy smile.

"Help Jake when he comes…trust no one but him and Nick. Evidence…still hidden here. Help them," he managed to choke out, his voice growing fainter. He squeezed her hand, but his grip weakened. "Tell my boys…I loved them."

Anguish filled her. Paul's two sons had all but abandoned him, yet his last thoughts were still of them. "Don't go, Paul," she pleaded, even as his hand grew limp. "We need you here!"

She stumbled to the telephone on the nightstand, desperation driving her. Fate had taken Bobby from her. Surely she wouldn't be expected to give up her friend, too. Her hands were trembling as she grabbed the receiver and punched in the 9-1-1 emergency number.

She spoke quickly, her words rushing out as fast as her tears. By the time she put the receiver down, her entire body was shaking. Suddenly Annie felt her stomach harden and she braced herself. It wasn't labor, she assured herself. It was one of the Braxton-Hicks contractions she'd been having these past few months. More a dress rehearsal as her body got ready for the actual birth, hopefully several weeks away.

She took a deep, unsteady breath, trying to calm herself down. She'd stay with Paul until help came. If there was a spark of life left in him, she didn't want him to be alone. He deserved better than that.

Annie started back to Paul's side when she heard footsteps behind her. With a gasp, she spun around just as a man walked into the bedroom.

The stranger stopped in midstride. "Who are you and what are you doing here?" he demanded. His voice was cold and held a deadly edge.

Her eyes wide, she tried to make out his features, but shadows hid his face. The only thing she could tell for sure was that he was tall and well-built. As he moved closer to the window, moonlight flashed in his eyes, making them blaze as if fueled by an inner fire.

Keeping the bed between them, Annie moved closer to the telephone, her back to the wall. "I'm Annie. Who are you?"

"Why is the electricity out, and where is my father?" His voice held an unmistakable air of authority, commanding her to answer.

Fear pulsed hard and fast within her, but his words broke through to her. "...Your *father?*"

"I'm Jake Black Raven." His voice was too controlled to pass as natural. "What's going on here?"

Jake. The twin who never played by the rules. Paul's description of his son echoed in her memory. He moved like a shadow, all grace and confidence, but there was deadly intent in each step.

"What on earth are you doing here? Was Paul expecting you?"

Ignoring her question, Jake threw the curtains open wide,

but the clouds muted the moon's glow and the room remained in partial darkness. "Where's my father?" he demanded.

"By the dresser, but he's badly hurt." Right now he needed to be with his father. Her question could wait.

Jake moved quickly. As he saw Paul's lifeless body, he dropped to his knees. "No!" His voice was an agonized whisper. "What happened?"

"I found him like this," she answered gently, sharing his pain. "Your father was attacked by Ralph Ortega, a man who was supposed to be his friend. He was dressed as Santa Claus for the party. But something must have happened. I've already called the police and an ambulance," she added.

"Ralph Ortega? I knew him years ago. Why would he do this?"

"I don't know."

With shaking hands, Jake felt for a pulse in vain. Gently, he closed Paul's eyes. "It's too late for an ambulance."

As the wail of a distant siren rose in the air, Jake stood and slowly walked back to the door. "I'll show them into the house. That responsibility is mine now as his son," he added, his voice hushed and strangled.

Alone, Annie knelt by Paul's body, her heart breaking into a million pieces. Tears fell freely down her cheeks as she grieved for the friend she'd lost.

Feeling the baby stir inside her, she placed one hand over her stomach. Once again, in the face of death, life cried out to her, demanding she remain strong. Gathering her courage, Annie said a silent prayer and stood. There was only one thing she could do for Paul now. Her testimony would be needed to bring his killer to justice, and she owed it to him to see this through.

Saying a final goodbye to her friend, she went downstairs to meet the police.

# Chapter Two

Annie sat at the dinner table as Captain Daniel Mora of the San Esteban Pueblo Police Department paced in front of her. Each of New Mexico's nineteen pueblos had their own police force, but Captain Mora's uncompromising stand on crime had made him almost a legend. His gaze darted back to her often as he asked question after question.

"You said the man was dressed as Santa, fake beard, cap, and everything, right?"

She nodded. With the lights back on now, she could study Mora freely. He was small of stature and seemed to possess an unlimited amount of energy.

"Then you said he threatened you with a knife and rushed out the door," he finished. "Now, think hard. Did you hear a vehicle drive off after that?"

She paused then, after a moment, shook her head. "I don't remember. I wasn't paying attention to anything outside. I was terrified and my only thought was to find Paul." She rubbed her shoulder where the killer had collided with her. "Captain, I've already told you everything I remember. I can't do anything more to help you right now. But I can still do something for the pueblo children—I can see to it that they all get their presents. This is the beginning of the Christmas season. Paul bought gifts for all of them and, despite everything, I know he wouldn't have wanted the kids to leave empty-handed."

"And neither do I. But I'm conducting a murder investigation and that's my primary concern at this time." He paused, then drilled her with his gaze. "Are you sure you have no idea what 'evidence' the deceased was referring to or where it might be?"

"I honestly don't. I do know that he had locks put on the doors recently, though. Someone was going through his stuff and snooping in drawers," Annie told him.

"Did he have any idea what the person was looking for?" Mora's eyes narrowed.

"He never said, but Paul didn't seem too worried about it." She paused, then in a shaky voice added, "I guess he should have been."

"And your relationship to Paul Black Raven was?" Mora questioned, eyeing her pregnant belly.

Annie tried to keep her temper in check. "We were good friends. That's why he hired me to restore the old bunkhouse. In exchange, I got a place to live rent-free here on the pueblo, though I'm not Tewa or a member of any of New Mexico's Pueblo tribes." She paused, then gave him a long, pensive look. "But I don't understand. Why all these questions? You already know who killed Paul."

Captain Mora shook his head. "We found Ralph Ortega down the highway, beaten and tied up by the side of the road, nearly frozen to death. He was in his underwear."

Her eyes widened and comprehension dawned over her. "When I asked Paul why Ralph had done this to him, he said, 'not', then he went on to say something else, so I didn't connect it. But I guess he was really trying to tell me Ralph was innocent." She paused, a new horrific thought taking shape in her mind. "That means the killer is still out there, and he could be anyone," she added, suddenly understanding Paul's warning to trust no one except his sons.

Mora nodded. "We'll find the trail to the killer, but first we have to gather all the information and hard evidence we can."

As she heard the sound of children crying, her heart twisted inside her. "Captain, please let me go take care of the kids. I'm needed out there."

"All right, but stay available for the next several days. I'll have more questions."

She reached the door when she heard Jake's unmistakable voice. He was in the room behind her, answering the officer questioning him. Annie turned her head and looked back through the partially open doorway. Jake was sitting, controlled and composed, in a tall-backed mission-style chair. Her heart drummed in her ears and her skin tingled with awareness. Though she knew he was under an incredible amount of pressure, he exuded the confidence of a man who knew his strengths as well as his limitations and was comfortable with both.

As if sensing her gaze, he glanced back and, for one brief moment, their eyes met. A rush of warmth spread over her and her pulse quickened. Alarmed by her own response, she quickly turned her head, breaking eye contact. Annie started down the hall when Captain Mora suddenly called her back.

"One more question," he said, meeting her at the door. His voice was low so only she could hear. "Do you know what brought Jake Black Raven back at this particular time after being away for so many years?"

"No, I don't. You'll have to ask him." The question had also been on her mind, but he hadn't answered when she'd asked earlier and she hadn't spoken to Jake since the police had arrived. The captain had made sure of that. She suspected that Mora was just insuring that his two witnesses wouldn't discuss the events before he could sort out the facts.

"Before you go outside, Mrs. Sandusky, you'll want to wash the blood off your hands." Captain Mora added gently, "It's okay now. The samples my officer took earlier should be sufficient."

A shudder ripped through her. In her haste to salvage a little bit of Christmas for the kids, she'd almost made things worse. Her stomach in a knot, she turned and headed directly to the bathroom to use the sink.

A few minutes later Annie stepped out into the *sala*. The Christmas tree now twinkled in the massive living room, but did nothing to lessen the gloom that had settled over the house. Picking up the sack of gifts from beneath the tree, Annie went outside to talk to the stunned guests.

Having received the news from the officers on duty, parents clustered in the parking area outside, trying to come to terms with what had happened. The children cried, impatient and frightened by events they couldn't understand.

Tired and cold, but doing her best to hide her discomfort, Annie began handing out presents to the children and wishing them a happy holiday season. The glow in their eyes as they accepted the small, brightly wrapped packages helped brighten her own spirits. At least for the kids, this dreadful evening would always hold one happy memory.

As she worked, Annie saw that Martin, the ranch foreman, had arrived. He'd undoubtedly seen or heard the police vehicles and had rushed over from his home on the adjacent property.

Martin gave her a nod, then went to talk to the police who, aided only by flashlights, were searching the grounds in the dark.

It was close to midnight when she was finally allowed to return to the bunkhouse. She hadn't seen Jake again, but she'd heard that Mora and his officers were still questioning him. People had often compared Mora to a bloodhound who never gave up once he caught the scent of a trail. He was certainly living up to his reputation now.

Exhausted, Annie slipped out of her shoes and eased down onto the bed, too tired to even try to get out of her dress. Yesterday, her biggest concern had been getting her latest carving finished so she'd have money to buy a few more things for the baby. Now she wasn't even sure where she'd be living a week from now.

She closed her eyes, wanting to stop thinking and just rest. As the gray mists closed in on her, she drifted off to an uneasy sleep.

IT WAS WELL PAST DAWN by the time Annie woke up, relieved to have escaped the nightmares that had plagued her all night. Sun streamed through the part in the curtains, making her hide her eyes. With effort, she struggled to overcome the gravity barrier her midsection posed these days as she tried to get up. The more her body grew, adapting to the baby inside her, the more cumbersome the slightest activity became.

A shower helped her come fully awake. After a quick breakfast, she sat at the rustic pine chest of drawers that served as her bill table and began to figure out her budget. Listing her debts against another column showing what she could expect to earn from her work, was a sobering exercise.

She took a deep breath, trying to calm herself, but when she let it out, it sounded more like a shudder. If Paul's sons shut down the ranch and sold everything, forcing her to move out of the bunkhouse, she wasn't at all sure how she'd manage. She would, of course, try to work double time to finish the promised carvings, but she'd also need to find a second job. Unfortunately, she seriously doubted there would be many employers willing to hire a pregnant woman this close to term.

She was pacing up and down the wood plank floor, lost in thought, when she heard a vehicle pull up outside. Annie watched from the window as Jake Black Raven stepped out of a brown-and-tan pickup.

Last night she'd only caught glimpses of the man. In the full light of day, he was even more devastatingly handsome than she'd realized.

She followed him with her eyes as he strode up to the front door, his cream-colored wool sweater contrasting against his copper skin, coal-black hair and piercing eyes. Despite his easy strides, there was an air of masculinity about him that was impossible to mistake. A prickle of warmth ribboned deliciously through her, but she firmly brushed the feeling aside, attributing it to just another crazy surge of hormones.

Composing herself quickly, Annie opened the door. "Please, come in. Take a seat anywhere," she said, leading the way into the room. As she sat on the wooden chair, she looked back at him. He was standing a few feet away, his gaze on her swollen belly. The surprise on his face was easy to see.

Annie suddenly realized that in the darkness and in all the confusion of the night before, he'd never seen her body clearly, let alone noticed the fact that she was pregnant. Their gazes had met once when she'd turned her head and looked back at him through the partially open door after Mora had finished questioning her. But she'd been facing away from him at the time.

Then Annie saw Jake's gaze focus on her left hand. Silently she cursed the fact that she'd taken off her wedding band. Pregnancy had made her hands swell and the ring had become uncomfortable.

She looked directly at him, knowing what he was thinking. As with many at the pueblo who didn't really know her or her relationship to Paul, Jake was probably wondering if the baby she was carrying was his father's. When she'd moved in, her pregnancy had not been noticeable. Jake was obviously too tactful to ask, but, if his thoughts continued along those lines, he'd soon begin questioning if someone acting out of jealousy, or perhaps on her behalf, had committed the murder.

She almost began to tell him the plain and simple truth, but then stopped. As a foster kid, she'd spent a lifetime being scrutinized and judged by people she scarcely knew. That experience had taught her one thing—explaining herself was a waste of time. A person who distrusted her would never value her word, either.

As he sat on the sofa and she saw the wariness on his face, sympathy filled her. She told herself his reaction was only natural and she had to cut him some slack. "I'm very sorry about your father," she said softly. "Everyone in the community will miss him."

"Thank you," he said, his voice heavy. "It's still difficult for me to accept this. I always thought of my father as indestructible." He stood, apparently uncomfortable on the old leather cushions that seemed to swallow people up.

She studied Jake's expression as he walked to the window and looked out toward the main house. He'd stayed away for so long and now it was too late. She'd been led to believe from the things Paul had said that there'd been some kind of argument and that the boys had struck out on their own right after high school. But why had they abandoned their father so completely? She doubted that the argument had been entirely Paul's fault. It seemed out of character with Paul's gentle nature.

As the moments of silence stretched between them, Annie remembered how much Paul had enjoyed talking to her about Jake. In the last few months she'd learned all about the boy who'd tamed the wildest horse in his father's stable with nothing more than soft words and an iron-willed determination.

Paul had often said that Jake had been the twin most like him, always challenging any obstacles in his way, and accomplishing what he set out to do. Hearing the stories about Paul's first-born twin, she'd fallen a bit in love with Jake herself, though only in the sense one might admire a legend.

It was hard to say where the truth stopped and a father's pride began, however. Less complimentary stories about Jake also abounded in the pueblo. He'd left his father's ranch at eighteen and now, twelve years later, he was the head of one of the most successful residential construction firms in the Rocky Mountain area. But, unlike Paul's gentle stories, gossip on the pueblo also claimed that Jake had turned his back on everything that made him a Tewa. Some said he had a cash register for a heart and cared for little except the bottom line. He'd driven more than one man out of business by undercutting him, and it was his single-minded dedication that had placed his firm at the top.

She studied Paul's son now, trying to learn everything she could about him. Depending on the stories she chose to believe, he was either a devil or a saint. Experience told her the truth probably lay somewhere in between.

JAKE STOOD, looking out the window as he waited for Annie to return from the kitchen with the cup of chamomile tea she'd offered him. Hearing her footsteps, Jake turned and took the mug from her hands.

"Now what can I do for you, Jake?" she prodded, then took a sip of the steaming liquid.

"We have to talk. You were the only witness to my father's murder." Though there was nothing he could do to avoid it, he regretted having to discuss this with her.

Speaking to this beautiful, gentle woman about a vicious murder seemed wrong in itself.

"I should tell you that I wasn't a witness. I found your father *after* the fact."

"But you were the last person to see him alive." She nodded and he continued. "From the kinds of questions I was being asked by the police, I know my father said something to you before he died. I'd like to know what it was." To have to talk to a virtual stranger, however beautiful, in order to find out about his own father stung. He kept his tone quiet and even, but the flicker in her eyes told him that, somehow, she'd sensed the effort it took.

Annie recounted what had happened, then added what she hadn't told Captain Mora because of its personal nature. "Your father wanted you and Nick to know that he loved you both very much."

Jake felt his muscles tense. Years back he'd yearned to hear that from his father, but now, they were only words— a message conveyed much too late. Darkness and regret filled him, leaving a bitter taste in his mouth.

"Tell me about this hidden evidence he mentioned," Jake said.

"I wish I could. Paul asked that I help you, but I have no idea what the evidence he spoke about was or where I can find it."

"Someone viciously attacked and killed my father," he said, the words tearing a hole in his gut. "Based on his last words, we can conclude that he believed his killer was one of the people he knew well and trusted." Jake's eyes came to rest on her. Her pregnancy only seemed to add to her beauty and vibrant femininity. Although, despite the circumstances, she seemed composed and calm, just beyond that, he sensed something fragile about Annie. Whether it stemmed from sorrow, or fear, or maybe even guilt, he couldn't say.

"I hope you're not thinking that I killed your father," Annie said sharply, looking him straight in the eye.

"I know you didn't kill him," he answered, noting her anger. Even the possibility that anyone might believe she'd harmed his father was a personal affront to her. "The evidence fully supports your innocence. Captain Mora said that the killer's clothing would have been completely splattered with blood. You had blood on your hands and a bit on your clothes when Captain Mora questioned you, but that was the extent of it. Also, I'm certain that my father would have been able to wrench a knife away from you. He was in remarkably good shape, from everything I've been told."

"Paul was in excellent shape."

Now, he saw disapproval in her eyes. He could almost hear her unspoken words telling him he would have known exactly what physical shape his father had been in if he hadn't stayed away for so long. But, like many others, she had no idea why he'd really left.

"So what's your theory?" he said.

"I wish I could give you and Captain Mora an idea of who might have killed Paul," she added, "but I just don't know. The Santa hair and beard covered the killer's face well and, at the time, I really thought it was Ralph."

"Then tell me this. Who were my father's enemies?" He saw her flinch. She didn't like talking about his father in this dispassionate way. Whatever feelings she'd had for him were real and went deep.

She paused, lost in thought. "Your father wasn't an easy man to deal with. He had his own way of doing things and that probably annoyed some people."

She wasn't hard to read on this, Jake thought. He could see that it had been difficult for her to say anything negative. "He played by his own rules, I know, even if it meant others would get hurt in the process," he said, then took a long breath. "Can you give me some idea of where I should begin looking for this evidence? Mora suggested that someone had been going through the house looking for it and that's why my father had put locks on the doors."

"That's true," Annie said. "I'm sorry I can't be more helpful on that score, but what I can do is help you search. After he fired his last housekeeper, I sometimes gave him a hand with the cleaning and I know where he kept almost everything, including his private papers. We could start in his office."

"The police have given me limited access to the downstairs portion of the house. We can go over now, if you're free."

"First I'd like you to answer one question for me."

Intrigued, Jake watched as boldness crept into the woman's eyes with the same assuredness she used to brush the fall of soft brown hair from her shoulder. "Go ahead."

"You've been gone for years, so I've heard. What brought you back home so suddenly?"

He gave her a surprised look. "I assumed you already knew."

"Paul never said a word about it to me," she admitted honestly. "Your father was my friend, but we respected each other's privacy. I knew something had been troubling him for the past month or so, but he never offered to talk about it and I didn't ask."

Jake nodded, looked toward the carving once again, then met her eyes square-on. "Everyone close to my father learned to respect his privacy. He'd have it no other way. But now I have to do the unthinkable—go through all his personal things. It's become my duty."

Too many unanswered questions added weight to his sorrow now, and at the center of everything was this young beauty who had clearly been a part of his father's life. No matter what it took, he'd find answers soon. And, if the gods were merciful, learning the truth wouldn't add to the pain he already kept hidden in his heart.

ANNIE TOOK THE tea cups back to the kitchen and washed them out in the sink. Although she'd known this would be hard on her, she could understand why it was even more difficult for Jake. Yet it was impossible for her to read the feelings that lay behind Jake's hooded eyes. From everything she'd seen and heard of him so far, she knew Jake was a man whose emotions ran deep—a man who was unaccustomed to opening himself to anyone.

Instinctively, she knew that Jake had secrets no woman would ever coax from him. She silently noted that he still hadn't told her why he'd returned. She wasn't going to let the matter drop, but getting that information from him would be tricky. Jake didn't seem like the sort who could be forced into doing anything.

Annie returned to the living room where Jake waited, picked up her coat from the back of the sofa where she'd left it last night and followed Jake Black Raven to the door.

"There's something you need to know," she said, stopping in midstride. "I have every intention of finding out what happened to your father, and not because I was there when he was murdered. The fact is, he was a very kind, loyal friend who helped me out when I needed someone. I won't forget that. Paul deserves to have his killer brought to justice and I'm going to do all I can to see that it gets done. It's the least I owe him." She paused, as Jake turned from the door, then added, "But there's more to it than that. I have to do this for myself, too. The killer knows I saw him. Though he was in costume, I have no way of knowing how threatened he feels by me, and I won't have something like that hanging over me and my baby."

"Maybe it would be better for you to leave town for a while."

"I'm safer here surrounded by friends, and with my nurse midwife nearby, than I would be in an unfamiliar place filled with strangers."

"You have a point," he agreed, taking her coat from her.

Holding Jake's gaze, she continued. "Even though you don't know me and have no reason to trust me, the fact is we need each other to find out the truth. As I've heard it, you haven't been back here in over a decade. That means you've lost touch with many people you'll want to question. You could use my help getting those doors open again." She placed her hand over her stomach. "And I can use your help doing some of the legwork, like tracking down whatever leads we manage to uncover."

"You'll have many other things to worry about with the baby coming and all," he said, helping Annie on with her coat, then following her out the door. "I think you'd be far better off not getting involved in the investigation and letting the police handle it."

She could sense he was trying to protect her, but she didn't need that from him—or anyone else. She could take care of herself. "It was your father's last wish that I help you and that's exactly what I'm going to do—with or without your consent," she added pointedly, letting him know precisely what to expect from her.

"So I have no choice?"

"No, not really. But I thought it would be impolite to not warn you," she said with a tiny smile.

Standing beside his truck, Annie braced herself by holding on to the open door. She carefully put her foot up on the running board, but the ground was slippery with mud and she lost her footing.

Jake gripped her waist, quickly supporting her. "Easy there," he murmured close to her ear.

For one heart-stopping moment, Annie was filled with

an awareness that was purely feminine and wildly exciting. His touch, so gentle yet so strong, made her pulse race.

*Desire.* The knowledge stunned her. "Thanks for the help," she mumbled, stepping up into the cab and settling herself onto the seat. She felt his gaze on her as she worked the seat belt around herself, positioning it low on her hip and below her stomach.

"You're very welcome, Annie," he said quietly.

It was the first time he'd called her by name. The way he'd said it, with that deep, masculine drawl, sent a delicious shiver up her spine. Unable to resist the temptation, she looked up at him. The intensity of his gaze ribboned around her like a gentle embrace, though it took her a moment to recognize the look in his eyes for what it was. It was the sensually charged appraisal a man gave a woman he found attractive.

Her breath caught in her throat and a purely instinctive response made all the sensitive nerves in her body dance. For the first time since Bobby's death, Annie felt suddenly beautiful and vibrantly alive.

## Chapter Three

Jake drove carefully, aware of the woman beside him. Annie Sandusky was quite a looker. Soft brown hair framed her face and cascaded around her shoulders. Even in last night's muted light, he'd known she was a beauty. Her features were delicate and well-defined.

Yet nothing had prepared him for seeing her standing in front of him clearly in the full light of day. Her pregnancy and, in particular, all the questions her condition raised, had taken him completely by surprise.

Late last night he'd had a few moments to speak to Martin, his father's ranch foreman. He'd learned then that Annie Sandusky had lived at the bunkhouse for several months. Had his father, who was more than twice her age, fallen in love with this white woman and brought her here to his pueblo? It didn't seem likely. His father had been a deeply religious Tewa who had always felt marriage outside the tribe was a mistake. If the child had been his father's, Jake was certain Paul would have married her. Thoughts circled around his mind like a hawk searching for prey, but he had no answers.

"Your father spoke about you often," she said, interrupting the silence between them. "He was proud of you."

"Did he actually say that to you?" he asked skeptically.

"Not in so many words, but believe me, he was."

Annie's eyes shone with a gentleness he'd never seen in anyone before. He felt the tug on his senses and quickly looked away, disciplining his thoughts. Despite what common sense told him, it was possible Annie was carrying his father's child. The thought sobered him. The attraction he felt toward her was, at best, totally misguided.

"Your father *was* a good man," she stated defensively.

He glanced over at her, but didn't comment. He could see the disapproval in her eyes as she looked back at him. It was clear that her loyalty to the father had already affected her perception of the son. In Annie's eyes, Jake suspected he was viewed as nothing more than the ungrateful son who'd turned his back on his father and his Tewa heritage.

Somehow, he seriously doubted that his father had told her the entire story. It was ironic that the firmness of her belief was founded in the one person who had shattered his own ability to trust.

"You know what had been bothering your father, don't you?" Annie observed thoughtfully. "Did Paul ask you to come back because he wanted your help?"

Her steady gaze seemed to penetrate through him. Annie was steel and velvety softness all rolled into one devastating package. "Yes. He contacted me. I almost didn't come, but it was the first and only time in his life that he ever asked me for anything."

"So you came back to help him." She nodded in approval.

"I did it for myself, not for my father. I wanted to show him the value of a son he'd cast aside."

She shook her head. "I don't claim to understand what happened between you, your brother and your father, but I know that Paul loved you and Nick deeply. His last thoughts were of you."

"Guilt isn't the same as love," Jake countered quietly.

"You probably don't know this, but he was the one who sent *us* away."

Annie said nothing for a moment. "Paul once mentioned that he'd always worried you two would never get out of his shadow—or each other's—unless you left the ranch and went out on your own. If he drove you two away, I'm sure that was the reason."

He shook his head. "My father wasn't that noble. Simply put, he was a tyrant. His opinion was all that counted, as far as he was concerned."

"The Paul I knew wasn't like that at all," she protested. "I think the problem is that your memories are a teenager's, a boy at odds with his father. I'm sure your opinion would have changed had you come back home years later and met him as an equal—man to man."

Jake shook his head. Annie couldn't have known his father that well if she truly believed all that. People didn't change. He wanted to tell her the truth about his father and how he destroyed the people he professed to care about most, but changed his mind. There was no point. She had enough to contend with already.

Out of the corner of his eye, he saw Annie place one hand over her stomach. Even the possibility of his father having a relationship with this woman, young enough to be his daughter, made his chest tighten painfully. But he couldn't really blame his father, if it were true. Had the situation been different, Jake knew he would have tried to get close to Annie himself. Her gentleness and her courage drew him.

"Tell me about your baby's father. It doesn't seem right for you to be alone," he said, unable to suppress his need to know.

Anger flashed in her eyes. "I'm a widow," she said flatly. "And I'm not as alone as you think. I have friends at the pueblo, like Martin, and Elsie, my nurse midwife. My baby and I have each other, too.''

It was obvious she'd resented his question. Her tone made it clear she had no intention of discussing it further with him. But, more importantly, she hadn't actually answered him...

''Do you know if Ralph Ortega was able to give the police a description of the man who attacked him?'' she asked, forcing the conversation back to the more immediate problem at hand.

''Not as far as I know,'' Jake answered. ''All I heard was that Ralph told Captain Mora that he was hit over the head and then, when he regained consciousness, he discovered he'd been tied up and almost stripped bare. The only thing left of the Santa outfit was the toy sack. Ralph was suffering from hypothermia when he was found, and he's now listed in guarded condition.''

A few minutes later they'd parked the truck and made their way up the walk to the front door of the main house.

Annie hesitated at the entrance.

''Will you be okay coming back in here so soon after what's happened?'' Jake asked. ''If you'd rather, I'll take you back to the bunkhouse.''

''No, I can handle it.'' Taking a deep breath, Annie stepped inside. ''This house will never be the same again without Paul,'' she added sadly.

Jake felt a heaviness in his chest. Annie was right. His father was gone, and no matter how hard he tried to deny it, a part of him mourned the loss. Tearing his gaze away from the yellow tape blocking the stairs, he headed for the study.

Annie walked in behind him and sat. Jake couldn't help but notice that her rose-scented perfume was the only thing that softened the austerity of his father's domain. He looked around, wishing he were any place but here.

"You never told me why your father asked you to return home," she pressed. If they were going to be in this together, Jake was going to have to be more up front with her. She couldn't allow him to duck the issue any longer.

He paused and, with obvious reluctance, sat in what had always been his father's favorite chair. "Have you considered the possibility that my father was trying to protect you by not telling you about this? If that's the case, I'm not sure I have the right to say anything now. Your condition…is delicate," he finished at length.

"Being kept in the dark seldom helps anyone," she said sharply. "I can take care of myself a lot better if I know what I'm up against."

Annie had a point and he knew it. But a part of him still felt the need to protect her. She was extremely vulnerable right now, whether or not she wanted to admit it.

"Let me tell you something you may not be aware of," she said. "There has been a lot of speculation and gossip about my relationship with your father ever since I moved into the bunkhouse and my pregnancy became obvious. People have made a lot of assumptions based on hearsay, and it's totally unfair. I've done nothing wrong."

Annie looked directly at him and, as she did, Jake felt the pain and frustration behind her words. The sudden connection between them stunned him. He'd never responded to any woman in this way before. A link he neither wanted nor understood was forming between them.

"Some people are convinced that I know every detail of your father's life," Annie continued. "And that's where the problem lies. If the death of your father hasn't satisfied the killer, if there's something else he wants or needs, he's going to come for me next."

"You're right." Jake stared at his father's desk pensively, before deciding to tell her what she needed to know. "I received a letter from my dad last week," he confided.

"He told me that he was being cheated by a close friend and, for that reason, wanted to handle the matter himself instead of turning it over to the cops. He said the situation was serious and asked if I would come and help him out. He said he needed to talk a few things over with me."

Jake let his breath out in a hiss. "I told Captain Mora about my father's letter, and he asked to see it. Unfortunately, I threw it away, and it's long gone. Once I made the decision to come, I didn't think it was necessary to hold on to it."

"Did your father tell you who he suspected?"

"No. I figured he was planning to let me know when we met in person. My father wasn't the kind to lay all his cards on the table."

"What about your brother Nick? Did your father contact him, too?"

"I don't know. Nick and I don't talk much these days."

"We have to find out. He also needs to know what's happened, if he doesn't already."

"I've tried calling, but I haven't been able to reach him so far. By the way, does he know about you?"

"What *exactly* do you mean?" she asked, her unflinching gaze on him. "What's to be known about me?"

Annie wasn't going to give an inch, Jake could see that. She'd mentioned unfair gossip and, he had to admit, it seemed unlikely that she'd been his father's lover. "That you were our father's friend, and that you live at the bunkhouse here on the property," he said. "By the way, the last time I saw the bunkhouse, that place was in shambles. When was it fixed up?"

"After I moved in. I did the work. I put in shelves, repaired the adobe walls and stained the wood. The rest of the hired help, Martin and the part-time wranglers, all live in their own homes, so it was just sitting empty and dilapidated. Your father hated waste, and figured that allowing me to live there while I fixed it up was a good solution all the way around.''

Jake's memories came crowding to the forefront of his mind. The bunkhouse had been their mother's artist studio. One evening his father had gone in there and, in a rage, destroyed all her work. His mother hadn't touched her paints and easels again; she'd never been the same after that.

Anger began to simmer inside him. And now, years later, his father had given this woman the job of restoring the studio and had allowed her to pursue her own artwork there. The knowledge knifed at him. It was the ultimate in hypocrisy. ''Did my father ever tell you what happened there?''

''All Paul ever said was that those rooms had seen a lot of sadness and the time had come to move forward.''

It made little sense to Jake. His father had denied one artist, but made it possible for another to work there. Then again, in some crazy way, maybe his father had been trying to balance out the past. Jake just didn't know anymore, and his father wasn't around to provide any answers.

Annie got up, reached into the closet behind the massive walnut desk and brought out a large box. ''This was his stack of unanswered correspondence.'' She placed it in front of Jake, then went to a tall, walnut file cabinet and pulled out some ledgers. ''I think these are this year's ranch accounts, but I'm not sure how up-to-date everything is. Your father sometimes had me help him with the paperwork and filing taxes, but basically he played catch-up once a month.''

''That was his way,'' Jake answered, remembering how many times bills had been overdue, not because of lack of funds but because his father had been busy with the horses or something else.

Jake stared at the ledgers Annie had set in front of him,

wondering if he should bring in his own accountants or honor what he knew would have been his father's last wishes and do it himself. He opted to take care of it alone. He didn't want any more strangers delving into the family's business matters until he knew more about what was going on. It would have been easier, though, if his father had moved into the modern age and done his bookkeeping electronically. "Is Patrick Kelly still my father's attorney?"

"As far as I know," she answered from her position at the window overlooking the corral. "But I doubt he ever did much except draw up papers when a horse was sold or a stud or mare was leased. Your father didn't discuss his business with anyone. He didn't even use a computer, because he said that if he had a problem, he'd have to call in somebody to come look over his shoulder. Maintaining his privacy was almost like a game to your father, one he enjoyed. Had Paul been born in the Middle Ages, he would have had a million winding secret passages all through the house."

Jake smiled. "That's not so far off the mark, but my father was no dark, romantic hero. He was just a man who lived alone, even in the midst of people."

She nodded pensively, but didn't comment.

"Do you know if my father had a will drawn up?"

"He mentioned something about updating his will a few months ago, but that's all I recall. He didn't talk about it other than that."

Jake nodded. That fit with his father's love of privacy. "If we can't locate that will, we may have a serious problem. Without one, probate can hold things up for a long time." He and Nick would have to try to juggle their father's estate in addition to their own businesses for as long as that process required. His gut clenched. He wanted to get back to Denver, to the life he'd made for himself there. Here in Northern New Mexico, on pueblo land, no matter where he turned there were either questions or memories he'd hoped to forget.

"Patrick Kelly is on vacation," she told him, moving to stand beside the massive desk. "I heard he's an avid skier, so he's probably on the slopes somewhere. I'll track him down for you. I'm sure he's left word with his office staff."

"If we find the will, do you think there's a chance you're mentioned in it?" he asked.

"I have no idea. But for the record, that's not the reason I'm offering to help you," Annie said curtly. "I just figured you had enough on your hands trying to get in touch with your brother, taking care of funeral arrangements, and honoring the pueblo's own death rituals. If you prefer to handle it all on your own, just say so."

He saw anger flash in Annie's gray-green eyes. Her cheeks were flushed and, though it was hardly possible, she looked even more beautiful. But what attracted him even beyond her looks and intelligence was her fighting spirit. Despite her soft voice, she never seemed to back down except to regroup.

And that was why, as far as he was concerned, Annie Sandusky was a walking danger zone. He was attracted to her, which only spelled trouble. Growing up on the ranch under his father's thumb he had learned that it never paid to form attachments. Attachments only gave someone else power over your feelings.

That lesson about life had served him well, too. His lifestyle in Colorado suited him to a tee. He had few, if any, worries. He either lived in one of the homes his company crew was readying for the market, or, if that wasn't possible, in a furnished apartment. He didn't even own a potted plant. The last thing he needed in his life was to find himself attracted to a pregnant woman who'd undoubtedly become dependent on him.

Still, as his gaze strayed over Annie where she stood, he

felt a yearning he couldn't define. Wondering about his sanity, he began to sort through the large stack of correspondence in front of him.

"All I can see here are bills. Just how he recorded his income, and when checks came in, I haven't a clue. It's going to take days to go through everything." Jake set the mail down and picked up the current ledger, shaking his head.

"I have a feeling we'll find our first clue hidden here among all this paperwork," Annie said somberly. "But you're right. It'll be like looking for a needle in a haystack." Hearing footsteps, she turned around and smiled as a Tewa man in his late fifties came into the room. He had wide shoulders and a strong build that attested to long hours of hard physical labor at the ranch.

"After all that's happened, I wasn't sure if you'd come in today, Martin," Annie said, reclaiming her seat in front of Paul's desk.

"I never left. I slept in the room next to the kitchen." He glanced over at Jake. "Good morning. I'm sorry I didn't get more time to talk with you last night, Jakey."

Jake had always hated the nickname, but from Martin he would have taken almost everything. Without hesitation, Jake stood and hugged the older man. "I should have known you were here. I went out to the stables earlier this morning, but the animals had already been fed and watered."

Martin nodded. "I take care of the horses shortly after dawn. But my job has always included more than that. Your father was a Made Person, one of the tribal leaders who directs our rituals. According to our ways, that means he was a mediator between the spiritual and the human worlds. I was his *Towa é*—his war captain assigned to guard him whenever he left the pueblo. Now, as his *Towa é*, there are responsibilities that I have to attend to. Do you remember what has to be done?''

Jake nodded. ''But the police won't release the body this soon. They need to do an autopsy.''

''The Winter Chief, the man who is in charge of all the pueblo ceremonies done this time of year, has already spoken to Captain Mora. The Office of the Medical Investigator has promised to do what they have to quickly so that the body can be returned to us. If your father's soul is not released according to our rites, twelve days from the day he died, he'll return and call others to join him. Many will die.''

Jake struggled to remain patient. Traditions and religious customs at the pueblo required attention to even the minutest detail. The endless demands never failed to make him feel suffocated, though he knew the ancient rituals were meant to accomplish exactly the opposite. They were the means for bringing the tribe together again after a tragedy.

''The winds were strong before sunup this morning,'' Martin continued. ''That means his spirit is already growing restless.''

Jake returned to his father's desk. ''Until they release the body, there's nothing that can be done. The laws of New Mexico apply here.''

''But since you were the first twin to be born, you're the head of the house now. People will expect you to see to it that our customs are upheld. There'll be a lot for you to handle, too, but at least you won't have to face it alone. Tewa ways demand that two of us remain in the house at all times until the burial rites are completed. If the house is unoccupied, your father's spirit will return and stay. I'm a war captain, and I'm loyal to this family. I'll stay by your side. I won't allow anyone or anything to endanger you.''

Jake shook his head. ''I understand the traditions of the

pueblo, but I don't need a war captain to guard me. I'll finish what needs to be done, and see to it that my father's killer is found. After that, I intend to give the land back to the tribe, and sell all the ranch's assets. My home's in Colorado now.''

"You'll do what you feel you have to," Martin said. "If you need me for anything, I'll be close by." The foreman left as quietly as he'd arrived.

Jake knew Martin had no intention of giving him some space. His mind was made up, and nothing would change it now. He would remain Jake's protector.

Jake looked at Annie. "I want you to know that you don't have to worry about finding a new place to live right away. First, my father's affairs have to be taken care of, his property settled, and the land turned back to the pueblo, and I don't expect any of that to happen before the case is closed."

He paused, then remembering how his own father had turned him out with practically nothing, added, "I don't want to pry, but will you have enough money to relocate when the time comes? If not, I'll be glad to help. I know you want to stay around friends, but once your baby is born, you may be ready for a change. I own other properties in Colorado. If you need help finding rent you can afford…"

She gave him a wry smile. "I don't need charity, if that's what you're really asking. I can take care of myself *and* my baby when it arrives."

Annie was proud, and that was one emotion he understood very well. Jake tried to hold her gaze, but she had suddenly decided to show interest in some books on the shelf above his head. Frustration tore at him. Women usually liked him, but he had no idea how to charm a woman that was so…well, *pregnant*. That, admittedly, was one of the primary reasons he was determined to help her, too.

And, if it was his father's child she carried, he owed her something more—he didn't know just what at the moment.

"Before I get bogged down going through all these papers, I'm going to try once more to get hold of Nick," he said at last.

"In that case, I'll give you some privacy and go talk to the part-time wranglers Paul hired to work with the horses. Those men knew your father as well as anyone. The horses were your dad's passion." Annie smiled sadly. "He used to say that he could always trust his horses, that their body language never lied."

Jake shrugged. As usual, the old man had left something out. Horses signalled their intent, but not always far enough in advance to benefit their rider. He was about to point that out, but one look at her face stopped him.

"Your opinion of your father is different from mine, Jake. But one thing I can say with certainty is that the animals understood your father, and he them. Even the high-strung stallions never gave him problems. He could get a horse to do anything for him, without ever laying a whip on him."

Jake remembered how his father had trained the animals. He'd been relentless, wearing the horse's resistance down with slow, psychological pressure. In the end, he'd always win. He'd done the same with Nick and him.

Jake leaned back in his chair and had started to reply when someone knocked at the door. It was Martin again. "The police are here. Captain Mora has a warrant to search the house and all the out buildings, including the bunkhouse."

"For the murder weapon?" Jake asked.

Martin nodded. "And anything else the killer may have left behind. They're working in the bunkhouse now. They'll be here next."

# Chapter Four

The thought of the police ransacking her home made her turn as white as a ghost. "My carvings!" Annie sucked in her breath. "If they damage my current project, I'll lose my income. I can't start all over with only nine days left before it's due."

"Your carvings will be all right, Annie," Jake said, rising from his chair and moving to stand in front of her. "That's not what they're looking for." Her fear touched him. He knew what it was like to struggle to make ends meet. He'd been there himself not many years ago. He resisted the urge to put his arms around her to try to soothe her fears, knowing she'd never tolerate it.

"I also have several knives. They're about the only tools used in chip carving. If they're damaged, or confiscated, I'm going to be just as hard-pressed to finish my work on time. Those knives are like extensions of my hands, and my imagination, when I work with the wood."

"But none of your carving tools could be the murder weapon. I saw my father's body," he said, his voice subdued. "The type that was used to kill him had a long, sharp blade, like a butcher knife."

"Yes, you're right," she answered, sorrow heavy in her voice. "I remember the murder weapon very well. The killer threatened me with it.'' She sucked in a long, shuddering breath. "But I just can't sit around here and hope for the best. I have to go over there and make sure my work isn't damaged or my tools misplaced when they move things around. If I'm not ready for this gallery showing, my entire career could be put on hold." Annie stood slowly and with effort. "I'm going to the bunkhouse right now. And, one way or another, I'll track down Paul's attorney for you. Patrick Kelly really needs to be here to help you, especially with the will."

Hearing someone else at the door, Martin motioned for her to stay where she was. "Let me get that first. People have been stopping by and leaving food all morning. But it might be Captain Mora and you'll probably want to stick around to hear what he has to say."

Martin stepped out and a moment later the police captain came into the room. Martin followed him in, then stood silently just inside the doorway.

Jake noticed that Mora was neither surprised nor offended by Martin's failure to give them some privacy. Martin had been completely loyal to his father, as everyone knew. No one would question him extending that loyalty to Paul's son. But Jake knew things weren't always the way they seemed. What appeared to be loyalty could have been motivated by something else entirely. The thought disturbed him, so he brushed it aside for now.

"The FBI will be monitoring this case closely. I already have an agent waiting for me at the office," Captain Mora said without preamble. "Jake, if either you or Annie knows anything about the murder, this is the time to tell me."

Jake shook his head, then glanced at Annie, wondering how much she'd say.

"I told you everything I know or remember," she said. Mora met Annie's gaze with a steely one of his own.

"Things must be very difficult for you right now. You've probably got a million things on your mind with the baby coming and all. Just remember not to make it worse on yourself by allowing old loyalties to drag you into the middle of a criminal investigation."

"Those old loyalties are based on respect and gratitude for a friend. I'm staying involved because I need to pay Paul back by helping find his killer. I would never withhold information."

Mora's skepticism was evident on his face.

"I'll continue to cooperate any way I can," she said, "but I sure hope your men haven't damaged any of my work as they searched. I need to finish the carving I'm working on and to get paid for it, because it will be my last big piece for a while."

"My officers were careful." Mora glanced at Jake. "We've already searched this house from top to bottom, but I have a special team going over the grounds now. We'll be here for some time."

"Take as long as you need. I want the answers as badly as you do," Jake answered.

As soon as Captain Mora left the room, Jake looked at Annie. He could see the tension in her beautiful eyes. She looked even more vulnerable now, obviously worried about her livelihood. All the things that had given her a sense of security, such as her home and her art, were being threatened.

"Why don't you take my truck and drive back to the bunkhouse? I know you're worried about what's going on down there. Come back whenever you're ready. There's no hurry."

"Thanks," she said with a hesitant smile. The loan of his truck was the kind of help she could accept. "I appreciate it."

Jake watched as Annie walked out of the office, head held high. There was a quiet dignity about her he couldn't help but admire. He didn't want to like Annie—she was a bundle of trouble—but he couldn't help himself. She was a fascinating blend of fire and ice, strength and vulnerability.

Alone now, he sat back and looked around. Even though his father was gone, this room still held his mark. It made Jake uncomfortable to stay here, but he remained seated where he was, almost in defiance. Memories crowded his mind. These walls had seen a lot of unhappiness over the years. His father had ruled this house with an iron fist, and what he couldn't tame, he defeated.

Jake and Nick had spent years trying to live up to their father's expectations, especially after their mother died. But nothing they'd ever achieved had satisfied him. Eventually he'd kicked them both out at the age of eighteen, a month after high school graduation. He'd given each of them five hundred dollars, which at the time had been just enough money to get by on for a month, if they were careful. Angry and surprised at the sudden expulsion, they'd both left, vowing to never return.

In retrospect, Paul Black Raven had gotten precisely what he'd wanted for his sons. Two boys with a desperate need to prove themselves had gone out into the world and succeeded, each in his own way.

With reluctance, Jake picked up the telephone and dialed his brother's number. Distance and time had worked to make the differences that had always existed between them even more pronounced. He and Nick seldom spoke these days. Talking only led to arguments. He'd almost been relieved yesterday and earlier today when nobody answered his calls.

As he waited for ●meone to pick up the phone, Jake

thought about his brother. Nick had always viewed the world from a different perspective. He'd never been able to see the big picture, because he'd always concentrated far too much on the small pieces of the puzzle.

Jake remembered their mother comparing them to fire and ice, both invincible in their own way. Jake was said to blaze over anything that stood in his way while Nick weighed his options critically to come up with ways to achieve his desired goal. He would freeze out anything and anyone in his way by anticipating and countering their every move. But, as everyone knew, fire and ice could not co-exist. Despite their physical similarities, their own natures had relegated them to opposite corners.

On the tenth ring, just as he was about to hang up, Nick at last picked up the phone. Tension filled Jake as he heard his twin brother's voice for the first time in months. He identified himself, though he knew it wasn't needed.

"I'm surprised to hear from you," Nick answered, his voice nearly identical to Jake's. "I've never known you to call in the middle of a workday. Is something wrong?"

"Yeah, little brother," he said, filling Nick in on the basic facts of his father's death. "I've got things covered here for now, so if you need some time to make arrangements before you head back, I understand. I'll handle things for both of us."

"Like hell you will," he stormed. "I'll be there the second I can find someone to cover for me here in Phoenix."

Jake heard the dial tone and, despite everything, smiled. Nick would never believe it, but he hadn't been trying to be patronizing. He'd only been trying to help. He shook his head slowly. Nick had spent his adult life putting people back on their feet by providing job training for those down on their luck. He'd offered tough alternative programs in Arizona and had produced remarkable results. Yet, despite

Nick's legendary control over his temper, Jake could still get under his brother's skin.

Staring out the window lost in thought, Jake was startled when he heard Martin's voice behind him. He turned around quickly, wishing Martin wouldn't pad around the house as silently as a cat. "Yes?"

"The Winter Chief is here to take your father's ritual bowl to its resting place."

"I'm not releasing anything. Not until I have a chance—"

"The police have no objection. They respect our traditions—as you should," Martin added sternly.

The bowl had been his father's most important ceremonial object. Since ritual items owned by someone of his father's standing could not be used again, they were retired to a lake or mountain shrine by the priests.

As Jake met Martin's gaze, he decided this was a battle he didn't want to fight. If the police had no objections, neither did he. Knowing where his father had kept the sacred bowl, he went to the bookcase and reached for the top shelf, bringing it down. "Here. Give it to the Winter Chief and tell him to do with it whatever needs to be done."

Martin took the hand-shaped pottery bowl reverently. Decorated in traditional patterns, it had been hardened in a carefully controlled piñon fire. "Your father worked hard to be a good man," he said somberly, "though, admittedly, he seldom did things the way we would have wanted."

Jake said nothing, knowing any argument was futile and out of place now.

"You never really understood him," Martin added, "but maybe you will as you go through his papers and learn more about him. The real problem between you and Paul was that you were very much alike. You were both fighters, and strong-willed." •

Martin looked around the room sadly. "When you finally accept the similarities between you, and allow yourself to think like him, you'll find the clues that'll lead you to his killer."

Before Jake could ask him anything more, Martin was gone. Jake pursed his lips, annoyed. In some ways, Martin had been more of a father figure to Nick and him than their real father. But the man could also be the most annoying human being in New Mexico.

Still thinking about what Martin had said, Jake reached for the *xayeh* that had always been kept on the shelf beside the bowl. The souls of their ancestors were said to be part of the stone that served as a guardian to the family. As he held it in the palm of his hand, a faded memory began taking form in his mind.

One night, a lifetime ago, he'd snuck into the house after curfew. He'd been heading for the stairs when he'd caught a glimpse of his father taking books down and hiding something up on the high shelf. Jake hadn't lingered. Back then nothing had been as important to him as not getting caught. But now, with Annie's words about hiding places still ringing in his mind, he felt compelled to look.

Setting the *xayeh* down on the desk, Jake reached up and cleared the upper shelf. As he did, the outline of a small, hinged compartment carved into the wall itself came into view.

For a moment Jake didn't move, reluctant to open the panel. Violating his father's privacy went against everything he'd been taught. But his father was past caring, and his murder demanded justice. Knowing he had no choice, he pulled the tiny handle.

Reaching inside the boxlike enclosure, he withdrew a small, leather-bound notebook. As Jake leafed through the pages, he found a listing of every address he and Nick had ever lived at since the day they'd left. It was then that he realized their father hadn't really abandoned them. He'd kept tabs on them all through the years. The news stunned him, giving him a new perspective on the father he thought he'd known so well. The knowledge that he'd been watching their progress all these years was unsettling. Had his father cared more than he'd let on? Jake wasn't sure anymore.

Hearing the sound of footsteps and unfamiliar voices right outside, Jake moved quickly, putting the notebook back where he'd found it and replacing all the things that concealed the niche in the wall. He didn't want anyone else to know about the address book until he'd had a chance to study it and show it to his brother.

A moment later Martin stepped into the room. He glanced down at the *xayeh* that still lay on the desk, and gave Jake a knowing smile. Jake wondered if Martin had known about his father's special hiding place all along, but there was no way to find out without tipping his own hand.

"The police will be finished soon," the foreman said. "Just remember they have a right to whatever information will lead them to the killer, but nothing more. I would advise you to honor your father's privacy even in death." Martin placed a tray with a sandwich and a glass of cola with a twist of lemon in front of Jake. "Your father and I got used to having lunch together recently. We took turns fixing the sandwiches. Today was my turn."

Looking down at it, Jake smiled. "You remembered how I like my soft drinks."

"Of course. I know this family almost as well as I do my own," he said. "And now I better get going. There's a lot of work to do today," he said, heading out the door.

As Jake sat behind his father's desk, a gnawing restlessness plagued him. For the first time in his life, he was beginning to understand the weight of responsibility his father had shouldered. If the ranch was turned back to the pueblo, which owned the land, Martin, for one, would lose his job. He wondered what would become of him then. The man had worked for the Black Raven family for almost thirty years. And there were others, as well, such as the wranglers, who were only able to keep their own small farms thanks to the extra earnings their employment here provided them.

And now, to make matters even more complicated, there was Annie to consider, too. The woman had become part of Jake's every thought, whether he liked it or not. As it stood, the bunkhouse was her home. She'd worked hard to make it so, and she deserved to have a place to live. If he sold everything he inherited and the ranch closed down, what would happen to Annie and her child?

The inescapable truth was that his father's legacy involved far more than a ranch on pueblo land, a houseful of furniture, and a small herd of quality horses. "Old man, what have you gotten me into?" he whispered. Silence was his only answer.

# *Chapter Five*

Annie finished straightening up the room she'd turned into her studio. The police had created a lot of clutter as they'd searched through everything, but at least they'd been careful not to damage her carvings or carry off any of her tools. She was grateful to Captain Mora for that.

Annie looked around the whitewashed adobe interior with a heavy heart. She'd expected to stay here for at least a few years, but now everything had changed—all except for the baby that was due in less than a month. With each passing day, she felt closer to the child inside her. It was funny how a tiny baby who hadn't even been born yet, had changed her entire life and her outlook on everything.

Annie walked into the former tack room off the bedroom area, the place she'd turned into the nursery. All along the wooden beams where riding gear would normally hang, she'd placed wooden cutouts of teddy bears and other cartoon characters from the pages of a children's book. She'd made the pale buttercup curtains. The hand-crafted cottonwood-and-pine crib in the center of the room was a gift from one of the women at the pueblo. It had taken Annie months but she'd managed to fill the nursery with all the little treasures she'd hoped her baby would love.

Now, with Paul Black Raven gone, the bunkhouse had

ceased to be a haven for her and the child. The nursery would have to be cleared out and she'd be forced to move on.

Depressed, she walked back to her bedroom. She was glad now that she hadn't spent any money on Christmas decorations. She'd need every cent, from the looks of it, these next few months. Annie eased beneath the down comforter. Her back ached and her ankles were swollen again. These days the slightest thing wore her out. She closed her eyes and snuggled into the warm bedcovers, planning to rest for just a moment.

CARS DRIVING BY the bunkhouse one after the other woke her from a sound sleep. The traffic didn't come as a surprise to her, in fact, she'd been expecting it. People from the pueblo and surrounding countryside were undoubtedly coming to pay their respects.

Annie struggled to her feet. She thought she'd only just dozed off but, as she checked the clock, she realized it was already evening. And, to make matters even worse, she still hadn't returned Jake's truck.

Trying to renew her energy, she showered quickly then slipped into her favorite maternity dress. The dark green wool was warm and perfect for such a cold day as today.

Locking the door behind her, Annie drove to the main house, found a place to park among at least ten other vehicles, then hurried to the front door. As she stepped inside, she was surprised to see how many people from the area were there. The *sala* was nearly full, and a half dozen or more visitors were standing in the hall.

Annie nodded to the faces she recognized as she looked around for Jake. She finally spotted him beside the kiva fireplace, speaking to Iris Ortiz, a middle-age spinster with a voice that always reminded her of a cawing crow.

Iris had worked for Paul as a housekeeper until early last summer. Paul had never told her why Iris had suddenly left his employ, but Annie had learned the story months later from Martin. Paul had apparently caught Iris reading his private papers and fired her. Like Martin, Annie suspected that Iris had been in love with Paul and had simply wanted to know more about him.

As she watched Jake now, Annie wondered how much he knew about Iris, but, as usual, it was impossible to read much from his demeanor. The only thing that betrayed the tension he was feeling was the stoniness of his expression, obviously the result of his self-control. When he gave a rare smile, the gesture never quite reached his eyes.

Annie reached for a cup of hot apple cider from the serving tray on the table and took several sips, trying to warm up.

Martin came over then, and, standing beside her, surveyed the gathering. "I have a feeling people will continue to drop by until late evening. Everyone wants to pay their respects to Jake since, traditionally, he's the new head of the Black Raven household."

"And, no doubt, they're also curious about him. Look at the furtive glances they keep sending in his direction."

"Everyone wants to know what he's going to do next."

Annie knew that the question was a critical one for Martin, too. "If the brothers decide to sell the horses and close up the ranch, what will you do?"

Martin shrugged. "I'll find another job, maybe closer to Santa Fe." He looked directly at her. "And you? Someday your carvings will bring you all the income you need, but you need time to make a name for yourself."

"I'll be able to get by for the next few months on the pieces I've already sold, but after that I'll just have to see how things go.'' She tried to sound matter-of-fact, but the uncertainty of it was still pretty daunting.

Martin continued to look around the room, silently noting the quick glances people gave Annie. ''You're under scrutiny here today, as well as Jake. Most of the people still don't know what to make of you.''

''You mean, because of that persistent gossip that I'm carrying Paul's child? At first I told them plainly that the baby wasn't Paul's, but the gossip continued. There's nothing more I can do. They can either believe me, or not. It's their choice.''

''I've gotten to know you pretty well over the past year, and I don't think you're capable of telling a convincing lie.'' He gestured toward Jake. ''But you've got to give him a chance. He doesn't know you at all. To earn his trust, you've got to show some trust in him, as well,'' Martin said before moving away to greet new arrivals at the door.

Annie was refilling her cup of cider when a wonderful shiver raced up her spine, leaving her body tingling. Obeying an instinct she didn't really understand, she turned to see Jake looking at her. His earthy eyes captured and held her gaze. He'd been looking at her and, somehow, she'd felt it as keenly as a lover's touch. He gave her a devastatingly sensual half smile that this time went all the way to his eyes.

As he crossed the room, her gaze stayed riveted on him. His loose-legged stride exuded masculinity. Men stepped back automatically, making room as he went by. The women cast him admiring glances. His presence and charisma were a devastating combination that delivered quite a sensual wallop.

Her heart drummed furiously with excitement as he drew near. Then Annie noticed Iris, the ex-housekeeper, trailing behind him, either unaware that Jake's attention had shifted away from her, or maybe because she was just too curious about him to allow him an easy exit.

"I'm glad you're here," Jake said, joining Annie at last. "I was beginning to worry."

Annie knew instinctively that his words had piqued Iris's curiosity. Trying to minimize the gossip that would undoubtedly be all over the pueblo the next day, Annie handed him his keys. "I'm sorry I took so long. Thank you for loaning me your pickup."

"I suppose I should extend my sympathies to you, as well," Iris said, interrupting. "Now that Paul…er, Mr. Black Raven is gone, your life will certainly be changing, won't it?" she added, looking pointedly at her.

"Except the fact that I've lost a dear friend, I don't expect anything else to change drastically," Annie said, determined not to give Iris tales to carry. "I'll still be living in the bunkhouse for the time being, working on my carvings, and I'm still going to have a baby. My life's pretty predictable, I'd say."

But Iris persisted. "To make a living out of your art, I expect you'll have to work long hours. It's expensive to raise a child, particularly for a single mom. Not that you intend to stay that way, I'm sure. My goodness, just look at yourself. You're young, pretty, and resourceful. I bet you've got your sights set on someone already."

"Please excuse us, Iris. There's some private business I need to discuss with Mrs. Sandusky." Jake took Annie's arm and led her across the room. "I was afraid you were about to punch that annoying woman," he added as soon as they were at a safe distance.

"And here I thought I was doing a great job of keeping a poker face."

"Others might have thought so," Jake answered. "But you and I seem to read each other pretty well."

His voice, soft and masculine, felt like an intimate caress. An intoxicating warmth flowed through her. ''It's just your imagination.''

''Is it?'' His whisper weaved past her defenses, leaving her feeling more vulnerable than ever.

As people began to approach, offering condolences, Annie found it impossible to leave his side, though she desperately wanted to put some distance between herself and Jake.

Finally, Jake took a deep breath. ''You know, there's something not right about these people. They say the right things, but their hearts don't seem to be in it.''

''Your father had many acquaintances but, from what I could tell, only a handful of friends.''

''Yes, I think you've put your finger on what was bothering me. My father had people who were loyal to him, and enemies, too, I'd expect. But friends…I'm surprised he knew how to make any at all.''

''Martin and I were his friends, and there were others, too,'' she said in defense of Paul. ''But he chose to keep his inner circle small. You didn't know him as well as you think, if you really believe he was incapable of making friends. He could be charming and incredibly kind.''

Suddenly a burly Tewa man with long hair wrapped *chongo* style at the nape of his neck strode into the *sala*. His footsteps were loud as he stepped across the brick floor, and his expression was that of a man looking for confrontation, not consolation. As people's eyes turned toward him, the room quickly grew quiet.

Curious, Annie studied the stranger, who'd seemed to bring everything to a standstill with his arrival. The man's features were sharp and disproportionate.

The newcomer spotted Jake and went directly toward him. The crowd gave way in front of him like sheep avoiding a hungry wolf. Excusing himself from Annie, Jake went forward to meet the man.

Annie couldn't take her eyes off the pair. Their handshake was brief and they spoke in hushed tones; she was unable to overhear their conversation, despite the lingering quiet.

"That's the twins' uncle, Thomas Ray," Martin said in a low tone, joining her. "He's their mother's oldest brother. I don't think he's stepped foot in this house since the day his sister died, almost twenty years ago. He and Paul never saw eye-to-eye on anything."

"Paul mentioned him to me once after I'd overheard an argument he'd had with him on the phone. I believe there was a long-running feud between them over a diary Saya had kept."

As they spoke, another Pueblo man, small in stature but not in girth, joined them. She smiled at Virgil Lowman, glad to have him there. She'd liked the man since the first day she'd met him at Paul's ranch. Virgil ran the small local bank where most everyone in the area kept their money, Paul included. Lowman was a tough businessman and financial advisor, but had a reputation for honesty.

"I never expected him to show today," Virgil said, looking at Jake and Thomas. "When Saya died, her family blamed Paul. They claimed that he'd broken her spirit and that her body just lost its will to live. Thomas was always the one who spoke the loudest."

Although Annie didn't want to hear anyone speak badly of Paul, she knew she had to listen to learn more about her friend. Someone had hated Paul enough to murder him, and the trail to the killer started with Paul himself.

"What happened between Paul and his wife? It must have been very serious for anyone to have made an accusation like that."

''Paul wanted to be the center of Saya's world and was terribly jealous. He hated the fact that everyone came to her for advice. She was everyone's confidante.''

''Did he ever mistreat her?'' Annie asked in disbelief.

''He never raised a hand to her,'' Martin interrupted in a firm voice. ''They were mismatched, that was all. Saya was a gentle creature by nature, who tried to help everyone she met, but Paul just didn't understand her. She needed his support, not constant criticism. The problem was that Paul wasn't the kind of person who did that well, if at all.''

''But that was such a long time ago, and Paul must have changed quite a bit over the years. He was one of the gentlest men I've ever known.''

Virgil nodded. ''You're right. Twenty years ago, I could have given the police a list the size of a phone book filled with people who hated him. But these days, it's different.''

As Virgil excused himself and moved away, Annie looked back at Martin. ''As far as you know, was Paul afraid of anyone?''

Martin raised an eyebrow. ''He feared no one, you know that. It just wasn't in his makeup.'' Martin stepped up to the table to help an elderly visitor who'd stopped by with a serving dish of homemade tortillas.

Elsie Muller, the pueblo's only nurse and Annie's nurse midwife, came up then and greeted Annie. ''You're looking well,'' Elsie said with a satisfied smile.

In the last few months, Annie had grown to know and like the middle-age nurse practitioner who took care of everyone who lived on the pueblo, whether they were traditionalists or modernists. Despite the fact that Elsie was not a Native American, her respect for the tribe's ways had won the pueblo people's confidence.

''It's been such a shock,'' Elsie said in a hushed voice.

"I can't remember the last time anyone was murdered around here."

"I used to think this was the safest place on earth. But I'm beginning to suspect that was mostly an illusion. It seems I've misjudged a lot of things. Yesterday, for example, I would have sworn I knew Paul very well," Annie said slowly. "Now, I just don't know."

"I heard Martin telling you about Saya. But he wasn't being completely honest with you."

"How so?" Her attention became riveted on Elsie. Because of her role as a nurse practitioner, she knew almost all the pueblo families and their secrets.

"Saya was my friend, and a gifted artist. Oil painting was her passion, but Paul never understood her devotion to it. One night, he confronted Saya in her studio and they had a terrible argument. I never did find out from Saya—or anyone else—what prompted it, but I saw the results. Paul had been in a rage. He never touched her, but he destroyed Saya's easels, brushes, and every painting she'd had. Saya's studio, the bunkhouse where you live and work now, was in shambles. After that night, Saya changed. She even gave up painting, something I never thought possible. But their relationship was shattered. As far as I know, they never spoke to each other again, except in public."

Annie thought of her own work. Chip carving was sometimes the only thing that kept her focused and moving forward with a purpose in mind. She loved the baby with all her heart, but her work was an intrinsic part of her life, too. Sympathy for what Saya had gone through and lost made her ache all over.

"Paul was really hard on the boys, as well, after that," Elsie continued. "And it got worse, especially after their mother died. Some thought that he was just trying to toughen them up, that he was afraid they'd be too soft because of their easy life. But I always thought that it was all part and parcel of whatever happened that night at the studio.''

''The Paul Black Raven I knew never even raised his voice,'' Annie whispered, still stunned over the revelation.

''As he got older, Paul realized he'd lost everything that mattered to him except this ranch. His wife had passed away and his sons were out of his life. He tried to change then, and actually succeeded in a fashion, but it was too late to undo the damage he'd done. He was all alone except for Martin, who'd remained a loyal friend and employee. Then, after many years of being without a family, you came into his life and became like a daughter to him. I really think that you were one of the best things that ever happened to Paul. Through his friendship with you, he finally began to learn that gentleness and kindness were signs of humanity, not weakness.''

Stunned by the revelations, her thoughts drifted back to her first visit to the bunkhouse. In retrospect, maybe she should have asked more questions instead of automatically assuming vandals had broken in and trashed the place. But at the time, no other explanation had seemed plausible. Splattered paint had covered almost everything, including the ceiling beams and floor and, in the debris strewn everywhere, she'd seen traces of canvas.

The sound of loud voices in the next room suddenly interrupted her thoughts. Annie recognized Jake's voice. He was one of the two men arguing.

''My priority is to find my father's killer,'' Jake was saying. ''Everything else is secondary. If you have a grievance, write it down and give it to my lawyer.''

The sound of crashing glass was followed by the dull thud of something slamming against a wall. Along with the others, Annie rushed toward the closed door of the study.

The apple cider she'd been drinking sloshed over the side of the cup as she hurried, but there was no time to find a place to set it down.

Annie weaved through the crowd of people and, without hesitation, knocked and simultaneously opened the door. As she entered the study, Annie saw that Jake had his older, heavier uncle pinned to the wall and was holding him there. A framed pen-and-ink sketch of a stallion lay on the floor among the broken glass.

Jake's strength surprised her. Even more impressive, was the way he was using only the amount of force necessary to neutralize his opponent. He was being as careful as he could be under the circumstances to not hurt his uncle. But the effort to keep himself in control was costing him. She could see the strain and tension etched on his chiseled features. Clearly, holding back was not something that came naturally to Jake.

Hastily placing her cup on the bookcase, she took a step toward the men, then stopped in midstride as Captain Mora came into the room, followed by half a dozen other men. Moving past her, Mora motioned Jake back and stepped between the men.

"What's this all about, boys?" Mora stood his ground.

Thomas glowered at Jake and wiped a drop of blood from the corner of his mouth. "You're just like your father. You have nothing of your mother in you. Look at what you've done to the sketch your mother made of your father's favorite horse."

Jake picked it up and saw that the glass had cut into the paper, tearing it. Sorrow and regret shadowed his features.

Mora glared at Thomas. "You know better than to come into this house of mourning with that attitude," Mora clipped. "If you don't leave now, I'm going to let Jake throw you out."

"I'm not leaving this place until I get what I came for," Thomas snapped.

"You'll probably have to wait until a will is filed before you can take anything out of this house. But I'm listening. What is it you want?" Mora asked.

"I came for my sister's diary. Her husband would never give it to us, though *we* were her family. It belongs to us, not Black Raven or his sons. My sister recorded her private thoughts in those pages and our family has wanted that diary since her death. It's the only thing that might answer all the questions that have continued to divide us, even to this day. It's our hope that it'll help us understand, once and for all, why she never came to any of us for help, even after it was clear to everyone that her marriage was destroying her."

"You're looking for absolution," Jake accused. "You want something that will say it was my father's fault and exonerate all of you. I'm sorry, but I still can't help you. I don't have that diary."

"Save your pity," Thomas snarled. "Just tell me where your father hid it, or if you really don't know, help me search for it."

"Do you have any idea where Paul might have hidden the diary?" Mora asked Thomas.

Jake shook his head. "It's a big house and I've only been back for a day."

Annie knew Mora was thinking of Paul's last words and his mention of hidden evidence. If Paul had a hiding place, they all needed to know where it was.

"My sister's diary is here someplace. Twice before, when Paul was outside working with the horses, I snuck in and searched the house. But there are too many places to look and I ran out of time."

"You want to press charges, nephew?" Thomas looked at Mora, whose eyebrows were raised.

"No. Not that you don't deserve it," Jake muttered.

Thomas met Jake's cold glare. "But *you* know where he hid things, don't you? I can tell you know something, boy. It's there in your eyes." He took a step toward Jake, then stopped when Mora blocked his way again. "You probably found the place when you were a kid. Very little slipped past you and your brother when you two were growing up."

"As I said—" Jake practically bit off the words "—I don't have my mother's diary, and I have no idea where it might be."

Captain Mora looked at Jake, his eyes narrowing. "Are you positive about that, son? Withholding evidence is a crime—just like breaking and entering." He glanced at Thomas.

"*If* I find evidence that pertains to the murder of my father, you'll be the first to have it."

Mora's eyes narrowed. "Evaluating evidence is my job, not yours. Your father had a tendency to take things into his own hands, and right now you're coming across as being just like him. But we have a killer out there who may feel the compulsion to strike again. Don't make me have to bury two Black Ravens."

When Jake didn't reply, Mora escorted Thomas out. Jake and Annie followed them as far as the hall, but then Mora glanced back at Jake. "Let me handle this while you tend to the others here."

As Mora went outside with Thomas, people clustered in small groups inside the house. A tense silence shrouded the room. Finally, when they all heard the sound of a vehicle rumbling noisily away, everyone began speaking at once.

While Martin calmed the guests, Annie motioned Jake

back into the study, which was now empty. "You have a very nasty bruise forming around your left eye, and a small cut over your eyebrow."

"I've had worse," he said, dabbing the blood with a handkerchief. "I work in construction. Trust me, I can take a punch."

"You can also raise a lump and get an infection." She went to the adjoining bathroom and came back holding some antiseptic and a box of Band-Aid strips. "Have a seat. And be careful of that glass still on the floor."

Annie stood in front of him and dabbed the antiseptic over his cut as gently as she could, but she felt him flinch as the liquid stung him. She looked down quickly to make sure he was okay, but when their gazes met the emotions she saw reflected in his eyes rocked her all the way to the core.

There was awareness of the miracle growing inside her in his gaze. But there was something darker mirrored there, too, an undercurrent of attraction and raw desire. She knew with every bit of intuition she possessed that Jake found her pregnancy only added to her femininity and beauty. Excitement and an aching sense of wonder and vulnerability pulsed through her.

Jake's gaze scorched her with its intensity as he touched the swell of her stomach, his palm smoothing over her in a light caress. The gesture was made impossibly intimate by the fire smoldering in his eyes. "You're so incredibly beautiful," he murmured.

She knew she should move away, but it was as if she were under a spell.

Jake gently pulled her down onto his lap and, framing her face with the palms of his hands, covered her mouth with his own.

She felt the impact of his kiss with every raw nerve in

her body. Passion traveled through her in spirals that made her feel deliciously weak. His hands were strong yet unspeakably gentle as he held her, his mouth coaxing and lighting fires too intoxicating to resist.

Time seemed to stand still. Everything faded away but the pleasures of his touch. She gasped as his hand cupped her breast, his fingers toying with her nipple and drawing a bead of precious fluid from them.

The exquisite sensations tore a soft moan from her lips. She had to stop now before logic and caution became nothing more than a memory. This was too reckless and just plain crazy.

She stood up abruptly, almost falling as she did, but he reached out to steady her.

Her breathing was coming in gasps and, as she looked down at him, she saw the same astonishment she felt reflected on his face. It had been too hot, too fast.

She moved back another step, fearful of feelings she couldn't explain. Needing to stay busy, she began to pick up the first-aid supplies.

"I need a drink," Jake said, standing.

Annie gestured to the cup of cider she'd left on the bookshelf. "Try that instead. It's healthier and, since it has no alcohol in it, it won't mess with your head. From what I've seen so far today, that's a definite advantage."

With a lopsided grin, Jake picked up the cup and took a sip. As he placed his lips where hers had been, a shiver ran up her spine.

With a grimace, Jake suddenly put the cup down. "I think someone spiked this, but I can't say I share their tastes," he said with a cough.

Annie looked at him in alarm. His face was becoming flushed and his lips were quickly turning blue. "Jake?"

Jake tried to stand, but his knees buckled and he dropped back onto the cushions, obviously weakened.

"Martin, Elsie!" Annie yelled at the top of her lungs. "I need help!" Annie sat next to Jake, trying to keep him from collapsing.

As her gaze fell on the cup, a shudder ran up her spine. Someone must have come into the study during all the confusion and added something to her drink. It was the only explanation. Horrified, she realized she and her unborn baby had been the intended victims and by offering Jake a drink, she'd sealed his fate.

# *Chapter Six*

Jake slowly opened his eyes. Where the heck was he? He looked around and tried to focus on the faces of the people around him, but he couldn't get his vision to clear. Then, like an instant photo slowly developing before his eyes, he saw Annie standing by his bedside.

Annie covered his hand with her own. "Easy. You're all right now."

The warmth of her touch flowed over him, heating every inch of his body like welcome rays of sunshine after a storm.

Seeing old Doc Cassidy and Elsie there, too, Jake realized that he was at the pueblo clinic.

"You're a very lucky man," Doc Cassidy said, coming forward to check his pupil response. Apparently satisfied, he stepped back and surveyed his patient. "Do you remember what happened?"

Jake's eyes narrowed as he tried to recall all the events. "I drank some cider, then it suddenly felt as if my head was going to explode. It kept getting worse until everything went black."

The doc nodded. "From what Elsie was able to put together, someone added the contents of your father's nitroglycerine prescription to that cup of cider. We're not sure how many tablets you actually ingested along with your drink. What saved you was that the pills were old and that they're meant to be taken beneath the tongue, not diluted in liquid. The effect was much reduced.'' He went to the door. ''I'll check on you again in a half hour. The police want to talk to you and I've got two other patients waiting.''

Jake tried to sit up but Annie placed her hand on his bare shoulder and pushed him back. ''Take it easy for a while. You deserve a rest.''

Someone had removed his shirt, and the touch of her hand on his bare chest sent a tremor through him.

''Have you been with me all this time?'' he asked.

She nodded.

As he looked into her eyes, he saw the worry and concern she'd felt reflected there. But something else also glimmered in those twin hazel pools. For several seconds he struggled to identify the emotion he'd seen, then it suddenly hit him. Annie was feeling guilty. ''This wasn't your fault,'' he assured her.

''I gave you *my* drink,'' she said, her voice breaking halfway.

''There was no way you could have known.'' She stood beside the bed, tears moistening her eyes, and it was all he could do to not pull her toward him.

''The doctor said the overdose could have been fatal. I nearly cost you your life,'' she told him.

Jake took Annie's hand and brought it to his lips. ''You got me the help I needed, and that saved my life. I'm glad you were there for me, Annie—before I took the drink as well as afterward,'' he said, gently reminding her of the kiss they'd shared. He was rewarded when she blushed and looked away.

Hearing a knock on the door, Elsie glanced up from the

chart. "That's probably Captain Mora. I refused to let him in before, but he's pretty eager to question you about what happened. Are you up for it?"

"Sure," Jake said, still holding Annie's hand. She tried to pull away, but he gave her a wink and refused to let go, betting that she'd give in rather than make a scene.

She leaned down and whispered in his ear. "I'll stay here with you, if that's what you want, but you've got to let go of my hand. There's enough gossip about me in this pueblo."

"Maybe someday you'll let me give them something to *really* talk about," he said, letting go of her at last and giving her a cocky grin.

"Maybe, someday," she answered softly, a twinkle in her eye.

Captain Mora entered the room and, giving Annie a nod, pulled up a chair. "I'm glad you're both here. You were together when this happened, so you might be able to help each other remember something vital. Everyone I spoke to claims to not have even noticed a cup of cider in the study."

"And I bet that's precisely what the person who did this was counting on," Annie said. "People were focused on Jake and his uncle, so the culprit had a clear field. Depending on when he actually tampered with my cup, he might have even had an empty room to work in. We stepped out when you were leading Jake's uncle outside."

"I remember," Mora answered.

"That cup was meant for Annie," Jake said. "Maybe we need to start with a possible motive."

Annie took a deep breath then let it out slowly. "I've been thinking about that. Maybe the killer was hoping to get rid of the one person most likely to identify him—me. I did see him, though admittedly he was in that Santa costume at the time. He probably hasn't realized that I was more focused on the knife he was waving at me than on his bearded face.''

''Getting rid of a witness makes sense, but an attack of this kind suggests a spur of the moment decision.''

''Maybe the killer heard Thomas mention Paul's special hiding place,'' Annie suggested. ''Once he learned that Paul hid evidence, he might have assumed that I would know where it was, or could get my hands on it. Like a lot of people, he may have assumed that Paul and I were a lot closer than we were. So, rather than risk having me become an even greater threat, he decided to act immediately. My guess is he must have seen the medicine cabinet through the open bathroom door and went in looking for something to use as a poison. Or he may have already known Paul was on heart medication, and this was probably where it was stored.''

Mora nodded. ''It fits. But, if we're right, he's going to try again, soon.''

''We have to come up with some countermeasures,'' Jake said.

''I'll order increased patrols in and around the ranch,'' Mora said. ''But, for now, that's all I can do.''

''My wranglers can keep an eye on the bunkhouse, too. I'll be willing to bet that they won't mind working overtime this time of year.''

Mora handed them each a sheet with a list of names. ''These are the people I remember seeing at the house. Can either of you add to this?''

Annie studied the list then, at last, handed it back. ''I can't think of anyone you haven't included.''

''Same here,'' Jake said, returning the paper and sitting up slowly.

Elsie came back into the room and looked at him matter-of-factly. "I see I was right. I just spoke to Martin and warned him that you'd be on your way back soon—whether or not we recommended that you spend the night here."

"There's no need for me to stay," Jake said firmly.

Annie helped him slip on his shirt. He accepted her help not because he needed it, but because he wanted it. Admittedly, he would have much rather had her help him undress than dress, but he'd take whatever he could get.

As her fingers brushed his shoulders, he had to suppress a groan. Her touch, however fleeting, had a devastating power over him.

"At least I know you'll be getting to bed early tonight," Elsie said.

He looked at her in surprise, wondering what she'd managed to read in his thoughts.

"Martin will see to it, even if he has to hog-tie you," she added, to his relief.

"By the way, Captain Mora, I'd like to have you or your men check out the bunkhouse before we drop Annie off," Jake said.

"No problem."

"You don't think he'd try again tonight, do you?" Annie asked Jake, then glanced at Mora.

Jake answered first. "Not really, but it's better to head off problems at the pass. If the police check out the bunkhouse, the word will get out that we're watching your back."

Discharging a patient from the pueblo clinic was not a lengthy process. Before long Annie was driving Jake's pickup back to the ranch, while Mora followed them several car lengths behind. "I think I should drop you off at the main house first," she said. "You've been through a lot."

"No thanks. I'm fine." He liked having her worry about

him. The realization unsettled him. Normally he would have felt smothered. "I want to be there when Mora goes through the bunkhouse," he explained for his own benefit more than for hers. "There's very little chance of all of us missing something important."

Jake saw Annie shudder and the gesture knifed at his gut. "You won't be left unprotected. You have my word on that. Between the ranch hands and the police patrols, you'll be safe."

He noticed that her hand was curled around the steering wheel so tightly her knuckles had turned pearly white. He reached out and covered her hand with his own. "You can move into the main house anytime you want, too. I'll watch over you there myself."

She gently slipped her hand out from under his. "I've stood on my own for a long time. I can't let anyone, even this killer, take my independence away from me. But I will accept your offer to have the wranglers keep an eye on the bunkhouse."

"Consider it done."

They arrived at the bunkhouse ten minutes later. The roads were icy and the temperature had dropped dramatically. Annie shivered as they walked to her front door. All she was wearing was the wool maternity dress, but without a coat, it wasn't much protection against the bitter cold.

Jake slipped off his leather jacket and draped it across her shoulders.

"No, you need it more than I do," she protested.

He draped his arm over her shoulders, keeping his jacket securely around her. "I'll feel better if you're wearing it. Humor me." He gave her a playful smile.

"All right," she said, giving in with a soft sigh.

The sound ripped through him, triggering his imagination. He wondered if she'd ever sigh softly that way for him in sensual surrender. His body hardened painfully. He willed himself to shift his thoughts away from her.

Annie hurried with the lock, opening the door as Captain Mora approached. Trying to duck the bitterly cold wind, she went inside quickly before Jake could stop her. Suddenly she stopped in midstride. A red felt Christmas stocking lay on the table by the door. A slow horror unfurled inside her as Annie stared at the Christmas stocking. Trying to save money, she hadn't purchased any Christmas decorations this year, though she'd made some for Paul's Christmas tree.

"That's not mine," she stated, her voice taut.

Jake followed her line of vision. Her name had been scrawled on the stocking with white chalk and a note peered out from within the folds.

She'd started to reach for it, but Jake pulled her back. "No, don't touch it."

Mora walked around her and, with a gloved hand, picked up the stocking and pulled out the note. Handling it only by the edges, he unfolded it.

Mora read the message out loud. "'Christmas can be deadly. Mind your own business.'"

Annie swallowed. "Short and to the point," she said.

"I'll see if I can lift some prints off this, or ID the source used for the letters on the paste-up note. I have a feeling they're from our local paper. With luck, this note will give us a few leads."

When Annie didn't comment, Jake glanced over. Her face was deathly pale. "Are you okay?"

She shook her head. "My door was locked, remember? And there's no sign of a break-in. If he just strolled in and left this for me, he's either got a key or he's an expert locksmith."

"Do you keep your door locked at all times?" Mora asked.

She shook her head. "Not normally, no, but I did leave it locked this evening. After what happened to Paul, I thought it was foolish not to start using my key at night."

Mora checked the lock. "This isn't a secure system. I could flip it open with a credit card. Get a dead bolt."

Annie nodded. "But what about the note? Clearly it was a warning to not help the police."

"He miscalculated," Mora said with a shrug. "You had little to do with the fact that I'm here and this is now in my possession."

"I would have given it to you, anyway, but the way things went down may just serve to annoy the killer even more."

Hearing footsteps, she turned as Martin entered. "I spotted the vehicles here and thought I'd better walk over and find out what's going on," he said. "I've left two wranglers at the house, so it won't be unattended."

Jake filled him in, then added, "Under the circumstances, Annie will have to leave the bunkhouse and come to the main house."

"Not if you have people keeping watch tonight," Annie said. "Besides, I can't just leave my carvings, and it would take quite a while to pack everything up." She looked at Captain Mora, then back at Jake. "With all the people around, there's no way this guy is going to return tonight, and I've got to go to bed soon. I'm exhausted, my feet are swollen, and my back's killing me. I need to get some rest."

"Okay, then. I'll stay here and sleep on your sofa tonight," Jake said.

"What? You can't be serious!" The thought of him sleeping so close to her made every fiber in her body dance with awareness. "I mean, the couch is terribly uncomfortable," she said, hoping to hide what she'd been really thinking.

He smiled at her, and there was something in his eyes that told her with assurance that he'd not only guessed her thoughts, he was quite pleased with them. Annoyed that she'd given herself away so easily, she looked away.

"You'll go back to the main house, Jake," Martin said firmly. "You wouldn't be able to throw off a three-year-old in your condition. I'll stick around here with two of the men and watch the bunkhouse."

"Sounds like a plan," Annie said.

Mora nodded in agreement. "I'll also get my boys to patrol the area closely tonight. But tomorrow, I want you to get a decent lock installed."

Annie nodded. "Of course. I'll do that right away."

Jake dropped down onto the sofa wearily. "The lock is my responsibility. I'll get it done. But right now, I'm beat. It's time for me to call it a night."

Annie rushed to his side immediately, one step ahead of Martin. She just couldn't forget the part she'd played in his near-fatal poisoning.

"Are you feeling okay?" she asked.

He remained quiet for a moment, then finally nodded. "I'm low on energy, that's all. Nothing a good night's rest can't cure." He started to get up, but his knees buckled and he dropped down heavily onto the couch again.

"Do you want me to call the doctor?" she asked quickly.

He shook his head. "No. I'd only have to hear another litany about the dangers of ignoring medical advice."

"Which you're too pigheaded to listen to, right?" she observed wryly.

He gave her a heart-stopping smile. "Isn't this a bit like

the pot calling the kettle black? You don't exactly listen to advice, either, you know.''

"Okay, here's what we'll do. You shouldn't move around any more than you absolutely have to, so you can sleep here tonight like you wanted. But you'll take my bed. I'll take the couch. Martin and the men can keep an eye on things for us both.''

Jake gave her a cocky grin. "I thought you might come around to my way of thinking.''

She stared hard at him, suddenly wondering if she'd been manipulated. Noting he was as white as the stuccoed walls, she recanted. "Just take it easy.''

Mora spoke into his two-way radio and, as he made arrangements for extra patrols, they all grew quiet. Finally, finished with the transmission, he said good-night to all of them. Martin followed him to the door.

"I'm going to round up the boys,'' Martin said. "We'll be close by, Annie. If you need anything, just draw back the curtains. We'll be in here in a flash.''

It seemed strange, but from the moment she and Jake were left alone, the very air around them seemed to become charged with electricity. As she walked back, she saw Jake looking around. His eyes came to rest on the photo of her and Bobby.

"That was my husband,'' she said. "It was taken last year, before he was killed in an accident.''

The news took him by surprise. "I'm sorry, Annie,'' he said softly. "Do you still love him?''

"A part of me always will, but the baby has helped me focus on the future, not the past.'' She brought out some blankets from the linen closet. "Letting go was hard, but Paul helped me shift away from my grief and focus on my work. He became like a father to me, at a time when I needed one.''

She'd answered some of his questions. He knew now that his father's relationship with Annie hadn't been sexual, but it also pointed out how little he knew about her. "Tell me more about yourself and Bobby."

She shook her head. "My past is my own. I don't want to talk about this anymore."

"I'm sorry."

"It's okay. I'll sleep on the couch," she said. "My bed's got plenty of blankets, but let me know if you need extra."

"The only way I'm sleeping in your bed is if you're there with me," he murmured.

His voice caressed her, soothing and tempting her all at once. She looked away and tried desperately to concentrate on something else.

"Go sleep in your own bed, Annie," he said at last, his expression gentle. "I'll be fine out here. And I'd rather be closer to the door."

"Do you expect trouble?" she asked quickly.

"No, not at all." He grinned slowly. "It's a man thing, that's all. I'd rather be the protector than the protectee. Male ego and all that."

His smile, so purely masculine, tore past her defenses. Everything feminine in her awakened. Aware of the danger, she braced herself to resist the temptation he posed.

Annie went to the bedroom and brought him her pillow. She'd make do with her coat tonight, though she wouldn't tell him that. She handed him the pillow and, as he leaned back against it, spread the wool blanket over him.

His gaze swept over her, lingering on her face, then dropping to her full breasts. When she finished straightening the blanket, he reached out for her hand.

"Thanks," he said.

His touch made her melt inside. She felt desired and safe,

feelings she'd never expected to experience again, particularly now that she was a widow and very pregnant.

"Annie," he whispered as she began to move away to turn off the lights. He wouldn't let go of her hand.

Moonlight filtered through a small part in the curtain, filling the room with a soft glow. She turned around and, even in the semi-darkness, her eyes found his.

"Thank you," he whispered.

She smiled weakly and broke free of his grasp, turned off the lights, and walked into her bedroom, closing the door behind her.

ANNIE WOKE UP suddenly as the baby kicked and shifted. With a sigh, she stood up and began pacing, knowing that the rocking motion as she moved would quiet the baby. Minutes ticked by slowly as she battled exhaustion. It seemed she'd been up for an eternity when the door to her bedroom opened slightly. She froze, her heart hammering. Then, a moment later, Jake appeared in her doorway.

He was shirtless, his jeans riding low on his waist, zipper down, as if he'd dressed in a hurry. Awareness shimmered between them.

"I heard footsteps, and I thought something was wrong."

"You shouldn't be up," she said, going over to where he stood, intending to help him back to the couch. But her good intentions were a mistake.

As she stood inches before him, his gaze seared over her, branding her flesh. "Do you know what you do to me?" he asked, his voice a tortured whisper.

Annie was barefoot and vulnerable, wearing only a thin nightshirt that did nothing to hide her body. Yet the raw power of her femininity called to him like a siren song and everything male in him responded.

He pressed his palm to her cheek, and she leaned into him instinctively. Before she could even take a breath, his mouth covered hers. The world began spinning, a million pleasures weaving through her. As she clung to his shoulders, he unbuttoned her nightshirt, tenderly caressing her breasts.

He slowly smoothed his palm down her body, passing the swell of her stomach, then dipping lower until he reached the center of her femininity.

"No," she begged, her body trembling with desire and urging her to not step away. "We shouldn't…"

She held her breath as she felt him touch the soft petals of her body then, with a groan, he pulled his hand away without reaching for the sweetness he'd needed.

"Don't," she managed, her voice unsteady. "We're playing with fire."

"There's something special happening between us. Don't tell me you don't feel it. I won't believe you."

"But we can't act on it," she pleaded quietly. "Neither of us is ready."

"Do you remember how it felt when I held and kissed you?"

Her knees were wobbly. It was all she could do to stand her ground. "That was a mistake."

"Then why did it feel so right?"

She had no answer. But even if she'd had, she was certain no words could have penetrated the sudden tightening at her throat.

"Don't make me regret letting you stay here tonight," she said at last, her words a soft plea in the darkened room.

"I won't take anything you're not prepared to give me freely," he said, his voice deep with passion.

As he moved away, a sadness pierced her soul. Only longing filled the emptiness inside her now.

He paused at the door, glanced back at her one last time, then left her room.

Taking a deep, shuddering breath, Annie sat on the edge of the bed. She'd wanted to surrender to her feelings and give in to Jake, but her life was too unsettled now. She couldn't afford to allow anyone to distract her from what she had to do. Everything depended on her ability to focus wholeheartedly on her work so she could ensure a secure future for her baby.

Slowly, Annie lay back down on the empty bed, the chill of the night her heart's only companion.

JAKE OPENED THE back door and stood outside in the darkness. It was bitterly cold, but it was like an icy shower and just what he needed. *Annie.* The name fit her. The sound was as soft as the whisper of the wind and as feminine as the woman who'd melted under his touch. Passion twisted through him. He wanted her. She'd stood before him, barely clothed, her breasts full and heavy. He'd wanted to take each in his mouth until he drove her crazy with wanting, then leave a moist trail down her body and show her even greater pleasures. He would have given anything for the chance to make her blood sing as she did his.

He muttered a curse under his breath. This was crazy. He knew nothing about her, yet the woman continued to draw him in every way possible. One thing was clear. He couldn't stay here tonight. Even the thought of her just one doorway away made his body tighten with desire. He went back inside, knowing what he had to do.

Jake turned on the lamp, and had begun to write her a note when a light knock sounded on the front door. He answered it and saw Martin standing there, a worried look on his face.

"I saw you moving around in here," he said. "The living room curtains are thin. Are you okay?"

"Yeah, but I won't be staying here tonight after all," he said, taking his jacket from the hook behind the door. "Will you stick around and keep an eye on things?"

Martin didn't ask for an explanation. He simply nodded.

Jake strode past him, cursing his own weakness. Most of all, he cursed his father, who even in death seemed to control the lives of those around him.

# Chapter Seven

Jake had been sitting in his father's study since dawn, sorting through the accounting books. He was searching for some financial irregularity or unusual expenditures that would point to whomever might have had a motive to commit murder. His progress had been slow, though his only interruption had been a call from the Medical Investigator's Office. He'd been told that his father's body would be released today. Shortly after that, he'd left word for the Winter Chief who'd help him plan out the funeral rites. Everything else was on hold until Nick arrived.

Hearing a knock at the door, he glanced up and smiled, seeing Annie. "Come in."

She entered the room looking even more beautiful than she had last night. Her cheeks were flushed from the brisk air outside, and her brown hair caressed her shoulders.

"We need to talk," she said, her voice quiet and determined.

"I know. I'm sorry about what happened last night," he said, then shook his head. "No, that's not true. The fact is I liked holding you, Annie. Very much."

Her eyes widened at his unexpected bluntness. "I—" She swallowed. "It can't happen again."

"But it may," he said softly.

"It can't, Jake. We have to be realistic. I'm going to have a baby very soon. I'm not looking for a casual relationship."

He saw her point. He'd spent a lifetime avoiding emotional commitments; it had become a way of life. He'd watched his parents' marriage deteriorate—he'd seen firsthand the big price of love, and he wanted no part of it. But his feelings for Annie wouldn't let him just walk away. "The attraction between us is real, Annie," he whispered. "And these things usually follow their own course."

She shook her head. "I don't live my life that way," she said, her tone final.

Jake said nothing. Life just wasn't that simple, whether or not she chose to believe it. Seeing the set look on her face, he decided to not pursue the matter for the moment.

Annie glanced down at the ledgers scattered across the desk. The Rolodex card file was almost on the very edge, and she pushed it back so it wouldn't fall off. "Have you found anything in those books that'll give us a clue to the killer?"

He shook his head. "It's hard to piece anything together. My father wasn't much on office organization. His banking records show that there were substantial cash withdrawals every month. But I'm not sure if that's significant or not."

"Have you spoken to Virgil Lowman?"

"Not yet. I doubt anyone will be at the bank this early. It's barely nine. I thought I'd pay him a visit after they open. Why don't you come with me? You know Virgil, and that might help me. You'll be able to sense if he's holding back on me better than I could. I figure he may be reluctant to answer some of my questions out of respect for my father's privacy—that is, unless he sees them as pertinent to the murder."

"I'll help you any way I can, but Virgil's pretty easy to read. From what I've seen, he speaks his mind."

"But he's also a businessman, which means he knows when to withhold information. If he didn't, he wouldn't be running that bank, or be in a position of trust."

She conceded the point. "I'll keep my eyes and ears open for you."

"In particular, I want you to let me know if you see or sense any change in Virgil's attitude when I ask him questions about my father's investments. He was my father's financial advisor, so I intend to push him pretty hard."

"Don't push too hard. You need his cooperation. If you make him angry, he's likely to shut you out altogether. Virgil must have respected your father, but I'm not sure how much of that he'll extend to you simply because you're his son."

He nodded. Many, including Annie, didn't know the real reason why he and his brother had left and never returned. Few would ever understand the sense of betrayal and abandonment they'd felt when they'd been abruptly cast out of their own home.

"I'll tread carefully," he said, "but I have a right to any information that pertains to my father and I intend to get it."

"Just remember, your approach may determine your success—or failure."

He nodded. A cool head. He'd need it—on every level. "In the meantime, will you help me search around the office? I'm looking for any papers that indicate expenditures or shifts in funds that seem unusual or extreme. And if you run across anything that looks like my mother's diary, I'd appreciate you letting me know. I've searched for it, but I haven't had any luck."

An hour later, after a fruitless search of Paul's office,

they left for the bank. It wasn't long after their arrival that they were shown into Virgil Lowman's office at the pueblo's small bank. The leather seats were stiff, but they matched the stuffy atmosphere of the office. Jake sat and regarded Lowman with a level gaze.

"I've been expecting your visit," Lowman said, sitting across from them. "I know you'll want access to your father's accounts and his safe-deposit box, but until the will is read or there's some kind of court order, I can't help you. Captain Mora already asked about the deposit box, but he doesn't have a court order, and apparently he doesn't have enough to get one."

"You think he would have been able to, with the murder and all," Annie commented, surprised.

"Paul was the victim, not the killer, and from what Mora said, he specifically mentioned that the evidence he left hidden was at the ranch. A search warrant has to be specific, so Mora would have to specify what he's looking for and explain why he believes it's in the safe-deposit box. If he presses the matter, he'll be able to get a warrant eventually, I'm sure, but that's not his plan. I think he intends to wait until the will is read and then be present when Jake opens the box. Believe it or not, it'll probably be faster that way." He looked at Annie. "Do you have a direct interest in this?"

Jake knew that Virgil was referring to her baby. He watched Annie's expression, but it revealed nothing of her thoughts.

"I'm here because Jake asked me to come, and because Paul was my friend and the best way I can repay him is by helping his son." She held his gaze boldly, knowing she'd sent him a clear message. "Does my presence make you uncomfortable?"

Her bluntness took Lowman by surprise. "If Jake wants you here, then it's okay with me," he said.

"Then let's get back to business," Jake said. "Are there any discrepancies in his accounts I should be aware of?"

"All his money can be accounted for, to the penny."

"Did he have many investments?"

"Some of your father's money went for the purchase of stocks and bonds. It was a routine procedure he asked us to handle once a month on his behalf. The bank complied," Virgil said.

"To the best of your knowledge was the ranch on solid financial ground?"

"Your father had one of the most successful businesses on this pueblo. It wasn't a huge operation, but it was as large as he wanted it to be. His horses were always in demand. Buyers came from all over the southwest. He could have expanded the ranch's operation several times over, but he chose to keep it at the level it was." Virgil paused. "Paul used to say that the reputation of the Black Raven Ranch rode with every animal he sold. Quality was everything to him. That's why the Black Raven name and brand carries so much weight in these parts. That's the real inheritance he passed on to you and your brother."

Jake said nothing. His father had always been protective of the ranch. He'd built the business from scratch, starting out with only two horses. The ranch had been everything to his father and that had been part of the problem since it had left little room for anything else.

"If the ranch had a financial Achilles' heel, what would you say it was?" Jake pressed.

"I think Paul himself was the ranch's biggest asset and also its greatest liability," Virgil said. "He could have cut corners taking care of those horses and paid his wranglers a little less so he could increase his profits. But he never did. Money was never your father's priority. I've heard he even gave out unofficial loans on occasion and allowed people to pay him back whenever they wanted. To him, money was a by-product of the operation. It was the business itself that held his interest, not the money he made.''

"I can understand that," Jake admitted grudgingly. He was the same way, and that bothered him. He'd always prided himself on being nothing at all like his father.

"Do you know where we might find a copy of my father's will?" Jake asked after a brief silence.

"If you can't find it at the ranch, you'll have to ask his attorney, Patrick Kelly. That's an aspect of your father's life I knew nothing about."

"I've been trying to track down Kelly for Jake," Annie said, "but I've been told he's on vacation in Europe. His office is having a tough time finding him."

"Have patience. Things take a little longer during the holiday season. He'll be in touch," Virgil assured them.

But patience was something Jake had precious little of these days. He'd left his business in the hands of his head foreman and he missed the daily challenges of running his own company. Here on the pueblo he was his father's son—nothing more, nothing less. It wasn't enough for him. He'd worked too hard to build a life of his own.

"Is there anything else you can tell me?" Jake asked.

"Not really. Most of what I know about your father is based on our business association and that, by its very nature, had its limitations."

"I've noticed that he made substantial cash withdrawals every month. Any idea what that money went to?"

"None I'd care to speculate on. I suggest you go through his accounting books back home until you track them down, if he entered them at all."

After thanking Virgil for his time, they headed back to

the ranch. "The key seems to lie with those accounting ledgers," Jake said. "But it's going to take me forever to add up all those columns and try to reconcile everything."

"Maybe Nick can help. Will he be coming soon?"

"I have no idea. I can't speak for Nick." He paused. "I can't speak *to* Nick. He and I look alike, admittedly, but that's where the similarities end. We'll just have to wait until he shows up."

"Was it always that way? I mean, were you and Nick ever close?"

"We were always competing against each other in school, and had different groups of friends, but I suppose we had some fun times. The last Christmas we had together was just before we graduated from high school. I remember going out on our horses to cut down a Christmas tree. Dad said we'd have to get it ourselves if we wanted one. His attitude annoyed us so much we got an enormous spruce, reaching all the way to the ceiling in the *sala.* He had to spring for an extra string of lights, but at least he helped us decorate it. That was a surprise. He even put on the ornaments our mom had painted for us when we were kids." He paused, then lost in thought, added, "I wonder what ever happened to those."

Annie smiled. "Paul hung them on the tree himself the day before he died. You might want to take a closer look sometime."

He lapsed into a thoughtful silence until they were at the ranch. "Do you mind if we make a stop by the stables first? I need to talk to Rick, Martin's nephew."

"No problem. Is it about the case?"

"In a way. He's worked for my father ever since he turned eighteen. He's thirty now, and probably knows quite a bit about the ranch. I figure he'll probably have a different perspective than Martin would on things, and that may be useful to us.''

As they left the truck, her movements were slightly clumsy, but instead of being put off, Jake found them endearing. Wondering if he'd ever have a sane thought again, he entered the stables.

A tall, thin man around Jake's age, wearing jeans and a denim barn coat, came out of an empty stall.

"Hey, Rick," Jake greeted.

Rick set the pitchfork against the wall and shook Jake's outstretched hand. "It's really good to see you back at the stable, Jake. Did you want me to saddle up one of the horses?"

He shook his head. "I'll be going for a ride one of these mornings, but not today. I came here hoping to talk to you."

"Can we talk while I work? I'm running behind and I need to bring down some hay. I could use a hand, too, if you're willing." Rick gave Jake's clothing a speculative glance. "Never mind. You're wearing your good clothes."

Jake pulled off his wool sweater and shirt, stripping down to a long-sleeved undershirt. "Let's get to that hay. And while we're stacking bales, tell me how business has been going here."

"Not much has changed since you left, in that respect. It's just a matter of keeping the horses in top shape and getting good prices for them."

As Annie looked at Jake, a delicious warmth ribboned around her. His muscles pressed against the thin fabric of his undershirt as he worked with purpose and power. Raw masculinity defined everything about him.

As the men began to move the bales of hay from the upper floor of the barn, she watched the good-natured competition between them. She could see the determination that drove Jake. He moved quickly and efficiently as he kept up with Rick, tossing bales down onto the ground floor.

When the men came down the ladder to restack the bales, she saw that Rick was wearing leather gloves, but Jake had no such protection, using only a big hook and his bare hands. His hands were reddened from the abrasion, but he didn't seem to notice. He went up to one of the horses who had waited impatiently for his feed and stroked his neck, his touch gentle.

Annie stood quietly, scarcely breathing, remembering how those same hands had felt on her naked skin. Desire flowed through her. She'd never thought it could happen to her—this craziness, these longings that ripped through her with such fierce intensity. Yet she couldn't deny the truth. Jake was stealing her heart a little at a time.

Hearing someone behind her, she turned her head. Martin entered the barn and, seeing Rick place a flake of hay in one of the feeders, glared at his nephew. "Where in the hell have you been? It's way past these animals' feeding time. I cleaned out the stalls and filled the water troughs over an hour ago."

As Jake came out of one of the other stalls, his slacks covered with hay, Martin looked at him in surprise. When he turned to look at Rick once again, his gaze was stone cold. "And you asked Jake to help you?"

"It's okay, Martin. I wanted to," Jake said. "It's been a while since I got a chance to work out here in the barn. It felt good."

Martin didn't take his eyes off Rick. "You and I will talk later."

As he left the barn, Rick muttered a curse. "Translated, that means there'll be hell to pay."

"Rick, would you like me to talk to him?" Annie asked.

"We were the ones who interrupted you, not the other way around."

"Nah. I can handle it," he said, then gave her a quick half smile. "He and I have been arguing back and forth for years. It's all part of Uncle Martin's nature. He used to fight with Paul, too, but you know about that. They each thought they knew what was best for the horses, and they argued about it all the time." He stopped speaking, then looked at Jake quickly. "But Uncle Martin never disregarded Paul's orders, believe me. My family's always been loyal to yours."

Jake nodded as he brushed off his pants, then picked up his sweater and shirt.

"I better get going," Rick said. "I've got to fix some fencing. Be seeing you."

After Rick left, Annie watched Jake for a moment. He stood by the barn doors, back erect, muscles tight, like a man bracing for a fight.

"Is something wrong?" she asked.

He nodded. "I know from my father's accounting ledgers that he spent two thousand dollars for hay less than a month ago. But there's less than five hundred dollars' worth in this barn."

She exhaled softly. "And as much as you hate to even think it, you're wondering if Martin has been pulling some kind of scam," she said, finishing his thought. "Let me set your mind at ease on that score. Martin would never have cheated your father. If you have a question, why don't you just ask him about it?"

"That's not always the best way." He held her gaze, then dropped it to her swollen belly. "Questions aren't always answered."

"It depends on how they're asked. When a person is innocent, it can really hurt to have someone close doubt them or ask for an explanation. Go gently with him,'' she advised as they reached the truck and got in.

He wondered what made her such a sensitive soul. "Annie, will you ever trust me enough to tell me about yourself? Surely by now, you know I'm your friend."

"We can be allies, Jake," she said, "but never friends. The attraction between us makes that impossible. My life is too complicated right now—my baby, my work, and finding Paul's killer. I can't afford to think about anything else because I need to stay focused on those priorities." Even as she spoke, her heart ached with yearnings she couldn't deny.

"Then tell me how to forget," he said, his voice a husky murmur. "I don't want to remember what it felt like to hold you in my arms, or how you tasted when I kissed you."

His words flowed over her like molten wax, burning a path to her soul. She tried to answer him, but no words could slip past the lump at her throat.

He sat still, not bothering to switch on the ignition. "I don't know what's happening between us, Annie, and I sure as hell don't understand it. But what I *do* know is that my feelings for you are more than just simple attraction. I've known many women in my life, but any thoughts of them never followed me every waking minute, or made me think of tomorrow and all the days after that."

As their eyes met, a shiver ran up her spine. She looked away quickly. "I don't know what's happening, either, Jake, but I know that I can't give in to it. I don't want any more heartbreak in my life. I've had enough to last a lifetime."

Before he could stop her, she left the truck and started walking down the road to the bunkhouse.

Muttering a curse, Jake went after her, but she refused to let him even walk with her.

Jake let her go, feeling helpless and hating every second of it. She ambled slowly, the baby's weight keeping her slightly off balance. He wanted to go to her, to take care of her and keep her safe, but it was the last thing she wanted from him.

He watched her, making sure she was okay until she entered the bunkhouse. Finally he drove to the main house. He understood her pride and her need to stand on her own. He admired her for it. He only wished she hadn't made it into an obstacle between them. It didn't have to be that way, though he couldn't seem to convince her of that.

"Did you two have a fight?" Martin asked as Jake walked through the front door. "I saw her walk off by herself."

"Not a fight—not really."

"Having a child is a huge responsibility. For a single woman like her, it's even more so."

"I want to help her, but she flatly refuses to allow it. She thinks it's charity."

"Is it?"

"No, it's not," Jake snapped.

"Then why do you want to help her? Your motives would be important to a woman like Annie."

Martin, as usual, had managed to cut right through to the heart of the matter.

Jake said nothing, sorting his thoughts. "I like her," he said at last.

"You probably like a lot of people, but you don't go out of your way for each one of them. What's so special about Annie?"

Jake muttered a curse under his breath. "I know next to

nothing about that woman, but I'm still crazy about her. Maybe I'm just losing it. You think?''

Martin smiled slowly. ''They say recognizing that you have a problem is a good sign.'' With a chuckle, he turned and left Jake alone.

Jake paced, seething.

Hearing a knock at the door, he glanced up to see Rick standing there.

''Boss, I need to talk to you.''

''Come in.''

''I was wondering if there's any extra work I could do for you. There are already enough men watching the bunkhouse, but I still need to earn a little extra for Christmas.''

Jake contemplated Rick's request, wondering if he could find a way to help Annie without making her feel she owed him.

''There is something,'' Jake said slowly. ''But it has to remain completely confidential.''

''Understood.''

''I want to know more about Annie's background—where she went to school, who her parents are—things like that. Think you can find out for me?''

''Sure. I can ask a few people I trust. What is it that you're after? It would help to know.''

''I want to find a way to help her without putting her on the defensive or hurting her pride. To do that, I'm going to need to know a lot more about her.''

''I'll get started right away.''

''Give it top priority. Tell the other wranglers to cover for you with the animals and the ranch. If Martin asks you about it, tell him you're doing a special job for me.''

*Chapter Eight*

As the hours passed, one accounting problem continued to defy Jake's best efforts to explain away. He was a good businessman and he knew as much about accounting as the people he hired to maintain his books. But there seemed to be no way to reconcile his father's large cash withdrawals. For the past six months, he'd made withdrawals totaling more than thirty thousand dollars.

His head pounding, Jake leaned back in his chair and picked up the framed sketch that had been broken in the scuffle with his uncle Thomas. His mother had drawn the horse as a gift to her husband. It captured the personality of the fearless stallion his father had prized. His father had proudly shown the sketch to every visitor and his mother had never failed to blush at his praise. It was one of the good memories he had of his life here, yet he'd almost forgotten it, burying it under memories of the hard times that had come years later.

Glancing at the box of unanswered correspondence, he decided to work on his father's mail next. Some of the letters had yet to be opened.

As he went through the stack, one envelope near the top caught his attention. It had been neatly typed, and had a

Santa Fe postmark, but there was no return address. Curious, he tore it open.

Inside, there was one sheet of paper—a photocopied page from what appeared to be a diary. The date at the top was twenty years old. If his memory could be trusted, it looked like his mother's handwriting.

Though the idea of invading his mother's privacy repulsed him, he forced himself to read it.

I'm trapped in a prison of my own making. I can't leave my boys, and I know Paul will never allow me to take them with me. He wants me here, a caged bird too wounded to fly. A horrible silence lies between us every time we're together. It's like an icy hand over my heart. But even this would be bearable if I thought there was some hope of us ever being a real family again. The truth is I still love Paul, and I know he still loves me.

The rest of the page was blank except for a typewritten note.

Your payment was late, so the price for my silence has now gone up. Double the original amount, and consider it a bargain—unless you're willing to take the chance that your sons will forgive you for what you put their mother through.

Jake stared at the blackmail note, feeling sick. His father had been wrong if he'd thought that the diary could turn his sons against him. He'd done that himself years ago. No revelation about his marriage, which had required the consent of two adults, could have hurt them as much as being turned out of their home by their own father.

His parents might have had a troubled marriage, but despite their private battles, they'd always presented a united front to the outside world. His parents had instilled in him a code of honor that made him the man he was today. It was his duty to get the diary back from the traitor who'd used it as a weapon and a source of profit.

Obviously someone else beside his uncle Thomas had been interested in the diary, and he'd succeeded where Thomas had failed. Still, he couldn't help but wonder what was in that diary and why his uncle Thomas was so determined to get it. He had a feeling there was more to it than he'd let on.

The wind rose outside, and dried leaves and sand rattled against the glass. The voices of the dead would never be still until blood avenged blood. Destiny had brought Jake back to Black Raven Ranch. Whatever the cost, there would be no turning back now.

HEARING SOMEONE KNOCK, Annie set down her cutting knife and wiped her hands. It was nearly noon and she'd been working intensely on her newest piece for hours, lost in her craft. Her concentration broken, she sighed and went to answer the door.

Annie smiled at Elsie and invited her inside. "We didn't have a scheduled appointment, did we?" she asked, hoping she hadn't forgotten. With everything that had happened, it would have scarcely been a surprise.

Elsie shook her head. "No, we didn't. I was in the area, and since you're within a few weeks of your due date, I thought I'd stop by and do a routine check on you."

After Elsie's exam and her assurance that everything was proceeding well, Annie poured them each a cup of herbal tea. "I'm glad you came by but what's going on? You generally don't pass through this neighborhood."

Elsie took a deep breath then let it out slowly. "Annie, I know how you hate gossip, but there's something you really should know. I was over at Lucinda Crow's house when Martin's nephew, Rick, stopped by. I heard him talking to Lucinda's husband. As you know they're in their nineties and have lived on the pueblo all of their lives. If I wanted information, I'd go to them, and that was exactly what Rick was doing. But he was asking questions about you and your days at the foster home. Although it wasn't on pueblo land, it was closer to here than Santa Fe."

Stunned, all Annie could do was stare. "I remember the Crows. They used to visit all the kids and tell us stories about the Tewas. But I don't get this," she said. "Why would anyone—least of all Rick—want to know about my life at the home?" The answer hit her before Elsie could reply. "Jake," Annie said flatly. "This has to be his doing."

Elsie nodded. "I think so, too. From what I've seen, he cares about you, Annie. He may want to know more about you and, face it, you really don't open up to anyone."

"That doesn't give him the right to invade my privacy. I think it's time he and I had a little talk," she said flatly.

"Now you're furious." Elsie sighed. "Maybe I shouldn't have told you."

"I'm glad you did. And don't worry, I'll keep your name out of this. But it's time Jake Black Raven understood that he can't have anything and everything he wants."

After Elsie left, Annie walked to the main house. She was hoping the brisk air and physical exercise would help to calm her down, but so far, it hadn't helped. By the time she reached the main house, she was eager for a confrontation.

Annie knocked and simultaneously turned the knob to enter but this time the front door was locked. The discovery made her realize just how many changes Paul's murder had brought about in the peaceful pueblo community.

Martin answered the door and stepped aside, inviting her in. "Start bringing your key," he advised. "We have to keep the door locked for Jake's protection."

She nodded. "Yes, I suppose extra security is a necessity for all of us now. Where's Jake?"

"In the study, going over his father's papers."

"He and I are going to have a little chat. Don't worry if you hear loud voices."

Martin smiled. "What's he done?"

"You don't want to know. First let me yell at him, then I may be able to discuss it rationally with someone else." She strode into the study without knocking, then closed the door behind her as Jake looked up in surprise.

"What is it with you, Jake? Do you think that I have no right to my own privacy just because I live on your property?" She saw in his eyes that he knew precisely what she was talking about. "You sent Rick on a fishing expedition without any regard for my feelings or rights. You may be the owner of the building I live in, but you don't own *me*."

"Let me explain—" Jake stood, and began to cross the room.

"There's nothing to explain. And don't bother to deny that Rick was acting on your orders."

"I'm not, but it's not what you think. All I wanted was—"

"To get information I didn't want to give you myself."

"Well, yes, but there's more—"

"More? What else have you done? And how *dare* you take this upon yourself?"

She wasn't going to give him a chance to get a word in edgewise, unless he first got her attention. Jake suddenly gathered her against him, his fingers tangling in her hair and forcing her head back as he took her mouth with his own. His tongue filled her mouth, taking and giving her pleasure until she melted against him. When the fire inside him grew too hot to contain, he reluctantly eased his hold.

Annie's lips throbbed and her heart was drumming frantically. As she looked up at him, the wildness in Jake's eyes made a shiver course up her spine. She wanted to demand an explanation for his actions, but she couldn't speak. The urge to step back into his arms was almost overpowering.

"I see I finally have your attention," he said, his deep voice vibrating with needs too powerful to hide.

"There are easier ways to get my attention. Though, I admit, this was effective," she managed to unsteadily concede. Her lips were swollen and, as she ran the tip of her tongue over them, she could still taste him. She fought the almost desperate impulse to renew their kiss and let whatever happened, happen.

"You're a proud woman, Annie. You don't want anyone's help, and I can understand that. But I care about you. All I was trying to do was find a way I could help you, if only from the sidelines."

"I've always paid my own way, with money or with hard work. You don't have the right..."

"When you care about someone, your heart overrules your head and sometimes you end up doing things you know you shouldn't do. I'm sorry Annie."

His apology touched her deeply. In all fairness, she'd asked questions about him, too. "We all do things we shouldn't sometimes," she admittedly slowly.

He gave her a curious look then smiled slowly. "So you've asked questions about me, too?" he asked, reading her mind.

"A few," she answered cautiously, avoiding his gaze.

He laughed, obviously pleased with his discovery. "I bet that was hard to admit," he said, brushing his knuckles against her cheek in a feather-light caress.

His touch sent an intoxicating heat spiraling through her. Her breath caught in her throat. Aware of the danger, she forced herself to move away from him and sat alone on the couch.

"There's only one way to handle this attraction between us," she said, her voice unsteady. "Except for the times when we're actively working to find your father's killer, we have to stay away from each other. We both know that a relationship between us can't work. I have my baby and my work to think of. To me, family and commitment are what give life meaning. But for you, it's different. You preferred to stay away from those things when you were growing up."

"You might be right," he admitted. "But I do care about you, Annie."

"Then help me do what needs to be done."

Annie saw the pain flash in his eyes and her chest tightened. She was right and, deep down, he knew it. The last thing Jake wanted was an instant family. To him, all "family" had ever meant was heartbreak.

Jake sat at his father's desk, then took out the photocopied letter he'd opened and encased in a plastic bag. He slid the note across the desk to her. "Someone was blackmailing my father," he said, then added, "I have to turn it over to the police, so leave it inside the bag."

As she stood in front of the desk and read the excerpt from Saya's diary, tears brimmed in her eyes. Paul and Saya had been trapped by pride and circumstances. She couldn't even imagine their pain—two people living together and loving each other from a distance, knowing that what separated them would never be bridged. The similarities between the past and her present relationship with Jake struck her hard.

"They suffered so much, Jake, but they were both victims."

"And then someone decided to use my mother's innermost thoughts to make a profit." His face hardened. "I don't understand why my father ever paid this scumball a dime."

"I can answer that," she said slowly. "Your father wanted to seal the rift between himself and you and Nick. That was at the heart of all his dreams for the future. He really hoped that you and Nick would return for good someday and run this ranch. He was afraid the diary had the potential of destroying what mattered most to him."

"My father wasn't afraid of anything. Had you really known him, you would have understood that."

"Everyone has a weak spot. For Paul, it was his rediscovered love for you and your brother. He was committed to finding a way of getting all of you to reconcile."

"There's got to be more to it than that. My father just wasn't the type to pay blackmail money. What he would have done was find a way to get the diary back, no matter what it took."

"If you're right, then maybe he was just stalling by making a few payments. It's possible that the reason the blackmailer hadn't received his money this last time was because your father was about to turn things around. If only we could find the evidence Paul told me about."

"It could be anywhere. It doesn't even necessarily have to be in the house. It could be somewhere on the property. Let's face it, it could take a lifetime to find it. We don't even know what we're supposed to be looking for."

She started to answer, but then gasped, her eyes closing.

"Are you okay?" he asked quickly.

She nodded, took a deep breath and let it out again. "It's nothing. I get these contractions every once in a while. They're nothing to worry about. They're not the real thing."

"How do you know?" he demanded, going to her side in a flash.

She smiled. "Because they go away, and they're not really painful. They're more like an uncomfortable tightening."

"Let me call Elsie," he said, helping her back to the sofa.

"No, don't. I'm telling you, it's nothing. I'm fine again now."

"You sure?" The last thing he wanted to do was try to deliver a baby.

She laughed. "Stop looking so concerned. It's perfectly natural. They're called Braxton-Hicks contractions. They happen."

"Can I get you anything? Milk? Juice?"

"No, relax. I'm fine."

"You're in absolutely no discomfort?" he pressed.

"The only part of me that aches are my feet. They swell up like balloons these days."

He knelt in front of her, and carefully slipped off her shoes.

"What are you doing?" she asked in alarm.

He didn't answer. Instead he began to gently massage her feet.

The gesture took her completely by surprise. She knew she shouldn't have allowed him to continue, but his touch was so gentle and soothing she didn't want him to stop.

"You don't have to do that...but it does feel wonderful," she said with a contented sigh.

"I can do all kinds of wonderful things. You just haven't given me a chance," he answered, his eyes twinkling.

"Hmm. I'll try to remember that." She leaned back into the cushions, only half aware of footsteps coming down the hall. "It feels heavenly. You have such an expert touch." She closed her eyes. "More. There. Just like that. Oh, that feels so good!" Suddenly aware that the footsteps had stopped, she sat up slowly and reluctantly, expecting to hear a knock on the door. But the footsteps began again, only this time going away from them and fading down the hall. "That's odd," she said, glancing at Jake.

Jake smiled. "My guess is Martin heard you and decided not to bother us."

Her eyes widened. "Oh, no! Do you realize what he must have thought?" she asked, recalling her own words. "Poor Martin! He undoubtedly thinks we've both lost our minds."

Jake shook his head and grinned. "I have a feeling he would approve." He began to massage her feet once again. With a sigh, she leaned back and surrendered.

He felt her relax. "Why don't you tell me about yourself?" he asked softly. "It's not fair, you know. I'm sure my father told you a lot about our family, and you know far more about me than I do about you."

She conceded the point. "Your father loved to tell me stories about you and your brother, and what you were like when you were growing up."

"So, how about it? Will you even things out just to be fair?" he asked gently.

As he began to massage her other foot, she gave in. Annie told him about her days at the foster home, and her long relationship with Bobby. Last of all, she told him about Bobby's death. Sorrow was laced through her words. "I lost a friend, the only one I'd had since childhood. It really hit me hard. For a while I didn't even want to get up in the morning. Then I met Paul. He helped me focus back on my work. He allowed me to live in the bunkhouse in exchange for restoring it, and for the first time in my adult life, I had no rent or utility bills to pay. I chose to help him around the house after the housekeeper left, and did clerical work for Paul from time to time, too, but every other moment I spent on my carvings. It was more time that I'd ever hoped for. I can't tell you how much that meant to me.''

"My father made a good deal. You've done a great job of restoring the bunkhouse.''

"Paul could have hired anyone to do that, but he chose to help me out in a way I could accept. I'll never forget him for that.''

"He found a way to help you without injuring your pride,'' he acknowledged.

"Yes, I suppose, but it was more than that. Paul helped me because he believed in my work. To a struggling artist, that kind of validation means the world.'' She sat up and slipped her shoes back on as a knock sounded at the study door.

Martin came into the room at Jake's invitation. "The Winter Chief sent word that he's coming over to talk to you tonight about the funeral rites.''

Jake nodded. "I notified him when the authorities released my father's body. Now it's only a matter of waiting for Nick to arrive.''

After Martin left, Annie stood. "I better get back to the bunkhouse. I've got work to do on my carving. I still have a December twenty-second deadline and that's just eight days away.''

"Let me drive you back,'' Jake offered.

She shook her head. "Fresh air will be good for me," Annie said, then left without another word.

Jake knew she was pushing him away emotionally and strengthening the barrier that stood between them. And, as much as he hated to admit it, she was right to do so. He cared about Annie, but he wasn't prepared to be a family man. There was no guarantee that he wouldn't be as bad a parent as his father had been to his brother and him—and he couldn't do that to Annie and her child.

Alone again, he stood at the window and stared outside. The sun peered through the clouds, dappling erratic shadows on the ground. As he turned and walked back to the desk, he glanced around aimlessly. The silence in the house was oppressive and the room seemed unspeakably empty.

He'd never minded being alone, had never felt lonely, but now whenever Annie was gone, it seemed as if a piece of himself was absent. What on earth was happening to him? What magic did Annie have that urged him to turn his back on caution and rush headlong into what was surely a disaster?

He remembered the words in his mother's diary. Her greatest unhappiness had come from loving. Maybe the past was already repeating itself, inevitably bringing together another two people who could only cause each other pain.

He watched the winter storm that was brewing over the mountains, knowing it would soon reach them. All the signs pointed to it.

Then, as if in defiance of the angry skies, a bright, clear ray of sunlight stole out from between the dark clouds and peered into the study. As it shimmered over the *xayeh* on the bookcase, it created a rainbow that flashed on the wall in front of him. The colors danced over the whitewashed adobe walls before fading as the sun disappeared from view.

He smiled slowly. Some would have said that his ancestors had just spoken. By bursting through the storm clouds, the sun had reminded him that the inevitable was made up of many sides, and often held its own gentle surprises.

# Chapter Nine

Annie went to the main house early the next day. Martin had invited her to have coffee with him, and it was such a rare invitation she suspected it had something to do with last night. Maybe he was worried about Jake and her.

She was feeling a bit nervous as she knocked on the kitchen door. Martin greeted her immediately and invited her inside. The moment she stepped in, the aroma of fresh hot coffee and muffins baking in the oven made her mouth water.

"I hope you remembered that I'm eating for two," she teased.

"I made enough for an army, including Jakey and the wranglers."

"Will Jake be joining us?" she asked, looking around.

"Eventually, if only for coffee. He took one of the horses out as soon as he was up. That was over an hour ago, so I expect he'll be back before long."

She studied Martin's expression. "What's troubling you? This is more than curiosity about what you heard last night, isn't it?"

He shrugged. "You're both adults. Whatever happened is between you two."

"Nothing happened," she answered. "My feet were sore

and he massaged them. It felt wonderful," she said with a sheepish smile.

"At least you two are getting to know each other. To be honest, I'm for anything that'll help Jake see this ranch as his home. Any personal relationships that keep him here will be good for everyone."

She realized how much was behind the matter-of-fact statement. Martin's life was tied to this ranch. "Then what's bothering you?" she asked gently. "Why did you want to talk to me this morning?"

"I've been wondering if Jake and Nick will close down the ranch," Martin said, placing a steaming cup of coffee and a blueberry muffin in front of her.

"I've wondered about that myself." It made her sad to think of Jake leaving, but he had a right to follow his own dreams.

"Maybe after they've been here a while, they'll decide to stay and run the operation themselves," Martin said, giving her a hopeful look.

"Based on what I've learned about Jake, I don't think so."

"Well, either way, the brothers will have to wait until the will—if there is one—is read," Martin said. "Jake, for example, can only sell what's his and there's no telling how things will be divided. In the meantime, maybe he'll begin to appreciate the ranch. Taking one of the horses out is a good first step. The way I figure it, the longer he stays, the better our chances are of him changing his mind about leaving."

"What about Nick? Do you think he'll want to keep the ranch?"

"I don't know. Nick is very different from Jake. This ranch would never consume him, not like it could Jake, if he'd let it. Nick is an idealist who likes to fight for causes he believes in. He started the job training centers, I heard, because he discovered what it was like having no real job skills after he was on his own after high school. While working at two dead-end jobs, he put himself through business school. He knows what people need to get and keep a good job. I have a feeling that Nick will probably want to sell the ranch's assets to provide funding for one of his programs. The simple truth is that this ranch holds many bad memories for the twins. There are good memories for them here, too, but, as it often is, the bad has overshadowed the good.''

No matter how she looked at it, it all spelled the same thing. She had to start looking for a new place to live. If the land reverted to the tribe, she wouldn't be allowed to stay. She was only on the pueblo because of Paul's hospitality. ''I wonder what kind of time frame Jake has in mind. Liquidating the ranch shouldn't take too long, I think.''

''I plan to stay until the first of the year, maybe three weeks at the most,'' Jake's voice boomed from the hall. ''If my father's killer hasn't been found, I'll stay longer, of course. I'm not leaving until that's resolved.''

Annie jumped, and turned her head to see Jake standing in the doorway. ''How long have you been there?''

''I just came in.''

His coal-black hair was windblown and his eyes shone with a bright, inner fire. As she looked at him, her pulse began to pound and her skin tingled with excitement.

Giving her a knowing smile, he poured himself a cup of coffee and took a muffin from the tray. ''I have my own business to look after, so I'll have to start traveling back and forth after the first.''

Jake looked directly at Martin. ''I'd like you to be caretaker of this place until everything is settled, since that could take months. Then, after the ranch is disposed of, I'm hoping you'll come work for me. I can use someone with your management skills, Martin. You're familiar with construction, so all you'd need is on-the-job experience.''

Martin shook his head slowly. ''My family is here,'' he said slowly. ''It would be hard to leave.''

''You'd bring them with you, of course.''

He shook his head. ''My wife, yes, but the others...'' He let the sentence hang. ''Let me think about it.''

Jake looked at Annie. ''And my offer to you still stands,'' he said. ''My company could use a reliable caretaker. You'd live on-site in a company trailer while construction was under way. Then, when the job was completed, we'd move you to the next site at company expense. Think about it.''

She wanted to say no, but the fact was she couldn't afford to refuse any business offer that would give her a reliable source of income. Her options were limited and, with a baby on the way, she couldn't afford to take too many risks financially. ''You're being very generous. But it would be hard making room for my work in a trailer. Give me some time to think about it, okay?''

''Sure. There's no rush. Nick's not even here yet. I tried to call him again this morning, but there was no answer at his home. I tried the job training center he runs, too, but I kept being put on hold. After that happened four times, I gave up.''

Annie stood slowly. The baby had been restless lately, and after another sleepless night, she was even more tired than usual. But there was still work to do. ''I better go back. I've got a lot of work to do.''

As she headed out of the kitchen and down the hall, she heard Martin's voice as he spoke to Jake.

''Do you realize what a difficult situation you're putting

her in? As an artist, she's known locally, but out of state it's a different story. She'd have to work from the ground up to establish herself in Colorado. It would take time before she could get the same kind of prices she gets here for her work.''

"If I owned property here, I'd be glad to let her use it."

"You do. This ranch."

"It's the tribe's land, you know that."

"Not while there's a Black Raven here," Martin answered.

Annie listened for Jake's reply, but none came. She took a deep breath, trying to ease the tension that gripped her as she realized that was his answer. Lost in thought, she stepped outside, and walked to the gate.

Jake caught up to her a few seconds later. "Do you have a few more minutes? There's something I'd like to talk to you about."

She followed him back inside to the study, and sat on one of the straight-backed chairs, trying to ease the pressure on her back. "What's up?"

"I want you to think back carefully and try to remember exactly what my father told you about the evidence he hid. Are you certain that he gave you no indication of where he'd stashed it?"

"I'm positive. There was so little time," she said, her voice a sad whisper.

"I searched the study because it seemed the most likely room, and I did find one hiding place," he said, telling her where he'd found the address book. "But he must have hidden the evidence he spoke about someplace else because there was nothing else in there and all the address book listed was the places Nick and I lived at over the years."

She considered it for a moment. "Your father was a great fan of mystery novels and may have used one to inspire him. Is there any chance that the hiding place you found has a false bottom or side?''

He looked at her in surprise. "I don't know. I never checked. Let's look right now."

He reached for the top shelf, cleared off the books and uncovered his father's secret place. Jake tapped the back panel and it sounded solid, but the left end of the recess had a hollow tone. "We may have something behind this board." He pushed on both sides of the wood, hoping to find a catch, but nothing happened.

"Let me take a look," she said.

"You're not tall enough. You'd need to stand on something."

"So help me steady this chair," she said, sliding one toward the bookcase.

He helped her up, and although it was difficult for her, Annie managed to balance herself enough to lean forward confidently. Like him, she tapped the inner walls of the small crevice, then pressed lightly on the corners. Nothing happened.

"See? My guess is that they hollowed out more of the adobe wall than they needed when they built this hiding spot. The hollow area isn't very big at all. Now, come down."

"One more minute." She closed her eyes and ran her fingers over the smooth wood. Her sense of touch was sensitive. Sometimes while carving it guided her more reliably than her eyes.

Suddenly she felt it. There was a slight indentation in the center. She opened her eyes but found it was barely visible, even when she was looking directly at it. Following her instincts, she pressed against it. The wood panel popped open and fell into her hands.

The crevice beyond was barely large enough to hold the

cache it contained. "There's a folded sheet of paper and a ring in here."

He helped her down, then took the items from her hand. He stared at the silver ring in surprise. It was crafted with an intricate raven design in its center.

"Do you recognize it?"

He nodded. "This was my father's. I remember when my mother gave it to him on his birthday many years back. He never took it off. But then, one day, I noticed he didn't have it on. He said he'd lost it."

He opened the letter and, as he began to silently read it, raw emotions flashed across his face. Once finished, he handed her the letter, not trusting his voice.

Annie read it.

If you've found this, Jake, then it's because I'm no longer around. You've known about this hiding place for many years, so I assume it's you who's reading this note. I saw you sneaking past my office that night when you broke curfew and I know you saw me putting some things up here. You never returned for a closer look, which was what I expected. But I knew that someday your duty would force you back for another look. Fathers don't live forever.

The ring is yours. As my eldest, it's part of your legacy and something your mother would have wanted you to have. No matter where life leads you, remember that you're a Black Raven. Wear the ring with pride.

Annie watched as he slipped the ring onto his finger. She noted the surprise on his face as he found it fit perfectly. "Some things are just meant to be, Jake," she said softly.

Hearing the whinny of horses and voices of men working outside, she glanced back up at the shelf. "Let's put the books back,'' she said. ''Out of respect, I think we should continue to protect his hiding place.'' As Jake gathered the books, Annie climbed back onto the chair and started to close the door to the hidden niche.

When Jake turned around and saw her up on the chair, he muttered a curse. ''You shouldn't be climbing up there on your own. Come on. Time to get down.'' He grasped her firmly by the sides, then lifted her gently off the chair and placed her in front of him.

His strength surprised her, but the gentleness of his touch was her undoing. As she saw herself mirrored in his eyes, the power of his gaze swept through her, making her blood sizzle.

She ran the tip of her tongue over her dry lips.

His mouth parted slightly.

Annie knew she should step back, away from him, but a force she couldn't resist compelled her to stay where she was.

It was at that precise moment that the baby kicked— hard. She gasped.

''Are you all right?'' he asked quickly.

She nodded and, taking his hand, placed it over her stomach. ''Can you feel the baby moving? She's kicking up a storm.''

Feeling the baby's movements against his palm, he smiled. ''She? Looks to me you've got a future football player.''

''I suppose it might be a boy. I wouldn't let them tell me when they did the ultrasound. But, in my heart, I think it's a girl.''

A sense of wonder and tenderness shone in Jake's eyes. He began stroking her stomach, and to her surprise, his touch seemed to calm the baby, though it sure wasn't doing much to calm her.

Excitement pulsed through her as he slid his hand beneath her clothing. Touching her bare skin, he continued caressing the swell of her belly. His touch sparked fires all through her. As her breathing quickened, he captured her gaze, probing her mind and her feelings like a skilled lover.

"I wish I could undress you now. I'd love every inch of your body until you needed me as badly as I do you."

His words weaved a spell around her. Her breathing was ragged, and a delicious weakness spread through her.

Jake pushed her sweater away from her shoulders, then opened her blouse. "You're so beautiful." He unfastened her bra and pushed it out of his way.

Her breasts, round and full, spilled into his work-hardened hands. As he teased her nipples with his thumb he saw her face become flushed and her eyes darken with passion. Her soft cry pierced him. He lowered his mouth to her breast, sucking it gently until she arched into him, holding his head against her.

Jake heard her cry out his name as she clung to him. She was all heat and passion. He left her breast and, as she moaned, he kissed her, catching the soft, lost sound with his mouth. His tongue played over hers with gentle mastery, his taste filling her senses and shattering the last of her self-control.

Their kiss turned hard then—fire meeting fire. He was fury and lighting. Thoughts slipped away, replaced by textures and sensations too powerful to resist. It was heaven and hellfire all at once.

Slowly they became aware of strong footsteps echoing down the hall, coming toward the study. Jake let go of her reluctantly and stepped away to block the door with his body as she quickly pulled her clothing back in place. "It's all right, Annie, I'll take care of this, and—"

There was no knock. The door to the study was suddenly thrown open, and Jake barely managed to step aside.

Muttering an angry oath, he turned to face their unwelcome intruder.

Annie, quickly adjusting her blouse, stared at the doorway in shock. Standing there was Jake's mirror image. She looked from one to the other, amazed. Their features were identical and, although they each looked ready for a major confrontation, there was a marked difference in their expressions. Jake's eyes blazed with pure fire while Nick's seemed as cold as ice.

"Hello, Jake. Care to step outside for a minute?" he asked, his voice hard as he took off his sport coat and draped it over the back of a chair.

Jake smiled, but his grin was nothing more than an answering challenge. "Whatever you say." He glanced at Annie. "This won't take long, Annie. I'll be right back."

She saw them stride down the hall, matching each other step for step. She'd sensed a peculiar tension between them. It wasn't animosity, but something less intense, though no less volatile.

Annie stepped to the window as they exited through the kitchen and walked out to the backyard. Fascinated, she studied the two men. She'd assumed that all Nick had wanted was some privacy, but there was more going on. She watched and listened carefully.

Nick's muscles pressed against his tight pullover sweater as they stood eye-to-eye. Jake's stance was more relaxed, but his shoulders were rigid, betraying his tension.

"Okay, little brother. We're here. Now what?"

"I spoke to Captain Mora," he said bruskly. "It seems you knew that Dad was in trouble, but you never told me. Why?"

"There was no reason to believe he was in any danger. Besides, it was his place to tell you, not mine."

"Like hell." With a lightning-fast jab, Nick slugged Jake in the jaw, knocking him to the ground.

# Chapter Ten

Jake sat on the frozen ground and wiggled his jaw to make sure everything still worked. "Did you *have* to do that?"

"Yeah," Nick replied. "You deserved it. The second you found out that there was trouble brewing here, you should have told me."

Jake rose slowly, then in a lightning-fast move, kicked out, hitting Nick behind the knees, toppling him to the ground. "I'm not going to pound your face into the ground this time, brother, it's just too cold outside for a fight. But if you *ever* do that again, I'll make sure your jaw feels worse than mine." He offered his brother a hand up.

"Tell me about the woman," Nick said, getting to his feet. "She yours?"

"No, brother. And neither's the baby she's carrying. She's a widow." He filled Nick in on what he'd learned.

"I stopped by the police station and was told that you're heavily involved in the investigation. To top things off, Captain Mora told me he thinks you're withholding evidence."

"I am, but it's not what he thinks. I found something recently, and I wanted you to have a chance to see it before I let it out of my hands."

They went back inside the house and, as they walked

into the study, Jake saw the long, thoughtful look Annie gave them. Their different clothing made them easy to identify now that they were side by side. He was wearing jeans and a fleece shirt, while Nick wore corduroy slacks and a pullover sweater. As he looked at her, Jake wondered if Annie would have been able to tell them apart otherwise. It would have meant a lot to him if she could.

Annie looked at Jake and smiled. "Are you two okay?"

Jake grinned. "Yeah. My brother and I were just saying 'I love you' in our own special way."

"My brother has a limited vocabulary," Nick said, extending his hand and introducing himself.

"I know you two have a lot to talk about, so I'll get back to my work," she said, walking to the door. "I'll be back later."

Jake felt that peculiar tug in his gut as she smiled gently at him. She could destroy him with just one sweet look.

Aware that Nick was watching, he looked away from her and walked to the desk. "Let me bring you up to speed," he said as Annie shut the door behind her. He showed Nick the blackmail note, warning him not to take it out of the plastic bag, and filled him in about the rest.

"Mora was right," Nick said after Jake finished. "You're very involved. After everything I've learned, I don't blame you at all, but there's one thing I can't figure out. I get the feeling Annie's right beside you on this. What I don't understand is why?"

"She was like a daughter to Dad. She's also a threat to the killer because she was there when he was murdered. Since it's her friendship and loyalty to him that has put her in danger, I intend to do my best to protect her."

"All right. If she was under Dad's protection, she's now under ours," Nick said.

As Jake took back the blackmail note, Nick noticed the

ring on his finger. "That's Dad's ring. He lost it years ago. Where did you find it?"

Jake told him. "It was meant for me," he said, showing him the letter. As Nick finished reading it, Jake added, "But it's yours if you want it."

Nick shook his head. "No, in your own way, you were closer to him than I ever was. He was right to leave it to you. What I *would* like is our mother's diary. If Uncle Thomas wants it, and the blackmailer stole it and used it against our father, all the more reason to get it back into safe hands."

"I'll make sure we get it back," Jake vowed. "But my first priority is to make sure Dad's killer is brought to justice."

"No. What we have to do is concentrate on the rest of the picture while the police do their work. You and I have to take a really close look at the impact Dad's death will have on the pueblo. We can't just close down the ranch, sell what's left, and walk away."

"The problem is, we both have businesses to run. We can't stick around here indefinitely."

"True, but there's a matter of responsibility—to the pueblo and to the families who have depended on the Black Ravens for years. Whether we choose to live here or not, we are still members of this tribe."

"I won't stay at this ranch one minute longer than necessary," Jake said slowly. "There are too many memories here for me, Nick—mostly bad ones."

"I know. It's the same for me. But there's more to it than just you and me."

Jake started to answer when a knock sounded at the door. "Come in," he said impatiently.

Annie stepped inside, followed by Martin. "Captain Mora is here," Annie said. "He stopped me on my way to the bunkhouse and asked me about the will. I told him Patrick Kelly is our best hope of finding it.''

"Shall I show him in here?" Martin asked.

Jake nodded. "I guess you two said hello earlier?" he said, looking at Martin then at Nick, and noting the lack of surprise on either of their faces.

"Yes." Martin looked at Nick. "As I said, it's very good to have you back, Nicky."

After Martin left, Jake turned to his brother. "I'm going to give Mora the blackmail note unless you want more time to look it over."

"No, I've seen all I need."

As Jake glanced at Annie, something hard in him seemed to melt away. Her belly was huge and she looked so vulnerable just standing there, waiting for Mora. If the captain gave her a hard time, he'd have to answer to him for it.

"Sit down, Annie," Jake said, offering her a chair. "Let's see what else the police have to say."

Mora came in a moment later. Jake handed him the blackmail note and Mora studied it. "Any idea who the blackmailer might be?"

"None," Jake said and Martin shook his head.

"All right. I'll handle it from this point on," he said. "I came to ask if you needed any help with the funeral arrangements. I understand the body's been released."

All eyes were on Jake and he didn't have to look around to verify it. "The funeral will be small, mostly family. Thank you for your offer, but it's not necessary."

"The burial must take place tomorrow morning," Martin said. "If your father's buried after the sun has reached its zenith, there'll be many deaths."

Jake felt a tightening in his chest. He'd spent almost all his adult life proving himself as a man, not as an Indian male. The rituals, and the Tewa part of him that he'd tried so hard to leave behind, were now taking over his life, making demands he wasn't sure he could meet.

"I'll attend the wake, of course, but I don't think I'm allowed to accompany you during the rituals," Annie said sadly. "I'm not Tewa."

Jake squared his shoulders. He knew she wanted to go, and he had a feeling his father would have wanted her there, too. "*We'll* decide who comes to our family rituals. And because of your friendship with our father, you'll be considered family. But the wake is an all-night function, and the visit to the shrine requires a long walk that's mostly uphill. Do you think you could handle it?"

"Yes, I know I can."

"All right, then. You'll come with me." He challenged Martin and Nick with a glance, but they simply nodded in approval.

After Martin led Captain Mora out, Nick excused himself, needing to unpack, and Annie and Jake remained alone in the study.

"If there's anything I can do for you, just let me know," Annie said. "I know how much it hurts to have to say goodbye to a family member."

"I didn't think it would hurt—not at this stage. I thought I'd handled that already," Jake said, then realized what he'd just admitted. He looked at her quickly, but there was only understanding in her expression.

"You can't run away from sorrow," she said gently. "I know. I've tried many times."

Annie was cutting through his pain, touching his heart and making a place for herself there, though she didn't know it.

"Tell me how I can help you," she said again.

"Be there for me until my father's in the ground, and his spirit is released," he answered.

"I will."

Her softness, her very nature, reminded him constantly that he was a man and she was a woman and that they were much alone. As she walked away, he felt a familiar ache inside him. His feelings for Annie were deepening despite his efforts to fight them.

The knowledge unsettled him. His parents' marriage had shown him that feelings weren't enough in a relationship, and could destroy two hearts, no matter how brave or strong.

He wouldn't let that happen to Annie or to him. It was better to walk away, though it tore out a piece of his heart, than risk hurting the woman he'd come to love.

THE SPANISH-CATHOLIC-derived *velorio,* or wake, was held for close friends and family. Others in the village came to pay their respects, then left. Meals were served throughout the night, but most of the time was occupied by the singing of funeral dirges and prayers.

As the sun rose over the hills and the wake came to a close, funeral dirges continued to echo in Jake's mind. He was tired. The worst of it had been tending to his father's body. Tradition had dictated they dress the body. He wasn't even sure how he'd managed to get through it. During the grim task, Nick and he had supported each other in a way they hadn't since childhood. In just the past eight hours, the bond between them had strengthened more than he ever would have thought possible.

Jake looked at Annie. She'd remained by his side just as she'd promised. Her presence warmed him, taking away the chill that had wrapped itself around his heart. After the men left to prepare the grave at the cemetery, he led all those who'd spent the entire night at the wake, including Annie, down the frozen road.

Annie stood beside him at the grave site, his own source of comfort on this emotionally draining morning.

After the body was buried, and they began walking away, she placed her hand on his arm and spoke for the first time in hours. "Patrick Kelly has returned. His was the call I took earlier this morning. He said he'd be by later today, after the Tewa portion of the ritual is over. He has a copy of the will."

The news should have been a relief, but it wasn't. Now, more than ever, Jake felt torn between the need to find the killer and go, and his desire to remain with Annie.

Martin approached. "It's time for the releasing rite. It would have been better for both of you if you'd had a chance to rest first, but it can't be helped. We've lost too much time because of the police investigation."

"Nick and I are ready," Jake said, glancing at his brother, who nodded. He then looked at Annie. "Are you sure you're up to this?"

"I'll be fine," she assured him. "It means a lot to me to be included."

Her soft words were like a whispered song to his heart. The simple truth was that he needed her with him now. "Then let's go."

"A room has been cleared in the house in preparation for the beginning of the rite," Martin said.

When they arrived at the house, Jake led the way to the now-empty dining room. Several pots of food were laid out on the floor. As the senior male, Jake knew this part of the ceremony would fall to him.

Taking a portion of the food inside each basket with his left hand, he placed it into a new cooking pot made especially for the ceremony. He smoked native tobacco, blowing smoke over the pot, then made a sweeping motion over each person in the room. It was a step toward releasing his father's spirit, but sorrow weighed heavily on him as he worked.

Jake then took a piece of ''dead'' or spent charcoal from the fireplace and placed it under his tongue. The room was encased in silence as he wrapped himself in a blanket and waited for all the others to cover themselves, as well.

As he looked at Annie, he noticed there were tears in her eyes. He envied the closeness she'd shared with his father. It hadn't been that way between his father and him for many years, even though they'd been flesh and blood. With effort, he forced himself not to think of the bad times, but rather to concentrate only on the good. It was his responsibility to make sure his father's spirit knew he was being forgiven for all his past transgressions. That act was at the heart of the releasing rite and was what would allow his father's spirit to go in peace. Yet letting go was the most difficult task of all.

Jake took the pot and led the small procession up the hillside to the shrine. The climb was arduous, and the heavy hearts of those around him touched him, adding to his own burden. He looked at Annie, worried, but Martin was with her and she seemed to be handling everything well.

Weary from the climb and the sorrow, they finally reached the summit. Jake presented the ''feast'' in the pot to his ancestors, who were said to be waiting there. Then three feet from the shrine, he dropped the pot, breaking it, according to ritual.

The people lined up behind him as he drew four lines on the sand. Then spitting out a bit of the charcoal, and turning to the cardinal directions, he invoked the soul of his father, asking him to release his hold on the living.

He repeated the ritual several times on the way back. Then, at the house, the rite was performed again at the windows and the front door. It was there that he finally rid himself of the last of the charcoal in his mouth. The way back had now been muddied for his father's spirit.

"You are free to go. Help us by bringing us long life and abundance."

As Jake intoned the words, the procession breathed a sigh of relief. According to belief, his father would now dwell in peace in the land of endless cicada singing.

As they each prepared to leave, Jake thanked them in the manner dictated by custom.

Annie was the last to approach him. "May you have life," he whispered to her, his voice softening instinctively as he spoke to her.

"Let it be so," she answered as the others had. Aware that they were alone now, Nick and Martin were saying goodbye to people down the road, Annie gave his hand a gentle squeeze.

The warmth of her touch wrapped itself around him. No medicine could have healed his wounded soul better than she had with that simple gesture. He captured her gaze, trying to convey with that one look what he couldn't put into words.

Her expression softened and the smile she gave him was filled with tenderness. Without words, she'd told him everything he needed to know. In her face, he saw the expression of love.

# Chapter Eleven

Annie stood with Jake and watched the people walk away. Martin had just gone inside to fix them something warm to eat. As the clouds covered the sun and the temperature dropped, she turned to go inside, but was stopped by an out-of-breath Martin.

"Wait. Don't come any farther. We've had a break-in," he said.

"Stay with her," Jake ordered Martin, walking past Annie quickly. To Nick, he said, "Let's make sure the intruder is really gone." As he went down the hall, Nick followed just a step behind.

Annie stood by the open door on the portal, remembering the man dressed as Santa Claus who'd appeared out of the dark and knocked her down the day of the murder. Her skin prickled and her heart began to beat faster. But it was daylight now. There were no terrors hidden in the shadows.

"It's all clear," Jake said, returning to meet them. "Come inside and get warm. It's too cold to stay outside any longer."

Martin called the police and they responded within ten minutes. Mora and his men searched for evidence and dusted for prints, but it was clear from Mora's attitude that he didn't believe they'd turn up anything useful. The back door had obviously been kicked in.

Two hours later, after the officers had gone, they gathered in the study.

Annie glanced at Martin. "You were inside before any of us, Martin," she said. "Did you manage to catch a glimpse of the intruder?"

"Mora asked me the same thing, and I'll tell you what I told him. I heard a noise in the back as I opened the door, but by the time I reached the kitchen, the door was open and the intruder gone."

Looking at the chaos in the study, Annie felt her throat constrict. File cabinets had been opened and files lay scattered everywhere. Paintings had been taken off the walls and the contents of the desk drawers were strewn about on chairs and the floor.

"Did Dad keep any cash here?" Nick asked.

"Not that I know of," Jake answered.

"I don't think this is a simple robbery. I noticed the gun cabinet in the hall seemed untouched," Annie said.

"All the accounting ledgers are gone," Jake said, searching through and around the file cabinet.

He looked up at the bookshelf. Some of the books had been pushed aside, and others lay on the floor, but the section in front of the niche had not been disturbed.

Annie met his gaze, then nodded once in silence. That was "score one for them."

"Paul's bedroom has been ransacked, as well, but it doesn't look as bad as this place," Martin said.

They went upstairs and, as they entered Paul's former room, Annie spotted the indentations in the carpet that signaled that the nightstand had been moved.

"Let's start here," she said, directing their attention to what she'd noticed.

Nick and Jake moved the heavy, oak nightstand aside, but there was nothing behind it. Jake crouched by the wall and tapped the wood lightly. Near the edge of the wall there was a seam that looked like a crack in the adobe. Pressing on it with his fingers, he felt it give and a small hinged door came open. The carved-out space was empty.

"The police didn't find this spot or they'd have asked about it. Something was kept here at one time, though not recently," Jake said. "You can see a faint outline of heavy dust on the bottom of this hiding place. Whatever was stored there was small, but it was taken out of here a while back. See the lighter layer of dust deposited after it was removed? From the outline, I think it may have been a book."

Jake silently considered the possibility that it might have been the diary. Maybe the blackmailer had come back to the same crevice, hoping to find something else of value there.

"Unfortunately," Jake continued, "we have no way of knowing if the intruder found everything he wanted. The accounting ledgers are missing, and I'll probably find some other business papers gone, as well, but there's no telling what he was really after."

"There's also something else to consider. This person knew about the releasing rite being held this morning," Martin added. "The break-in was perfectly timed."

"Paul warned us that the killer is someone masquerading as a friend," Annie said.

Although they worked together to restore order to the house, it was hours before everything was back in its place. By the time they finally returned to the study, it was four in the afternoon.

Nick was silent, his expression troubled. Jake was harder

to read. He carried himself with fierce containment as he stood beside the window, staring outside.

"The killer has been one step ahead since day one," Jake said, breaking the silence. "Now he has proprietary information about Dad's business and finances. We've lost whatever answers or clues were in those ledgers and accounting books. We have to find a way to turn the tables on him before he gets away with everything."

Nick shook his head. "Tracking a killer is the police's job. Let them do their work."

"Our father was killed, and his important papers, including, possibly, the hidden evidence Dad left for us, are now gone. Those facts alone make it our business."

Nick was about to reply when someone came to the front door. Martin answered it, and returned with Patrick Kelly. The middle-aged Anglo attorney entered the room and shook hands with both Jake and Nick. "I'm very sorry to hear about your father."

Jake gestured for him to take a seat. "We've been looking everywhere for a will."

"I have a copy and brought it with me. It's important I review it with you all now because some of the clauses are time dependent."

"We're eager to hear what the will says," Jake said, motioning for Kelly to use the desk.

"Everyone mentioned in the will is here now, so let's get started," Kelly said, as he waited for everyone to take a seat before he began reading out loud.

Annie felt the tension in the room clearly. It was almost as if the air itself had grown heavier. Martin was the first person mentioned in the will. He had been left a respectable sum.

Patrick Kelly suddenly stopped reading and looked up. "The rest will be a lot more complicated and, to really understand it, you need to know what was going through your father's mind at the time." He held Jake's gaze. "More than anything else, your father really believed that if he forced you to stay here for a length of time, you would learn to love the ranch as he had, Jake."

Kelly then looked at Nick. "Nick, your father knew that, unlike Jake, you liked taking your time before making decisions. But he just wasn't confident that you could ever be persuaded to commit to the ranch for its own sake. That's why he felt the future of Black Raven Ranch rested in Jake's hands. Paul believed that Jake had a gift when it came to working with the horses, and that his love for the animals was the key ingredient needed to keep the ranch going."

Kelly looked at Jake. "But he also knew that you would resist staying. That's why he had me add the following clauses to this will."

He resumed reading the will, and no one moved. "Nick, Annie and Jake will have to live at the ranch house for one year before anyone, including Martin, can claim their inheritance," Kelly said at last, finishing.

Jake glared at Kelly. "I'll contest this. There's no way we can all stay and run this ranch together. I've got my own business to take care of and so does Nick. And Annie has her own life. Did Dad just forget all that?"

"No. He expected you all to find a way to do both. Any of you can leave for up to a week at a time, and still comply with the terms. One more thing. Paul insisted you all begin living at the ranch within a week after the releasing rite. Providing you agree to his terms, you will all inherit one-third of the estate at the end of twelve months. The land itself, of course, belongs to the pueblo, and reverts to them if everything is liquidated."

Jake stood abruptly, fists clenched. "My attorneys will

have this thrown out of court. I don't care about the money, but my father can't be allowed to control our lives.''

"I have to warn you that contesting this will carries immediate penalties. Should either you, Nick, or Annie choose to circumvent or otherwise act against its intent, then three-quarters of the estate's assets will be given to the pueblo. Martin will get the remaining portion. If Martin contests it, then all of you must move out within a week, and the pueblo gets everything.''

Jake looked as if someone had just punched him hard in the stomach. He sat again.

"I'm sorry, but I can't go along with any of this,'' Annie said, rising and walking toward the door.

"Think before you decide,'' Kelly said in his best, most persuasive voice. "This will buy you time to become better known regionally as an artist, and could provide immediate financial security for you and your baby.''

Annie felt trapped. If she turned it down, would she be sacrificing the needs of her child to save her pride? She needed a place to live and really did want to stay here, where she had friends and the nurse midwife she trusted. If she left, she'd be all alone, and broke. Worst of all, there was also no guarantee the killer wouldn't come after her, putting her and the baby in even greater danger.

Tears welled up in her eyes and she struggled not to blink, determined to not let them see her cry as she returned to her seat.

"Look at it logically, from a business point of view,'' Kelly said to all of them. "What Paul has really done is guarantee everyone a place to live and work for at least one year.''

Annie glanced at Martin, and saw the emotions that warred inside him play across his face. He'd wanted the ranch to survive and so had she. Many depended on it, but being forced to do something against their will was not the right way.

Kelly pulled a video tape from his briefcase. "I was with your father when he taped this." Kelly placed the tape in Jake's hands. "Let him explain in his own words why he's chosen to do this. I believe everything will make more sense to all of you then."

Annie, stunned, walked out of the room with Jake, Nick, and Martin. As they stepped into the living room, Jake led Annie to the massive entertainment center. "Don't worry, Annie," Jake said, loud enough for only her to hear. "We'll figure something out."

Jake shoved the tape into the machine, anger punctuating his every movement.

Annie heard the tape click into the machine, then as Paul's image flickered on the television monitor, she sucked in a breath. His easy smile, his gentle eyes, looked back at her now. Sorrow for the friend she'd lost filled her heart. "Hello, Jake. Nick. And Annie. I know you're here with my boys and Martin, and wondering why I've done this to all of you."

Paul leaned back in his chair. "Let me explain, and maybe then you'll understand. I know you two boys—now men, may never forgive me for throwing you out of the house, but it was the only way I could think of to end the misdirected competition you had with each other and force you to focus solely on your own futures.

"If you two had remained at home, with me constantly looking over your shoulders and forcing my opinions upon you, you wouldn't have come into your own as you have. Part of my legacy was forcing you to find yourselves as men—not as twins, and getting each of you to accomplish something on your own, if only to prove to yourselves how wrong I'd been."

Paul stopped a second, cleared his throat and looked away from the camera a moment, then continued. "You never knew this, but I've been watching you, Jake, and you, Nick, ever since you left the ranch. There were times I thought I should step in and help one or the other of you boys through a crisis, but I held back, and, sure enough, each time you prevailed. And, though you may hate me for my methods, you'll have to admit that you are now strong, self-reliant, successful men who owe nothing to anyone else for your accomplishments."

Paul took a drink from a glass of water, then resumed his statement. "I'm as proud as any man could be of his sons, and I only regret that we couldn't have been together again as a family for a while. I wanted that more than anything else in my life. But that has ended now, and it's time for the living to move on."

He paused, then continued. "Annie, if you're listening to this tape, then it must be before your baby's first birthday. After that, I'd intended to change the terms of the will depending on what I learned about Jake and Nick, and how your own career was going. I've done what I have partly for you, though you may not believe that. You see, I know that your pride keeps you from asking anyone for help and I wanted to make sure you and the baby would be looked after at this critical time in your life. I'm the closest to a father you've ever had, and I do love you. I ask you now to trust me."

Annie wiped the tears from her eyes. She did trust him. He'd been a loyal friend and mentor. And, admittedly, what he was asking her to do was in her and the pueblo's best interests. Whether it would benefit Jake and Nick would depend largely on them.

Paul paused, measuring his words. "Jake, you're my son, and I love you, but I see you making the same mistakes I made when I was your age. You need to let others into your life, to learn what it really means to care. Unless you learn how to open your heart, you'll end up as alone as I am, and that's the last thing I want for you. Annie's gentleness can teach you a lot and, if I'm right, she'll touch your heart in the very way you need most."

Paul paused again, stared at his desk, then looked up at the camera. "Annie, help my son stop running from the best life has to offer. You know about love. It defines everything about you—your courage, your passion. Help him embrace life as you have. I don't want Jake to end up like me, and there's a lot of me in my son."

"There's nothing of you in me," Jake answered the video image, then looked away in disgust.

As if he'd heard, Paul leaned back and smiled. "I can hear him protesting, though in his heart he knows it's true." He shook his head slowly then, after a brief silence, continued. "Nick, it's extremely important that you remain at the pueblo. You don't know it yet, but your greatest joy, and maybe your greatest sorrow, is here, waiting for you. Everything you believe about yourself will be tested. But I'm confident that you'll eventually embrace your destiny the same way you do everything else—with your whole heart.

"I know you won't end up as I have, Nicky. Everything that will define you as a man, the very things you love the most, are here, and all you'll have to do is find the courage to reach out for them. Your future, and a small surprise—" Paul suddenly chuckled "—will make your stay the most interesting time of your life."

Jake studied his brother's expression. Nick stood rock-still, guarding his thoughts fiercely.

"But it's you, Jake, I worry about," Paul continued. "Trying to be your own man, you're likely to talk yourself out of the things that matter most. What I'm giving you now is not a punishment. It's my final gift to you—a son I'll always love.''

As the tape faded to black, Annie shook her head. ''I know this is all well-intentioned, but Paul overstepped his bounds.''

''Now do you see that I was right about my father? He always manipulated everyone around him. He's even trying to do it from his grave.''

Martin stood. ''I'll abide by whatever you all decide. This is a family matter and that's the way it should remain.'' He walked out before Jake could stop him.

''As much as I hate to say it,'' Nick said, ''Kelly is right. We have to think this out carefully before we do anything. This ranch is the heart of the pueblo.''

''I can't cast all the hands out of their jobs,'' Jake said. ''Like it or not, my father pulled the right strings this time. I still intend to come up with a way around it, but I'll need time.''

''Which means we have to comply with the will, at least for the time being. It's the only way to buy time,'' Nick said. ''I'm in.''

''I vote we go along with it,'' Jake said, then looked at Annie.

''Me, too,'' Annie said, knowing she didn't really have a choice with the baby almost due. She also didn't want to deny the twins their inheritance, or go against Paul's last wishes.

Nick stood. ''Then it's settled.'' He walked back to the study where Kelly was waiting.

''At least by staying, we'll get to finish what we started,'' Annie said. ''The fact is, we still have to find Paul's killer and we can't do that without each other, and the safety of being here among friends.''

"I need your help, too," Jake said. "You know the people in my father's life better than I do."

They stepped back into the study and joined Nick and Patrick Kelly.

Kelly was pleased with their decision to comply with Paul's wishes. "Good. Then life can go on as usual for all those depending on the ranch," Kelly said, standing.

As Annie accompanied Kelly to the door, Nick glanced at Jake. "Your feelings for Annie are strong, but you both have a great deal of pride. Don't let that keep you from reaching out to each other, Jake. No regret is harder to bear than the one that comes from something left undone."

Jake heard the raw emotion in his brother's voice. Whatever was bothering Nick was clearly painful to him. He waited for Nick to say more but he never did. Not wanting to press his brother to talk about it before he was ready, Jake backed off. Instinct told him that when Nick spoke of love lost, he spoke from firsthand experience.

"Dad's attempt to make us do what he wants could backfire," Jake said. "Dad never learned that if you force something to happen, it could end up falling apart. In an attempt to bring us all together, he may be driving a wedge between us, and Annie and I may pay the greatest price. I have to find a way around this will, Nick, before any more damage is done."

# Chapter Twelve

It was sometime after ten but, as usual, Annie was too restless to sleep. She lay in bed listening to the wind rattle long-dead leaves against the window pane.

Turning her back to the window, she tried to will herself to sleep, but her blood suddenly froze as the moonlight cast the silhouette of a man on the wall. A man with a shotgun.

Annie moved off the bed, heading for cover and reaching for the phone just as two loud gunshots echoed in the silence around her. Glass shattered and her pillow jerked twice, feathers exploding from the fabric. She heard the sound of screaming, then realized it was coming from her.

Huddled with her back against the wall, Annie dialed Jake's number, but by then, he and Nick were banging at her door.

ONE HOUR LATER, after the sheriff had come and gone, Annie and Jake sat in chairs in the *sala* of the main house. A crackling piñon fire in the corner fireplace felt almost as comforting as having Jake there with her.

"Tomorrow you'll move into the ranch house," Jake declared. "I should have insisted after the poisoning attempt. This just confirms my father's killer has chosen you as his next target. Something you know, or are certain to uncover, is a threat to him. We've got to find out what that is before it's too late.''

Annie stood and walked over to the Christmas tree that she and Paul had decorated only a few days ago. Now Paul was dead, and she was next. ''How could everything go so wrong so close to Christmas? What happened to 'peace on earth, good will to men'?''

''We won't have any peace until we catch my father's murderer.'' Jake moved to join her, and studied the ornaments. He cupped a hand-painted glass ball with the lifelike image of a black raven soaring over a solitary pine. ''My mother made that for me when I was ten. See my name hidden among the tree branches?'' Jake pointed to the spot.

''Your father hung that one on the tree himself, and another he said was Nick's.'' She looked around. ''Here it is.'' This ornament depicted a raven above a rocky mesa. She looked at Jake. ''I wish you could have heard how soft Paul's voice got when he spoke about those days when you were all truly a family. He told me those had been the best years of his life.''

She could see the emotions warring inside Jake as he struggled between the love he'd once felt toward his father and the bitterness he'd learned in his latter years. Then Jake looked up at the angel on the top. ''That's new, yet it looks very old. Did you do that?''

Annie nodded. ''I made it a long time ago, but since I didn't have a Christmas tree, I gave it to Paul to use because I knew he liked it.''

''My father was lucky to have you as a friend.''

''Sometimes friendships are so short,'' Annie whispered. ''I don't know how many more loved ones I can stand to lose.''

Jake, standing behind her, pulled Annie tightly against him. ''You're not going to lose anyone, Annie. I promise.

There's love for you here, too. All you have to do is reach out.''

She shivered as his breath caressed her cheek. His strength tempted her to surrender, but she needed to stand on her own. "I'm afraid to reach out to anyone." She slipped from his arms and walked to the fireplace, suddenly cold. "Life is just too uncertain, and my baby will need more than promises."

"Christmas is a time for miracles, Annie. You're carrying one inside you now."

"I believe in miracles, Jake, but I believe in myself even more." Annie forced herself to meet his gaze. "I can promise you one thing. My child *will* grow up knowing about the Black Ravens and their rare brand of courage, and what that meant to me at the time I needed them most."

Jake watched her leave the room.

Feeling more alone than ever, he placed another log in the fire, and sat in the chair. Without Annie, he'd never really be warm again.

THE FOLLOWING MORNING Jake had Rick and the other ranch hands install lights with motion detectors against each exterior wall of the house, for extra security. The locks on the house were changed, as well.

Though Jake, Nick, and Martin were doing the heavy work, it took several hours to move Annie's things from the bunkhouse to the main house.

"Annie, I think you should reconsider the room you chose last night. There's no doubt someone is out to kill you," Jake reminded her. "It would be easier for all of us to watch each other's backs if we at least stay in the same section of the house."

"Jake makes a good point, Annie," Nick added.

"With the new dead bolt in the kitchen, and that massive

front door, any intruder would make a lot of noise getting inside this house,'' she answered. ''And if they try to approach a window, the motion detector lights will come on. I'll stay downstairs.''

Knowing he'd get nowhere insisting, Jake conceded. Annie had a will of iron that was a match for his. He was used to having his own way and whenever she challenged him, every masculine instinct he possessed came to the forefront. But it was hard to fight someone who stood her ground with such quiet dignity. He had no defenses against someone such as her—a gentle but indomitable spirit with a mind of her own.

Annie walked to the doorway of the two adjoining rooms she'd chosen, then gestured inside. ''This larger one will be my bedroom,'' she said. ''The other, the nursery. But I'll also need a room to work in, something with much more light than either of these.''

''I already have something in mind for that,'' Jake said. ''There's a room at the end of this hall that served as my mother's greenhouse. The south wall is all windows, but they can be shuttered at night.''

Annie followed Jake, checked out the greenhouse, then nodded. ''I'd noticed this room from outside the house but I'd never been in it until now. It'll need to be cleaned out, but it's perfect.''

It didn't take long for the men to set up the beds and position the furniture in the bedroom and nursery. Once the task was finished, they left, giving her the privacy she'd asked for. Annie spent the rest of the day fixing up the nursery, and trying to make the rooms seem like home.

ANNIE WOKE UP EARLY the next morning. She felt a momentary stab of fear as her eyes opened and she took in the unfamiliar surroundings. Then, remembering she was in her new room at the ranch house, she forced herself to relax.

Dressing quickly, Annie went to the kitchen to fix herself something to eat, enjoying the quiet of the early morning.

Jake came in a short time later. "Good morning, Jake. You're up early," she greeted.

He looked at her and smiled. "How did you know it was me and not Nick? Did Nick already come through here wearing different clothes?"

"No, but I can tell you apart."

Jake said nothing, but the smile he gave her left her body tingling.

Annie watched him as he prepared his breakfast, aware of everything about him. His shirt hung open, exposing his muscular chest and strong build. Sensing her scrutiny, he looked back at her, his eyes dark and intense. Small fires raced up her spine as awareness shimmered between them.

She tore her gaze from his, trying to make the effort look effortless and casual. "What are you doing up so early? Nobody else is up yet."

"I didn't sleep very well," he admitted, growing somber. "I've been giving a lot of thought to the theft of my mother's diary. I have no evidence, except for the pattern of dust, but I suspect it was hidden at one time in the spot we recently discovered inside my father's room. That means the blackmailer must have had both access to this house and plenty of time to search. And he must have been nothing short of fearless, or driven. The doors to the house were usually kept unlocked, but there was always someone around—ranch hands, Martin, or even Dad himself."

"Okay, let's assume the blackmailer is someone who normally had access to the house, or knew the layout well. Who does that include... Martin, me, and more recently, Nick and you. But if any of us had wanted to search for something, we would have done it more carefully. We have unlimited access. And, of course, none of us could have been responsible for the break-in the day of the releasing rite since we were all together at the time.'' She remembered then that Martin had come back before any of them to finish preparations. Annie was about to remind Jake of that, when he continued.

"There's also Virgil Lowman. He was my mother's friend and my father's trusted associate. And don't forget my uncle, or the wranglers who work here regularly. Then there's Iris, my father's former housekeeper and cook.''

"You think she might have taken the diary when she was fired?''

"She could have, though we really have no clear motive to indicate why she'd do that. So the main question remains unanswered. What kind of evidence did my father have that made someone forego blackmail and commit murder instead?''

"You're assuming the thief and the killer are one and the same.''

"I am,'' he admitted. "I've known most of the people on this pueblo all my life. I have difficulty believing that there are two crooks of this caliber so closely linked to my father—one a vicious killer and the other a patient thief. Our tribe is made up of gentle, peaceful people.''

He'd used the word "our'' and that surprised her, but not as much as the love and respect that had resonated through his words. "You have some fond memories of your life here. They're not all bad ones. Do you realize that?''

Jake nodded. "I've come to realize that lately. I've tended to remember the things that brought me pain more than the things that brought me happiness.''

"That's natural but don't forget the good times. If you do, you'll only end up cheating yourself.'' Annie washed her empty cereal bowl and placed it in the drain rack. "If you'll excuse me, I need to finish setting up my studio. I've only got four days to finish my carvings."

"The tables and chairs will have to be moved in there to give you more space. Let me help you with that."

As they entered the old greenhouse, bright and warm but full of clutter, Nick came to join them. "We'll need to take some of this stuff out of here so you can have room to work. From the looks of it, I'd say it's been used as a storage room since Mom died."

Annie looked at the potting bench, then walked to the antique rolltop desk that stood against the north wall. "Why would anyone put a beautiful piece of furniture like this in a storage room?"

"Dad probably moved it in here after Mother died just to get it out of his way. He has a desk of his own." Jake looked at Annie. "We'll move it out for you."

She sat on the wooden chair in front of it. "No, I can use it for my business papers. It's really beautiful. I've always loved these big oak desks." She pushed up the tambour lid and looked inside.

There was a sketchbook inside filled with drawings and studies of landscapes, animals and local structures around the pueblo. Each sketch was dated, but not signed, though it was obviously Saya's work.

Jake came to stand behind her. "Based on those dates, Mom must have kept up her art even after Dad destroyed the bunkhouse, if only with sketches. The last date is just a month before she died." Jake's expression grew pensive. "This desk must have been her hiding place. I wonder if Dad ever knew?"

"I think he probably found out after she died," Annie said. "He must have been the one who cleared out this desk, since the only thing still in here is the sketchbook."

Annie searched through the top section, but found nothing at all. When she got to the small compartments in the center, one was stuck. She worked the small drawer, moving it from side to side until it slid open. "A piece of paper was wedged in the back corner. That's why it wouldn't open. The drawer's not damaged."

Out of curiosity, Annie unfolded the paper. "It's a bank deposit slip dated twenty years ago. It has your mother's name on it."

Jake took it from her hand. "It's not from a joint account," he said after a brief pause. "It looks like Mom had a few secrets of her own."

JAKE SAT in the office with Annie and Nick, studying the three deposit slips they'd found after searching through the entire desk. "There's over four thousand dollars' worth of deposits here. But I don't recall seeing anything in my father's financial records that indicated my mother had a personal account. From what I know about my father, too, it seems unlikely he would have allowed her to have one."

"You should probably talk to Virgil Lowman," Annie said. "He might be able to shed some light on this."

Jake nodded. "I'll call him as soon as the bank opens, which should be in another forty minutes."

"This account was probably closed or turned over to Dad after Mom died," Nick said. "But I can't figure out why Mom had her own account. She didn't have an outside job, did she?"

"Not that I know of," Jake answered. "But maybe she sold other sketches, or found a way to paint in secret, and then sold her work so Dad wouldn't find out."

Nick paced around the room. "Give the deposit slips to Captain Mora and see if he can make anything of it."

Jake shook his head. "I don't want to turn anything over

to Mora that isn't linked to the murder. It makes no sense to give details of our family's personal business to a stranger.''

"Good point," Nick conceded, "but before you follow up on those deposits, there's something else that needs our immediate attention. I was talking to the ranch hands earlier, and I found out that their paychecks are long overdue. They hadn't said anything out of respect for our father's death, but they depend on that money and we've got to take care of them. It's only a few days now until Christmas and they need their checks. We'll have to find their last month's check stubs to figure out how much they should be paid, too, since the business records have been stolen.''

Jake looked at his brother in surprise. "I know the men need to get paid, and we'll get to it right away, but how can you stay so focused on 'business as usual' when the death of our father is still unresolved?''

"I want to see justice done, but I also know that it won't change anything." Nick paused, then met his brother's gaze. "I think that the real reason you're concentrating on finding the killer is because, without Dad, there's nothing for you to focus your anger on. Some part of you wants to prove that you're better than him. So instead of looking around and seeing what needs to be done right now, you're trying to right a wrong and catch our father's killer—the only person Dad couldn't control. I hate to say this, Jake, but, like Dad, you're stuck on your own agenda and can't see past it.''

Before Jake could reply, Nick walked out. His brother's words had hurt him, but Jake was determined not to let Annie see how much. Yet as their gazes met, he realized she already knew.

"Nick is wrong about me," Jake said, his voice hard. "I have to see to it that the man who took my father's life pays for what he did, because it's my duty as his son. Can you understand?''

''Yes, I can,'' she said, her voice gentle. ''But don't be angry with your brother. Nick looks at things differently, but neither one of you is wrong.'' She paused, then added, ''If you two could find a way to work together, you'd be practically invincible.'' She stood. ''But I'm speaking out of turn. That's something you two need to work out. And, on that note, I better get back to my studio.''

## Chapter Thirteen

She had just finished changing the angle of her small carving desk for the third time when Jake walked into the studio. As she looked up at him, she saw frustration etched clearly on his features.

"No luck finding Lowman?" she asked.

"No. Have you noticed that whenever you really need to get hold of someone on the phone, it's nearly impossible to do so?"

She chuckled. "You're talking to an artist who sells chip carvings to make her living. I know that feeling well."

Jake leaned against the door jamb and regarded her thoughtfully. "Your work is very close to your heart, isn't it?"

He sounded almost wistful. She gave him a quizzical look. "Just like your construction business is to you."

He shook his head. "No, to me, my company is all part of what I do, not who I am. This—" he waved to the angel carving and the other one she kept covered with a cloth "—seems to capture your soul."

"But, you know, sometimes I'm not at all sure that's a good thing," she admitted. "I'd probably be better off if it mattered less to me. But I can't just walk away from it, not for very long. It's all part of who I am and who I want to be.''

''Like your baby?''

''Yes. I want to be a mom. And I also want to be a successful artist.''

''It must be difficult meeting the demands of so many different loves.''

She nodded. ''True, but they all help me stay focused, and remind me what's really important and what isn't.''

He regarded her, lost in thought. ''Compared to yours, my life seems empty. But it's not, you know.''

''I think you *are* dedicated to your company. You couldn't have made it prosper without a lot of hard work.''

''Yes, but hard work doesn't depend upon dedication and devotion. I don't give my heart away easily.''

She felt herself drawn by the power of his gaze. It wrapped itself around her, squeezed the air from her lungs. Memories of his touch teased her imagination as he stepped toward her.

He stopped by the Christmas cactus she'd set out on the window ledge. Bright red blooms with white centers covered the glossy green foliage. He caressed the leaves with a feather-light touch that made her skin tingle as memories danced in her head.

''I've always enjoyed seeing these plants this time of year,'' he said, ''particularly the ones with the red flowers.''

''They're very hardy. Water them, give them sunlight, and they're happy.'' She picked up the pot and handed it to him. ''Here. Consider it an early Christmas gift from me to you.''

Jake took the pot, then shook his head. ''It's beautiful, but I can't accept it. My life-style is all wrong for houseplants. I'm never in one place long enough to really take care of something that's alive.''

As he set the cactus back on the ledge, sadness and loneliness filled her. That was exactly what was wrong between them. Their very natures pulled them apart even as their hearts drew them together.

He walked over to where she stood and cupped her face in the palms of his hands. His eyes burned right through to her soul. ''I know I should stay away from you, but I don't seem to be able to do that.''

When he pulled her into his arms, she didn't resist. With a groan, Jake took her mouth in a harsh, possessive kiss. ''If only you could accept the love I can give you,'' he whispered, his breath hot on her cheek. ''Just you and me, loving—any way you wanted, everywhere you wanted.''

More than anything she wanted to accept what he was offering her, but she knew she couldn't. As the baby stirred inside her, she found the strength to step back.

''What we share is passion, Jake, and that isn't enough. Love has to be right in order to survive.''

He didn't fight her. They both knew what needed to be done. ''Every time I look at you, Annie, every time I'm near you, my heart tells me to do one thing, my mind another.''

As he turned and left the studio, Annie sank into the chair. Tears spilled down her cheeks. Everything in life had a price, and the cost of loving Jake was pain and heartbreak. The reality was inescapable—with the baby on its way, she needed more than what was in his nature to give.

ANNIE WORKED furiously for the next few hours, then, needing a break, decided to go for a walk. Sometimes it was the only thing that helped work out the kinks in her back.

As she strolled in the direction of the stalls, she saw Jake gallop out of the corral on one of the stallions. She'd only caught a glimpse of the rider, but it had been enough. Jake and the animal were as one, their movements perfectly co-ordinated.

One of the ranch hands ran out of the barn, looked around, and spotted Jake in the distance. The man shrugged and walked over to Rick, who was topping off one of the horse troughs. "Nick just rode off on Equinox before I could give him the new feed bill. Remind me to catch him when he comes back from his ride."

"That wasn't Nick," Annie said, approaching.

"Are you sure?" Rick asked.

"Positive," she said, surprised they couldn't tell the differences between the twins.

"I can't tell one from the other," the ranch hand said with a helpless shrug, "unless I recognize their clothes."

"Me neither," Rick admitted. "I just play dumb until they say something that gives them away. How do *you* tell them apart?"

She considered the question, really wanting to help him out. But there was no answer she could give him that made sense. All she knew was that her heart raced whenever Jake came near her, but it wasn't so with Nick. "I don't know exactly, maybe it's in their expressions. But, to me, they're as different as night and day."

As she returned to the house, she suddenly understood the truth behind her words. The reason she could tell the men apart was simple. She'd fallen head over heels in love with Jake, and her heart would never be fooled.

With a soft groan, she went back to her studio. At least there, she was in a world she understood.

IT WAS AFTER DARK when she finally stopped working. The new carving showed a lot of promise. She had created the image of a woman reaching for a star that was just out of her reach. The yearning, the struggle for hope, was slowly coming out in the wood as her heart guided her hand.

Exhausted, she moved the piece to the center of the table and covered it with a cloth. The natural light was gone, and it was time to stop. As she went to the window to peer into the night, she found it impossible to see anything past the circle of floodlights that now illuminated the main house.

Then, suddenly, she caught a bright flash, like a single headlight just beyond the illuminated grounds. Curious, she squinted, trying to make it out despite the distortion created by the frosted glass.

The brightness died slightly, then seemed to expand in size. Unable to make it out clearly, she opened the window. At that same moment she caught a whiff of smoke. It lay heavy in the air along with the loud whinnies of frightened horses.

Only one thing could explain it—a fire in the barn. She rushed out of the studio and into the hall.

"Fire! There's a fire outside!" she yelled.

Jake had already seen it and was at the door, reaching for his coat when she arrived.

"Annie, stay here," Jake commanded. "You can't help, not in your condition. Call the fire department." He reached for a pair of work gloves.

Annie picked up the phone, and left the information with the pueblo's volunteer fire department.

She was about to tell Jake when Nick rushed in through the back door. "Martin's already getting the horses out, but we need help. Annie, can you spray water from one of the garden hoses? We've got to wet down the hay before we lose the entire barn."

"Of course I can." She grabbed her jacket off the hook.

"No, you can't," Jake protested. "You could get hurt."

"I know enough to stay out of the way of a scared animal. I *can* help. And you need an extra pair of hands."

Nick held the door open. "Let's go, Jake." He looked at Annie. "Don't feel pressured into coming. It's your call."

"I'm going." She followed the men out, though she knew Jake didn't like the idea. The moment she got a clear look at the barn, she knew that they'd need far more help than the four of them could muster.

The two brothers sprinted ahead, and she hurried as fast as she could. As she approached the stalls, Martin came out, leading a horse. He'd thrown his coat over the animal's head, covering its eyes. Several more were already loose, heading out to the pasture at a fast trot.

Annie grabbed the garden hose, which was kept coiled beside an insulated water faucet, and turned on the tap. She adjusted the spray nozzle as she pulled the hose toward the barn.

With Jake, Nick and Martin working in tandem, it didn't take long before all the animals were safe, but the flames were shooting high into the darkened sky through a charred break in the roof. She kept the garden hose aimed at the base of the flames, but she wasn't able to get as close to the fire as she wanted. The smoke was too thick, and twice she had to step back when she started to cough.

The men worked together, Martin manning another hose while the twins used shovels and rakes to isolate burning bales, trying to minimize the spread.

"As long as we can keep the fire from reaching the storage area on the other side of the stalls, we'll be okay," Jake yelled. "Keep the water going."

"There's a breeze building that will fan the flames and

spread this fire, no matter what we do," Nick yelled back. "We're not going to be able to stop it."

"We have to. We're on our own for now." Just as he spoke, the sound of honking horns revealed a dozen or more vehicles making their way along the main road. The first had already turned down the drive, and more were following.

"Our neighbors have seen the flames," Martin said. "Your father always helped them, giving away thousands of dollars of hay each year to those who were strapped for cash. They'll be here now that the Black Ravens need help."

Annie and Jake exchanged glances. They now knew what had happened to the hay. At least Jake could be at peace about that.

Men and women parked their cars a safe distance back, then ran toward them with shovels and buckets. They were quickly organized into teams and whatever was salvageable was hauled away from the flames. Two lines formed a bucket brigade from the horse troughs, passing water from hand to hand toward the fire. Those at the end doused the flames, and returned the buckets to be refilled.

By the time the fire department arrived, the fire had been contained. With extra help, it wasn't long before the flames were reduced to a few smoking embers. She looked at the gutted section of the building, and relinquished the hose to one of the pueblo men.

Exhausted, she moved over to a table where two women were providing cups of drinking water from a large jug and tending to people who'd inhaled smoke.

It was then she saw Jake. His cheeks were blackened with soot and his gloves were tattered and partially burned. He was catching his breath now that the fire was finally beaten down. Filling up a paper cup, she handed him some water.

He took a deep swallow before speaking. "Everything's okay now," he said. "And the horses weren't hurt."

His voice was like a warm embrace in the bitter cold of the desert night. "I'm glad." She gestured around her. "It appears that the Black Raven Ranch has a lot of friends."

He nodded slowly. "Maybe because it belongs to the tribe as much as it belongs to us. The Black Raven family has given it direction, but people from the pueblo are its lifeblood. And for the first time in my life, I'm really glad that's the way things are. The sense of unity and brotherhood we saw here tonight is what being Tewa is all about."

"It sounds to me as if you've come home for keeps," she said, her voice a bare whisper among the loud voices of the men still working.

"It's strange how things work out. I'm beginning to see that I've spent a lifetime running away from something I love. I—"

"Fire! At the house!" someone shouted.

Muttering an oath, Jake turned around quickly. Smoke was coming out of the study window. "I should have known! The fire here was a diversion. The main house was the real target." He tossed aside the paper cup and ran toward the house with Martin and Nick at his heels.

Two firemen grabbed fire extinguishers and followed them while others got ready to move the pumper.

Annie stumbled toward the house, tears running down her face. If she lost her carvings, then she would be completely broke after the baby arrived. She'd been counting heavily on the money the sale would bring.

This time, though everything was at stake for her, she was not allowed to help. The fire department took charge.

Fortunately the flames were easily extinguished, and it was less than ten minutes before the all-clear was given.

As a big fan was placed in the main entrance to extract smoke from the building, Jake came to join her. "It's okay, Annie. The fire was confined to the *sala* and my dad's study. Someone set the Christmas tree on fire, along with the curtains in the study, but the firemen were able to put it out before it spread beyond those two rooms. Some of the furniture is ruined and a lot of the books and papers in the study are a total loss."

"This was the arsonist's way of trying to make sure the evidence was never found," Annie observed thoughtfully. "I'm sure of it."

"Which means he didn't find what he was after, either," Jake answered. "But if the evidence was hidden in the study, then he may have succeeded in getting rid of it for good." He paused, catching his breath, then continued. "He was smart. The logical place to start the fire was in the *sala* with the Christmas tree. There was a chance the fire might have been blamed on the tree or the lights. What gave him away was that we were able to catch the fire in time to see that there was a separate fire in the study. The fireman who does arson investigations hasn't made an official determination yet, but there's little doubt the fires were set."

"None of us is safe now," she said softly.

"Annie, have you considered putting as much distance between yourself and this ranch as possible? My father never dreamed we'd be facing this when he made out his will, and we might be able to contest it on that basis."

She shook her head. "I have nowhere to go and, here, at least I have friends and my midwife. There's something else I have to consider. What kind of parent would I be if I ran away when trouble came, instead of standing up for what I knew was right? I can't turn my back on the principles that are at the foundation of everything I believe in, and expect to impart them to my child someday. I know what's right, Jake, and it isn't running away."

"You've got a lot of courage, Annie. You'll be a wonderful mother. Thank you for what you did here tonight."

"This was Paul's ranch," she said quietly. "It's now yours and Nick's and, at least for now, it's my home, too. I care about this place and I fight for whatever owns a piece of my heart."

"I envy the man you'll say that about someday, sweetheart."

His voice was a dark, husky murmur that made her skin tingle and filled her with yearnings too powerful to deny. Passion shimmered in his eyes, calling voicelessly to her, tempting her to surrender.

Annie wanted him to narrow the gap between them and kiss her, throwing caution to the winds. As their eyes met, Jake heard her silent wish and answered.

"Annie," he whispered, moving toward her.

Suddenly someone called out his name. He cursed softly. "I better go." Stepping away from her reluctantly, he turned and jogged toward Martin and Nick. The men met at the front door then, accompanied by a fireman, went inside.

As the cold wind whipped against her, Annie looked around, studying the concerned faces of those present, wondering if the killer was among them—because it was obvious Paul's murderer was someone he had known. One of them was a wolf in sheep's clothing.

# Chapter Fourteen

At the kitchen table the following morning, an uneasy silence reigned over them as they stared at the plate in the center of the table. There lay the few ornaments they'd managed to salvage. They'd fallen to the floor, the strings that once tied them to the tree having burned through first.

The firemen and Captain Mora had agreed from the evidence and the case history that both fires had been a result of arson. The police had checked for vehicle tracks, hoping to identify the culprit, but so many people had shown up to help it had been a futile exercise.

"I'm positive that money is at the root of everything that's happened to Dad, to us, and to this ranch," Jake said. "I'm just not sure how it all connects."

"I keep thinking of those cash withdrawals you mentioned," Annie said. "From what you've said, they were substantial amounts, and we still don't know what the money was being used for."

"You have to remember that hay and feed purchases were often handled in cash," Martin said. "It was the same with services like plowing up a field, or clearing the ditches. Most people around here are old-fashioned and wary of checks. But it's hard to keep track of money that's used in so many ways. Your father hated those accounting ledgers he was forced to use for tax purposes. Saya had kept the ranch accounts for Paul until she died and he hated having to take them over.''

"Dad still trusted her with the ranch, even after their troubles," Jake said thoughtfully, then lapsed into a brief silence. The importance of what he'd just learned stunned him. Despite their differences, Paul Black Raven had trusted his wife with what was most important to him—his sons and his ranch. "If Mom was used to keeping accounts, maybe that's why she opened her own. It gave her the freedom to manage her money any way she chose. What do you think?"

Martin gave him a neutral look. "That's not for me to say."

"Does it surprise you that she had her own account?"

Martin paused, then shook his head. "Saya never wanted to be completely dependent on anyone."

"Including my father?" Jake pressed.

Martin nodded once, then stood. "If you don't need me anymore, I'll be going outside. The barn needs a lot of work." He went quickly out the back door.

Nick stared at his brother. "Why did you bring that up? You know Martin doesn't want to get involved in the family's personal business. He has a place within our family, but he's not *part* of our family. More to the point, that's exactly the way he wants to keep it."

"I thought that was the best way to find out what he knew," Jake said.

"I'll tell you what I know. Dad was being blackmailed precisely because he didn't want us to know too much about Mom. I believe, even now, Martin would continue to respect Dad's wishes on that subject and tell us as little as possible."

"Point taken," Jake said, conceding. "I just wish we had that diary back."

Nick stood. "I'm going to do some work at the pueblo job center for an hour or so, because I volunteered to help out. But as soon as the lumber and nails are delivered, I'll come back here and lend the men a hand with the repairs on the barn."

As he walked out, Jake checked his watch. "I'm going to see Lowman this morning. I want to find out more about my mother's account." As he looked at Annie, he wondered if she knew how much he cared about her and how much he wanted to take her into his arms. He looked away, knowing he needed to stay focused. "I'd like you to come with me."

"I can't. I'm behind schedule on my work as it is."

"It could be dangerous for you to stay here alone, particularly after what's happened," he said. "All our hands will be outside this morning working on repairing the barn and stalls. That's our first priority, not the house. This place is still airtight and structurally sound, but the animals need a secure place ready for them when the weather turns foul."

"I'll stay on my guard, don't worry. The locks are still good, remember? There's also the gun cabinet down the hall," she said.

He gave her a skeptical look. "Would you be able to use a rifle or shotgun?"

"If I had to, yes. Your father taught me how to shoot. But I don't think it would come to that. If I hear an intruder, I'll call the men."

"With wood saws, and the electric nail guns, you might not be heard. This guy, whoever he is, is getting bolder. Torching our house seems like an act of desperation to me, don't you agree? Besides, Annie, I can really use your help. We don't know who the murderer is. We need to look at everyone and everything carefully. You can pick up subtleties and changes in mood faster than I ever would, and something like that could end up leading us to a vital clue.''

"All right," she said at last. "But I've got to tell you, I'm getting worried about missing my deadline for these pieces. It's only three days away."

"Will the gallery be upset?"

"It's not that. It's just that with Christmas almost here, I can get better prices. After the holidays, people are usually hit by a ton of bills and the money for luxuries is tighter."

"We'll get our business done and get back here as soon as possible," he promised, going to get their jackets.

Five minutes later they were on the narrow two-lane highway. "There's one thing we have in our favor," Annie said thoughtfully. "The person who set fire to the house has no way of knowing if he succeeded in burning the evidence or not."

"You're right. He knows less than we do—for once."

Annie sat up, focusing on the area around them. "Where are we going? This isn't the way to the bank."

"When I called earlier, I was told Virgil wouldn't be in until just before noon, but that he was planning to have a late breakfast at the Silver Slipper Casino. I figured meeting him there was perfect, since I'd rather catch him away from the bank where he'll be more relaxed."

"Where's the casino?"

"On another pueblo about a half hour from here. We should arrive just about the time he comes in."

As the miles stretched before them, Jake was acutely aware of everything about Annie. Her perfume was elusive and gently scented, like her. He felt a stirring in his blood. Though she was completely out of his reach, he couldn't stop wanting her, and not just in a physical sense. Annie was a remarkable woman. She had more courage than many men he'd met and when she spoke of debts of honor, she truly meant them, she wasn't just saying the words.

Although they arrived at the casino early in the day, the parking lot was almost full. Inside, a noisy crowd hovered at the tables and slot machines.

They soon found Lowman at one of the blackjack tables, a soft drink at his side. Seeing them, he played out his losing hand and greeted them with handshakes.

"What brings you two here? I thought you'd be working on the barn or home repairs. Do you need a loan?"

"No, actually we wanted to talk to you about another matter and decided it would be better to catch you away from the bank so we wouldn't be disturbed," Jake said, deliberately keeping his tone casual. The last thing he wanted to do was to alarm Lowman in any way. His gut told him that the banker knew more than he'd shared with them so far.

"Come on," Lowman said. "Let me buy you two an early lunch—or late breakfast."

"I understand you're a regular here," Jake proclaimed after they were seated in the restaurant area. He didn't really know if it were true, but he couldn't think of any place where a bluff was more appropriate.

Lowman laughed. "It all started when our pueblo asked me to look into the feasibility of opening our own casino. Now, it's just a good place to get lunch." He grew serious. "So tell me. What can I do for you?"

"I'm trying to put some pieces of my past together," Jake said, "and it hasn't been easy. Did you know my mother well?"

Lowman's expression softened and his eyes misted. "She was a great lady. She charmed everyone who knew her."

It was the sudden gentling of Lowman's gruff voice that alerted him. "Were you two friends?"

Virgil took a deep breath, then let it out. "We went to school together for years, and I'd like to think she considered me a friend," he said, his voice sad. "But your father was very jealous and protective of Saya. There was never time for us to just sit and talk, though we both would have liked that."

"Who was her best friend?" Jake asked.

"I think she was close to the mother of one of your high school classmates, but the woman died tragically with her husband years ago. Saya confided in me from time to time, and sometimes in Martin, but she was always careful around him. His allegiance was to Paul."

"And yours?" Jake asked as their sandwiches were brought to the table.

"I was a friend to both your parents," he said with a shrug. "But I never would have betrayed Saya's confidences."

"Just recently we found a deposit slip that indicates my mother had a bank account in her name. I was hoping you could shed some light on that. It seems out of character somehow."

Lowman's eyes focused on an indeterminate spot across the room. "I remember that. She called it her nest egg. I don't think your father even knew about it until after her death."

"So the account was turned over to him or Patrick Kelly as part of the estate?"

"That's usually how it works, but I don't recall. It was so many years ago. I'd have to check our records at the bank, and that might take a while."

"I'd appreciate it if you would," Jake persisted.

"I'll take care of it." Lowman checked his watch. "I

have to get to the bank now, but take your time eating and get dessert if you want. I'll have the bill put on my tab. And if there's anything else I can do, don't hesitate to contact me. I thought the world of your mother, and of your father, too.''

Afterward, as they walked to the car, Annie looked at Jake. ''I don't know if you picked up on this or not, but I believe Lowman was in love with your mother at one time.''

''I think that's overstating it a bit.''

''No, I don't think so.'' She considered her words carefully. ''Did you notice the way he spoke about her? Even his tone of voice changed. It was wistful. But I don't think your mom ever acknowledged his feelings. For some reason I was reminded of the kind of crush teenage boys have on the cheerleaders at their schools.''

''It's possible. My mother was a beautiful woman. I've heard my uncle say that she could have had any man in the village, but she fell in love with my father and, after that, no one else would do.''

''I wonder if Martin felt the same way about her, too,'' she mused.

The question surprised him. It was hard to think of Martin as being attracted to his mother in any way. ''I don't think that's possible. He was totally loyal to my father.''

''I'm not saying that there was anything inappropriate going on. I'm only suggesting that Martin may have had feelings for her, as well. Things like that tend to complicate even the simplest matters.''

''Are you now thinking that Martin might have had something to do with the murder?''

She shook her head. ''I'd be shocked if he did. Martin isn't a violent man. A more realistic possibility is that he's holding back information, trying to protect people who have passed away and are beyond the need of protection.''

Jake nodded. ''That could be. I'll look into that some more as I follow the trail of the missing bank account. If anyone, Martin included, is holding back information that might root out my father's killer, I'll find out sooner or later.''

''Let's just hope we get what we need before the killer does,'' Annie whispered.

## Chapter Fifteen

After they arrived at the ranch, Annie went straight to her studio. As she looked at her carvings, hope filled her. These would bring her a good price. She was certain of it.

As Annie worked, her concentration was complete. No other thoughts were allowed to intrude as she listened to her instincts and the wood chip carving began its final step toward completion.

Hearing a knock at the door sometime later, she jumped and spun around. Jake stood there, holding a fire-damaged glass Christmas ornament. "I'm sorry. I didn't mean to startle you. I just thought maybe you could do something with this," he said.

She looked at what had once been the beautiful ornament his mother had painted for him. "It's pretty badly damaged. I'm not sure it can be restored."

As he looked directly at her, she saw the sadness in his eyes. "This has been in our family for at least twenty years," he said. "I just thought that maybe…"

Annie could have no more turned him down than she could have stopped her heart from beating. She knew how small things could give comfort, becoming the center of memories too cherished to relinquish.

"I won't promise anything, but I'll see what I can do."

"Thanks," he whispered, his eyes never leaving hers.

His gaze caressed her as intimately as a lover's touch and, for a moment, magic shimmered between them.

"My father was right about you, Annie," he said softly. "Your gentleness encompasses everything you touch." He reached for her hand. "I really do need you in my life."

She gave his hand a squeeze, then let go. Even friendship couldn't be trusted when her body sang with needs only he could assuage.

He walked over and studied her angel carving. "This is really an incredible piece of work. There's something very lifelike about the emotions on their faces."

"If people who look at the piece can identify with the feelings I carved into the figures, then I've done the job I set out to do. It's hard to make people really *feel* anything these days, you know? We grow up learning how to shield ourselves from emotions."

"I didn't realize how much I do that until you came into my life."

Longing filled her as she looked at him. With a burst of will, she moved away. It was too hard to even think with him in the same room. "Will you excuse me? It's almost dark and I still have to go for my daily walk."

"Let me walk with you. I need some fresh air and I'd much rather not have you walk around alone anymore."

Knowing from the set look on his face that he wouldn't take no for an answer, and not having the strength to argue, she agreed.

They headed in the direction of the barns, walking slowly. As they reached the pile of charred lumber that had been stacked on the north side of the corral, Jake stopped and stared at the debris from the fire. "None of the animals was hurt, so I should be grateful. But when I look at the damage and the waste, I feel as if I've been punched in the gut.''

Annie wondered if Jake realized that his love for the ranch was coming through in every word he uttered. ''This is your home. It's natural to resent an attack like this.''

''Let's take a closer look inside the barn. I promised Martin I'd check the progress here this evening.'' Jake switched on some extension lights and the large kerosene heater the men had used earlier.

She walked with him through the barn until they reached the newly rebuilt stalls. ''At least this part is finished and you'll be able to stable the horses whenever you want,'' she said.

Jake climbed up the ladder to the hayloft. Only the remnants of a few bales remained, too scattered to be used easily for feed. It would probably have to be raked up and used for bedding instead.

''Be careful up there,'' she warned.

''It's okay. The flooring's been patched, as well as the roof.'' He began to sort through some scorched beams, trying to salvage a leather halter that had originally hung from a rafter.

''You better come down. I can tell from here that the flooring hasn't been reinforced enough. It dips when you walk.''

''Let me get this halter first. It's stuck under some damaged wood that was replaced but not hauled outside.'' As he knelt, trying to move a nail-filled board, the wood groaned under his weight.

Hearing the sound, Annie looked up quickly to see the board begin to sag down. She called out a warning, but it was too late.

The wood splintered and Jake started to fall through, but

he reached out desperately, grabbed a floor joist and hung on.

Her heart in her throat, Annie watched as he dangled from the loft. "Hang on!" Looking around for a ladder or something to break his fall, she noticed the pitchfork directly beneath Jake. It had been wedged in place between a small stack of undamaged hay bales, tines up. "Don't let go!"

She wrenched the pitchfork free, then moved the bales closer together. "Okay, you can drop down now. The hay will cushion your fall."

Jake hit the ground with a grunt, and rolled off the bales into a pile of straw bedding.

Annie watched anxiously as he sat up, brushing the straw out of his hair and off his face. "Are you okay?"

"Yeah. But thanks for spotting the pitchfork. I owe you one."

"This was no accident," she said. "That pitchfork wasn't just left there, it was carefully propped like a spear."

He looked up and studied the section of flooring that had given away. "That new wood was partially sawn through *after* the repairs were made. Had I fallen on the pitchfork..." His gaze captured hers again. "The murderer might have claimed another victim, if it hadn't been for you."

"But how could he have known you'd come here to the barn and climb to the loft when you did?"

"He couldn't have, not for sure. Anyone working here, like Martin, Rick or one of the wranglers, could have been caught in this trap. He's trying anything now just to slow us down or warn us off. The real problem is, he's getting desperate. This person isn't concerned about hurting innocent bystanders and that's what makes him deadly, not only to the Black Ravens, but to anyone connected to us, like you," he added, his voice taut.

"We're both okay. Don't think about what might have been. This was one disaster we managed to avert. I'm really glad I was here for you," she said.

She offered him a hand up.

Jake took it, but, as he pulled himself up, Annie slid on the loose straw and tumbled down, landing on her knees in front of him.

"I'm sorry, Annie. It's my fault," he said quickly. "My weight was too much for you. Are you all right?"

"I'm fine. The ground is as soft as...well, a bed of straw. It wasn't your fault at all," she said, feeling foolish. "I slipped, plain and simple," she said, scooting back to make some room between them. Her heart was pounding so loudly, she was surprised he couldn't hear it.

His expression gentled, though his eyes burned with an intensity that left her breathless. "Annie, how do I touch you the way you've touched me? You already have my heart," he said, his voice low and hoarse. "It's yours to take—or break. How do I make you feel what I do?"

Everything feminine in her responded to him. "You already have," she said, her voice unsteady.

"Then surrender," he murmured, narrowing the small gap between them.

"We shouldn't," she said, her voice trembling.

"No, we shouldn't. But we will. We have to."

His head dipped down and he took her mouth in a kiss so tender and so deep, all her resistance and logic vanished. She moaned his name, desperately needing the closeness and intimacy he was offering her.

Slipping her hands beneath his sweater, she caressed his smooth, bronzed chest. He was all masculine hardness and sinewy strength. His tattered breathing, his groans...all fueled her own growing passion. He needed her, and she needed him. Nothing else mattered now.

Primitive fires danced along her spine, giving her courage. She tugged at his sweater, pulling it away from him, but as she tried to unfasten his belt, she began to tremble.

He took her hands in his own and kissed them, then moved back and stripped off his clothing, allowing her to see him as he was. Her eyes were dark and heavy with passion as she looked at him, her gaze branding every inch of him. She was ready to become his and everything male in him knew it. With infinite tenderness, he undressed her, baring her until nothing stood between them.

Skin against skin, she surrendered to the love she could no longer deny. As the stars filled the skies outside, the heat of passion encircled them in safety and warmth. He rained kisses down her neck, loving the way she melted against him.

"Jake." Her voice was like a whispered prayer.

"I'm here, sweetheart. Feel my hands and my mouth on your sweet body. Let me love you in every way you've ever dreamed of—everything…everywhere…for you."

She felt his heated mouth suckle her breast as his hand moved inside her, parting her and invading her body. His strokes fanned the flames within her. She cried out his name over and over again.

Holding back was agony, but he wouldn't rush them. He started to push her back onto the straw but, as her swollen belly pressed against him, he suddenly pulled back.

"I can't hurt you or the child," he breathed in a tortured whisper. "But let me take you in the only way I can." He burned kisses down the length of her body, whispering dark words as he caressed her, seeking and probing, tasting and filling her emptiness. A fire too intense to bear raged inside her.

"Let it happen. Let me be the man you surrender to."

Pleasure after pleasure flowed over her until she came apart. She held nothing back, trusting in him and the love he'd shown her.

Once certain she could give him no more, he shifted and held her against his side, brushing a kiss on her forehead. Annie whimpered as she felt his hardness against her thigh. It had been so complete, yet not. Tears formed in her eyes.

"I need to be one with you," she whispered. "I know what it's like to be strong—and alone. I don't want to be strong tonight."

"I don't want you to regret this…" he said, his voice raw.

"The baby will be all right. And it will do the baby's mother a world of good," she whispered, pushing him back onto the straw and hay bedding.

He helped her sit astride him and, lifting her bottom, guided her as she lowered herself over him. Her body spread then tightened around him.

She felt too good. He had to hold back. His hands were shaking as he grasped her hips but, using every last bit of willpower he possessed, Jake allowed her to set the pace. Only when she got tired, did he take over, moving in the same gentle rhythm she'd set.

His eyes strayed over her as she sat on top of him, riding him gently. He caressed her swollen breasts and her belly, then moved down to the center of her. As she rocked her body back and forth over him, he began to caress her there. Her eyes widened and she gasped as new fires spread over her.

The love she felt in her heart made the pleasure he was giving her more intense and sweeter. Even with Bobby, making love had never been like this. She knew then that no other man would ever touch her heart the way Jake had.

As desire burned through her, her fingers dug into his powerful shoulders. "More," she pleaded.

He thrust up into her, giving her what she wanted, but careful not to hurt her.

"No, don't hold back," she urged, her eyes never wavering from his, taking him even more deeply into herself.

"Sweet Annie." His control vanished as passion made its own demands. She welcomed his thrusts, engulfing him in her heated warmth. The fire, the velvet...drove him to the brink of sanity.

As he arched his back, thrusting into her, she cried out his name. Her body shattered and a cascade of tender fires swept over her, leaving no part of her untouched.

It was a surrender that came from the soul. She'd given him everything, willingly.

Every muscle in Jake's body tightened. Every masculine instinct he possessed drank in the power of her gift to him. His chest heaving, his skin hot, he thrust upward one more time and, with a cry, exploded inside her.

Annie held on to his shoulders then, with a soft sigh, sagged against him, every bit of energy she'd had expended.

Jake wrapped his arms around her gently. Annie and her child were a part of him now—his family.

"It was..." Words failed her.

"For me, too," he murmured. "You taught me something about love tonight. Gentleness can be more powerful than I ever imagined."

Tears filled her eyes. He was still a man who loved freedom, something a woman and child would never be able to give him. But, for tonight, their souls had taken flight and soared together.

MINUTES PASSED SLOWLY. It was getting cold, despite the large heater in the barn, and Jake knew they would have to go back soon. But he couldn't will himself to stop holding her. She felt so right in his arms. As he brushed her hair away from her cheek so he could kiss her, he felt the moistness on her face. "Why are you crying? Have I hurt you?"

"No. It's just hay fever. We *are* on hay, you know," she said, keeping her tone light. She pulled away from him and smiled as the baby stirred. "And the baby's fine, though probably a bit miffed at us for disturbing her rest." She shifted so he couldn't see her stomach.

He tugged gently at her hand until her body was turned toward him. He could see the baby's movements clearly as the child pushed against her stomach. He touched her belly gently, almost in awe. The baby was part of the woman whose body he'd shared and the baby's life had irrevocably touched his own. Nothing would ever be the same. There were problems to be faced and solved, but he felt closer to Annie and the baby now than he'd ever felt to anyone. For the first time in his life, he wanted to have a family. Permanence held no terror for him anymore.

Aware of the way his gaze rested on her distended belly, and feeling self-conscious, Annie began gathering up her clothes quickly.

Jake reached for her hand and brought it to his lips. "I have never seen a more beautiful woman, Annie."

"Or a larger one, I bet," she said with a shy laugh, refusing to meet his gaze this time. "We'd better get back to the house before Martin and Nick send out a posse. It would be embarrassing to be caught naked in the barn."

Hearing voices coming toward the barn, she gasped. "Oh, no! It's too late."

Jake quickly pulled on his jeans and sweater and, while

she gathered her things, gave her a smile. "I'll intercept them, then I'll be back. Don't worry."

As she watched him go, Annie tried to tell herself that what they'd shared had been of no consequence. In reality nothing had changed. The fact was she'd still be facing the future alone.

It didn't matter how deep Jake's feelings ran, with his skin still warm with the glow of passion. Once he was faced with the constant demands the baby would make on her, he'd soon begin to feel trapped in a relationship he wasn't prepared for.

Paul had been wrong to demand they stay together for one year. In the final analysis, all he'd really done was take two people who weren't meant to be together, and show them a world they could never have.

# Chapter Sixteen

The following morning Annie went out for a walk alone. What Jake and she had shared last night, first making love, then going out for a late candlelight dinner, had touched her soul. Then they'd slept together, Jake holding her close all night. Yet the love they'd found was destined to slip right through their fingers, and that knowledge was tearing her apart.

Realizing that she'd been walking much too fast, she stopped by the corrals and tried to catch her breath. That's when she heard Martin talking to the wranglers.

"I understood Paul's love for this ranch better than anyone else. The truth is, I knew his thoughts as well as I knew my own. There wasn't much he could keep secret from me."

"Then why can't you help Jake and Nick find that evidence? Unless that's settled soon, there's going to be another death, mark my words," one of the wranglers said.

"It'll all come out at the right time. Don't worry," Martin said.

There was a tense silence, then she heard Rick's voice. "You know where it is, don't you, Uncle Martin." From his tone, it was plain that the question was rhetorical.

Martin didn't answer him. "That's enough chitchat. Get

back to work, all of you. I want the stalls ready for the horses tonight. Is that clear?''

A cold chill settled over her, and she didn't stay to listen to the men's complaints. She was almost sure that Martin didn't really know where the evidence was. But if she was right about that, why was he letting others believe differently?

Nick was coming down the stairs when she returned to the house. ''Are you okay?'' he asked, giving her a thorough once-over. ''You look as if you've been running.''

''It's just really, really cold out this morning,'' she said, slipping off her coat. ''But I'm glad you're here. I need to talk to you and Jake. Can we meet in the kitchen? That way I can also get something warm to drink.''

''Sure. Jake's in there now, I believe. I heard him rattling around a while ago.''

Jake smiled at her as she walked in. His gaze touched her tenderly and intimately. ''I figured you were out walking. You didn't overdo it, did you?''

The power of that one look left her tingling. Annie tore her gaze away and wondered if Nick would be able to sense any difference in the way they treated each other this morning. She glanced at Nick, but his attention was centered on the muffins someone had placed on the counter.

As Jake and Nick ate breakfast, Annie recounted the conversation she'd heard outside. ''I think Martin was deliberately misleading them. If he knew, I think he would have told us by now. But I don't understand why he's doing this.''

''I think I can answer that.'' At Martin's voice, they turned to see him standing just inside the kitchen. He sat at the table with them and took a muffin from the serving plate. ''Someone has targeted this ranch and family. I couldn't stand by and do nothing, so earlier yesterday I started spreading the story that I knew more than I was letting on. I think the pitchfork trap Jake told us about last night was meant for me. Unfortunately, you were almost the victim, but by letting people believe that I know where the evidence is, I'm hoping the killer will come after me instead of any of you. It's my way of trying to protect everyone.''

Jake's face turned a deep crimson as he struggled to control his anger. ''Martin, you should have talked to me about this before putting yourself in danger. By now the story's all over the pueblo. There's no telling what the killer will do next.''

''He won't kill me. He'll need to find out what I know first,'' Martin said. ''Hopefully, we'll be able to find out who he is and capture him before that happens.''

''Depending on what the killer knows, he may decide that you're already too great a risk to him alive,'' Annie said. ''I certainly can't identify him, but that hasn't prevented his attacks on me.''

''The wranglers will watch my back. I won't be alone until we repair the fire damage.'' Martin stood and walked to the door. ''Hopefully this is going to buy you all some time, and take some of the killer's attention away from Annie. While the killer is focused on me, I'll expect you to find answers.''

Nick looked at Jake after Martin left. ''I'm going to spend the day with the ranch hands as they continue repairing the barn. I'll keep an eye on Martin, as well.''

''I'll join you,'' Jake said, then gave Annie a worried look. ''On second thought, I'm not sure I should leave you here alone at the house.''

''As Martin pointed out, he's the target now,'' Annie said.

Nick shook his head. ''It's still risky. Why don't you

work inside repairing the *sala* and the study, Jake? I'll stick to the barn repairs. With all the men doing the outside work, someone's got to concentrate on the house."

Jake nodded. "Good idea. I really don't want to spend Christmas in a fire-damaged house if I can help it." He was beginning to realize that despite some bad memories, he still valued this place as his home.

After Nick left, Annie stood and excused herself, avoiding Jake's gaze. "I might as well get to work, too."

"Are you avoiding me, Annie? We shouldn't feel uncomfortable around each other, not after what we've shared," Jake said softly.

She took a deep breath and prayed for courage. To allow a doomed relationship to continue was wrong and she owed Jake and herself more than that. It was time to let go. "I'm not uncomfortable around you, Jake. But it's time to face things squarely. What happened last night was wonderful, but it was something neither of us intended. Now it's time to move on. I've got my own life to live. My career is on the brink, and I've got a baby on the way. You're not part of my future."

"Don't tell me last night meant nothing to you. I won't believe it," he growled.

"Of course it meant something. You're the best lover any woman could ever hope for," she said, forcing her tone to stay casual. "It was forbidden fruit, you know, and that made it even better. But now that we've sampled it, it's out of our system."

She walked away from him, her shoulders back and her head erect, but tears were streaming down her face. Her heart had shattered into a million pieces. Sadness, black and suffocating, engulfed her. It was over now. All that would remain were the memories and the pain.

JAKE WORKED TIRELESSLY, scraping damaged plaster from the interior walls where heat had caused it to crack and break away. Anger drove him relentlessly. He'd wanted to kiss Annie senseless and force her to take back her words, but he knew that was not the way to win her. Fear was at the root of her words—fear of him, of getting hurt, of seeing love turn into disappointment and sorrow. But he wasn't the same man who'd arrived a few days ago. He no longer only craved freedom. His heart was now leading him in a new direction.

Life had treated Annie harshly and instinct told him she'd need far more than words to convince her that his love was real. As he thought things through, he stopped to consider what he had to offer her. The answers that came to him weighed heavily on his mind. He had no real home; he moved from one place to the other every few weeks, depending on the contract work. What kind of life was that for her child, or for any woman who wanted roots and security?

He stood for a moment and stared outside. He loved this ranch, but this was still his father's world. He knew next to nothing about making a living from a horse ranch. A man supporting a woman and a child needed to be able to earn enough to provide for them.

Annie had done the right thing by letting go. It was all so logical and clear, but something inside him wouldn't let him walk away. He looked down the hall, fighting the urge to go after her.

Suddenly the lights flickered and he heard a commotion outside. Men were shouting, and some of the horses were whinnying and running around the corral.

Annie came rushing down the hall, her eyes wide. "What's going on outside?"

''Stay here, lock the door, and stand by the gun cabinet. I'll go out and see.''

He'd barely reached the front door when Nick came rushing in, almost knocking Jake down. ''Martin's been hurt. He was working on the hot wire around the fence. It appeared that one of the horses had kicked an insulator loose and shorted out the line.''

''Is he all right?'' Jake asked, his jaw clenched.

Nick nodded. ''I think so. It looks like a setup. Someone tampered with the lines, and ran a full charge through the chain-link fence. Martin grabbed it by accident trying to get out of the way when a horse spooked. The voltage threw him back and tossed him to the ground. He got off lucky, but his hands are burned. He was unconscious for a short time, too.''

''I'll call the clinic and notify Elsie and the doc,'' Jake said. Jake picked up the phone and, after a quick conversation, hung up.

''We need to take him to the hospital right now,'' Jake said. ''Elsie will ride with him in case the shock or burns have any side effects.''

Nick nodded. ''I'll need your pickup to drive him to Santa Fe. You have a camper shell over the bed of the truck. He can lie down there.''

''I'll get some blankets and a pillow,'' Annie said. ''Did someone put some ice on the burns?''

''Not ice—snow,'' Nick said. ''It was quick and handy.''

''I'll get ice. The last thing Martin needs is an infection.''

Annie wanted to ride in the back, but Martin and Jake refused to allow it in her condition, especially since Elsie would be going. Instead, she followed with Jake in Nick's Jeep.

After picking Elsie up at the clinic, they raced toward Santa Fe.

Annie avoided looking at him, and he knew that being alone with him was as difficult for her as it was for him. They were going to have a long twelve months ahead, she thought with a sad sigh.

It took about half an hour to get to the hospital. Then, an eternity passed while they waited in the lobby with Nick. When the emergency room doctor finally came out to meet them, tension was running high.

The doctor wore an encouraging smile as he approached. "He's going to be okay, but you'll have to make sure he doesn't use his hands for several days. He didn't get a good grip on the fence, so the injured area isn't massive or particularly deep. But the palms and fingers on both hands will require bandages, and they'll have to be changed often. He also received quite an electrical shock, so he'll have to take it easy. If he hadn't been in such good physical shape and been thrown away by the surge, I think his heart would have stopped."

Martin came out with an accompanying nurse, walking slowly. His eyes were dull, and his hands swathed in bandages. "Where do you think you're going?" Jake demanded.

"Martin can go home, *if* he stays put," the doctor said. "I've given Elsie instructions that she'll pass along to your local doctor. He'll know what to do if there's any kind of problem."

Martin grinned at the boys. "Let's go. There's work to be done."

The doctor shook his head. "That's precisely what you can't do, not for a while," he said firmly. "You can watch and give directions, but remember not to get around ice or snow where you can slip. Using your hands to stop a fall will just complicate things. It's important that you use your hands as little as possible."

Martin stood there a moment, looking down at his hands. His eyes took on a curious distant look.

"Is something wrong, Martin?" Jake asked. "Do you need a painkiller?"

"No." Martin shrugged. "I was just thinking. This incident has given me a mortality check. I won't live forever, and before anything else happens, there's something you and Nick need to know. You, too," he said, looking at Annie. "It's important."

It was his tone that scared Annie the most. She had a feeling Jake wasn't going to like whatever Martin had to say, and neither was she. Every instinct she possessed assured her of that.

AN HOUR LATER Jake led Martin into the den. Nick took a seat on the sofa and Annie took the chair.

"It's time for you brothers to learn what happened between Saya and Paul." Martin paused, then, gathering his thoughts, continued. "I've never repeated this story because it was told to me in confidence, but it's your right to know. Maybe it'll eventually help you understand the turmoil your father went through and why things fell apart in your family." Martin took a deep breath, then let it out slowly. "I'm the only one, except maybe your uncle Thomas, who knows why Paul destroyed Saya's studio that night so many years ago."

Jake leaned forward. "Tell us what happened. I know that night changed everything between them."

"Paul discovered that Saya was leaving the ranch twice a week to meet with her art teacher, a Pueblo man who was a renowned artist but also had quite a reputation as a womanizer. Paul didn't want Saya anywhere near him, but she refused to stop attending her classes. In a rage, Paul decided to pay the teacher a visit, determined to teach him a lesson about staying away from other men's wives. But Saya guessed where Paul was going, and, afraid of what he might do, called her teacher and warned him. The man grabbed whatever he could carry and took off before Paul could find him. He ended up in Arizona, I heard.''

"At least Paul didn't hurt the man," Annie said with a sigh of relief.

"Paul hurt himself most of all that night, destroying the trust in his marriage," Martin answered. "When he returned to Saya's studio in the bunkhouse, he was still angry. Saya held her ground, insisting she'd done nothing wrong. She told Paul that she'd guessed where he was headed and warned her teacher, fearing for all of them. If Paul had found and hurt the man, he could have ended up in jail. But Paul wouldn't let the matter drop. Saya refused to argue, and kept painting instead, ignoring him. Finally, Paul exploded. He trashed the studio, ruining months of her work.''

Martin paused and exhaled softly. "It was all such a waste. After that night, Saya quit painting, though she kept sketching because it was easy to hide her drawings. She never spoke to your father again, either, except when absolutely necessary or around you and your brother.''

"It almost sounds as if you were there that night," Nick said.

"I wish I had been. Maybe I could have reasoned with Paul. Your father told me everything the day Saya died, including Saya's last words to him, denying that she'd ever been unfaithful.''

Jake remembered the sketchbook and deposit slip they'd found from his mother's account. Perhaps it had been more than just a nest egg. "Do you think she considered leaving him at one time?''

"I'm sure she must have thought about it, but, deep

down, she knew she'd never leave Paul. The fact was, she loved your father deeply and, no matter how much he hurt her, that never changed.''

Silence descended over them. Finally, Annie spoke. ''You look exhausted, Martin. You really should get some rest.''

Martin stood. ''Can you drive me home, Nick?''

''Sure, let's go.''

When, at last, Martin left accompanied by Nick, Jake walked into his father's study. As his gaze took in the damaged desk, he remembered the many times he'd seen his father seated there, grumbling as always about the high price of hay.

Recalling the story that his father had routinely given away hay to the other farmers in the pueblo, he began to question how well he'd really known his father, or his mother for that matter. Perhaps if he had that mysterious diary, he'd find out the truth about them once and for all.

Annie came up behind him a moment later. ''This house has seen too much unhappiness.''

''Yes, it has. But there were good times here too, once. After my father's killer pays for what he's done, maybe we can all look to the future and finally put the past to rest.''

''When you restore this place, Jake, it'll mark a new beginning for Black Raven Ranch because you're its future.''

He watched her as she walked out, then added, ''As are you, Annie.''

## Chapter Seventeen

Jake spent the following morning helping the ranch hands and working alongside Nick. With Martin unable to assist and, instead, keeping an eye on the house, nothing seemed to go quite as smoothly.

By the time Jake was ready to take his lunch break, Annie was packing her finished carvings into boxes she'd acquired in the kitchen. She'd been up since dawn.

"Looks like you've been hard at work," Jake commented.

"But I'm finished—finally!"

Hearing a knock at the front door, she stopped. "Don't get up, Jake. Eat your lunch. I'll go answer that."

Annie returned a minute later. "I'm sorry to interrupt you, but Iris, your dad's former housekeeper, has dropped by. She's insisting that there's a white wolf fetish somewhere in the house that belongs to her, and she wants permission to search for it."

Without waiting for an invitation, Iris entered. "I don't want to bother anyone, but Paul gave me that hand-carved fetish as a gift. I had it here while I was working for him, but forgot to take it when I quit. Now I'd like it back."

Jake glared at her, annoyed at the intrusion. "If it was

something you treasured, why didn't you take it with you when you left his employ?''

"I didn't remember where I'd put it, and I figured I could come back later anyway. But I lost track of time. Then, with everything that's happened lately…'' She shrugged. "Anyway, it's mine, and I'd like to have it back.''

Jake looked at her pensively. The woman was as nervous as a cat in a rainstorm, leading him to believe she was interested in more than the fetish. He wondered if perhaps she, too, was after the diary. The existence of the diary was, thanks to his uncle Thomas, common knowledge. What people didn't know was that someone else already had it—the blackmailer.

Or maybe Iris had heard about the hidden evidence, and wanted a chance to try her luck at finding it. Of course, there was also the slim possibility she was actually telling the truth.

"I have no desire to keep what's yours,'' Jake told her. "If you'll leave a detailed description of the fetish with Patrick Kelly, our attorney, Annie and I will do our best to find the piece for you.''

Iris's expression changed from confidence to confusion, then abruptly to anger. She turned her head and glared at Annie. "It's always you in my way, isn't it? Your innocent face hides more than any of the Black Ravens realize. It was your fault Paul fired me, don't think I don't know that. You wanted him for yourself, so you undermined my position here and forced him to choose you. Now you've got your sights set on Jake.''

"What?'' Annie stared at her in shock. "You can't honestly believe that.''

"Paul was going to be mine, but you wanted him, too, and you're young and pretty. You did everything in your power to become part of his life. Everyone in the pueblo knows it.'' She looked back at Jake. ''You need to open your eyes before she twists you around her finger like she did your father.''

''That's enough,'' Jake snapped, his voice all stone and ice. ''I won't have you making wild accusations like that in this house.''

Iris faced Annie. ''I promise you one thing—you won't win at your game. You'll never find happiness here at our pueblo or in this house.'' With one last glance at Jake, Iris rushed past Annie and left the house, cursing the entire length of the hall.

''Don't let her get to you,'' Jake said, going to Annie's side. ''She's obviously upset, and was talking nonsense.''

''Maybe so,'' Annie said, ''but the hatred in her voice was very real. I wonder how many others share her opinion of me.''

''None who matter,'' Jake said gently. He tried to pull her into his arms, but she pulled away.

''No, Jake,'' she said firmly. ''I have to take my carvings to the gallery in Santa Fe today. There are a few people interested in them already, according to the owner. I'm hoping it'll turn into a bidding situation. I'll get a better price that way.'' She checked her watch. ''I've got to get going. I'm already late.''

''How about letting me drive, then take you out to lunch later in Santa Fe? I have to go up to meet with Patrick Kelly.''

''All right. I feel a little uncomfortable driving alone so close to term.''

''It's a wise precaution. Let me get your coat,'' Jake offered.

Five minutes later they were on their way. The roads were clear and dry, although there were patches of snow in the shady spots beside the highway.

Annie looked back at the box holding her immediate economic future. "I sure hope someone will appreciate all the work I've put into these carvings."

"They will. I've seen your carvings, Annie. You're very talented. Why don't you let me help you give your work the attention it deserves?"

"What do you have in mind?"

"I could place ads promoting your work in the local and Albuquerque papers. It'll give you the kind of exposure you need."

"Ads are expensive. It's not just space in the paper—you have to hire someone to do the layout." She shook her head. "I've thought of doing that myself, but the fact is, I can't afford it."

"That's why I was offering to foot the bill. Think of it as an early Christmas present."

She stared at him in surprise. "I can't let you do that."

"Why? It's not that big a deal. I'm just glad to be in a position to give you a gift you can really use."

"You don't understand." She paused for several moments, trying to find the right words. "I've had to work so hard to make it this far in my career. I want to go the rest of the way on my own. I've paid my dues. I spent hours studying, sketching designs, trying to create a pattern or image with a sharp knife, a piece of wood, and my imagination. To come this far alone, and then achieve success because of what someone else bought for me at a crucial time, would take away from everything I've managed to accomplish by myself."

Jake nodded slowly. He, better than most people could have, understood her need to prove herself. He'd felt the same way about his construction company.

Thirty minutes later Jake watched as Annie entered the well-known art gallery near the plaza. He'd offered to advertise her work for purely selfish reasons. His feelings for Annie were strong and it was clear to him now that what they really lacked was a bond to bridge the things that separated them. He'd thought that if he could become part of the world of art she loved, if he could help her in some small way, it would have been a first step. But he should have known Annie's pride would never allow it.

As he pulled back out into the street, he had to acknowledge the inescapable similarities between his parents' situation and his own with Annie. What was worse, in a lot of ways the past was repeating itself, and that was one thing he could not allow to happen.

JAKE LEFT Patrick Kelly's office later than he'd expected. As he walked west toward the plaza, he noticed Annie strolling the sidewalk on the north side of Saint Francis Cathedral. He doubled his pace, wanting to catch up to her, but as he drew closer, he noticed someone tailing her.

Jake struggled to make out the man's face, but the stranger was wearing a wide-brimmed cowboy hat that hid his features, and his thick winter coat all but obscured his build.

Determined to catch and question the man, Jake cut through a small courtyard that led to several connected shops and restaurants. Hurrying through a clothing shop, he dashed down a small interior stairwell, and came out behind Annie, on the other side of a waist-high wall. He ducked down, pretending to tie his shoelace, careful to hide his face.

As the man started to pass Jake, his gaze focused on Annie, Jake straightened suddenly and grabbed him by the arm.

Jake stared at the very familiar face of his uncle Thomas. "Why are you following Annie?" he demanded.

"Because, like your father, you're blind when it comes to this young woman. Someone has to find out where she fits into everything that's happened."

Annie came rushing up, having heard and recognized the loud voices. "What on earth is going on?"

"My uncle decided to follow you," Jake said, never taking his eyes off Thomas.

"Listen, Jake. Annie Sandusky is the only outsider at the ranch. She and Paul were close friends, and he must have confided in her. If anyone knows or can guess where Paul hid the evidence that points to the killer, Annie can. I'm willing to bet that Saya's diary is in the same hiding place, too. I was hoping that she'd eventually lead me to it."

Jake's eyes narrowed. "So you're mostly interested in the diary, not who killed my father. That's what's been bugging me about you, Uncle Thomas. What exactly does this diary contain that makes it so important to you? There's more to it than you've let on. And tell me straight. I'm running out of patience."

Thomas started to protest but then recanted. "All right. The plain truth is, Saya was very easy to talk to. People always trusted and confided in her, so she knew everyone's secrets. Her diary, depending on what she chose to write in it, could prove damaging to many in this community."

"I'm not interested in other people's family secrets," Jake said, "only in ours."

"If you do find the diary, what will you do with it? Will you read it?"

"I'll let you know if and when that day comes."

"I'll hold you to that," Thomas said.

After he left, Jake took Annie to his favorite restaurant on San Francisco Street, but neither of them could concentrate on the food. Their minds were on the case.

"I keep thinking that I'm missing a vital piece of the

puzzle,'' Jake said, picking at a beef enchilada with his fork.

''Your father was a highly intelligent man. We know he had a fondness for hiding places, but he would have been far more careful after Saya's diary was stolen from the cubbyhole in his bedroom. What if he hid the evidence in plain sight? It could be something we've seen a hundred times and never realized it.''

''I think my father would have really enjoyed that—fooling his enemies with such a simple strategy.''

BY THE TIME they arrived back at the ranch, Jake felt as taut as a bowstring. Hurrying up the walk to the front door beside him, Annie matched his pace.

The tension between them was palpable as they entered the study. ''Okay, any suggestions where we should start our new search?'' Jake asked.

''His desk. He would have wanted whatever he considered important close to him,'' Annie replied.

''Right,'' Jake acknowledged.

Three minutes later they were still staring at the massive desk, now blackened on one side by the fire. The items originally on or in the desk were still there, mostly in boxes now, though some had suffered from the flames or the attempt to extinguish them.

Annie located and opened the daily calendar, the appointment book, and the notebook-sized business checkbook.

Jake studied the correspondence from the In and Out baskets. He even checked the telephone itself, which was sitting on the floor, now working again after the melted cord had been replaced.

Standing to his right, Annie flipped through the circular Rolodex card file, which had escaped both fire and water.

"There's nothing here," Jake said at last. "Maybe we should concentrate on another room. I've searched everything else in the study while I was cleaning up and repairing the wall."

She continued flipping through the Rolodex file, checking card by card. "There sure are a lot of cards in the section for last names starting with XYZ. I don't know about you, but I can't think of even one person around here with a last name beginning with one of those letters."

Jake took one of the cards out of the ring. "What kind of name is 'X-1'?"

As he held up the card, Annie leaned forward, studying the other side. "Turn it around. There's a bunch of stuff written on the back." She checked the other cards in the file. "There's something on the back of a lot of them, especially in the XYZ section."

"They look like accounts," Jake said, reading the information carefully.

"What on earth have we found here?" she mused, more curious than ever.

"He's turned the backs of these cards into an accounting ledger of sorts. I guess he wanted to keep this out of the books the accountants would audit." He studied the entries for a long time. "Look," he said at last. "The sentence at the top of each card makes no sense unless you take the first letter of each word and put them together. Look at this—'My Appaloosa Ran Through Interesting Neighborhoods.'"

"Martin," Annie said after a moment.

"Exactly. The two columns below are debits and credits. On the left is the date and amount loaned. On the right, the payments. Martin borrowed twice. You can see from where he paid off the first loan that my father charged no interest."

"He must have coded the cards to keep them private, despite their easily accessible location," Annie said.

"If you just happened to come across these, they'd almost look as if he'd been figuring out some math problems," Jake said, pointing to the stray pencil marks on the side.

As they sat and began to review the entries, Annie glanced at the amount Martin still owed. "That's quite a substantial amount. It's got to be equivalent to a year's salary for him."

"I'd have to check to be absolutely certain, but I think you're right," Jake said. "According to this, he was paying it off, but, admittedly, at a very slow rate."

"Look at this one," she said, handing him another card. "It appears Iris borrowed money, too. That's quite a bit for a housekeeper to have to pay back. And it looks like she's only made a few payments in the past ten months."

"My uncle also borrowed a bundle of cash, but according to this he hasn't even made one payment in the six months since the loan."

"Do you think this was what Thomas was really after?" Annie asked.

"He was probably hoping we'd never find any record of the loan, but my gut feeling is that he told us the truth when he said that the diary is his greatest concern. On the other hand, the person who broke in may have been searching for this. That would explain why he took my father's business ledgers."

"That person could have been Thomas, at least the first time," she said. "He would have known we were at the funeral, and could have estimated how long the rituals would take. But there's something else to consider. It's quite possible that this *is* the evidence your father was talking about. Maybe Thomas or someone else listed here killed your father.''

''These are no-interest loans,'' he reminded her. ''There also doesn't seem to be any payment schedule included. Why would they kill him over this?''

''People sometimes grow to resent the person who tries to help them.'' She gestured to the phone. ''I think you should call Captain Mora and tell him what we've found.''

''Yes, you're right, but I hope this doesn't create problems for Martin. After everything he's done for this family, he doesn't deserve it. If Mora thinks this loan gives Martin a motive for murder, he might question him again.''

''It can't be helped. This is evidence that has to be turned over.''

Jake dialed the tribal police then, after a brief conversation, placed the phone back down on the floor.

''That was quick,'' she said.

''Mora's away on personal business until later tonight. He'll call me when he returns to the pueblo.'' Jake stared at the Rolodex file, lost in thought. ''I'm going to pay Uncle Thomas a visit right now. He has more explaining to do.''

Annie looked at Jake, concerned. He meant to get the truth, and his concentration was so total, it gave him an air of danger.

''I'm going with you,'' she said. ''The situation between you two could get out of control easily. Circumstances must have forced him to borrow money from Paul, and that was undoubtedly very hard on him. But, now, to have to explain this to you…'' She shook her head. ''You need information, not a confrontation. If I'm there, I can help keep things on the right track.''

Jake considered it. He didn't want to leave her at the house alone. Though Annie would never admit it to him freely, the baby was taking a toll on her energy. The closer she got to term, the more vulnerable she became. All in all, he'd rather have her with him.

"Okay, we'll go together," he said.

Jake picked up the Rolodex cards that pertained to Thomas, then walked out to the truck with Annie. He couldn't help but notice that her steps these days were slower as she struggled against the added weight of the growing baby. Yet, she was at her radiant best. She'd never looked more beautiful to him than she did now.

"Once word gets out that we know about these loans—and it will after we approach Thomas—the killer is bound to get nervous and that'll make him even more dangerous," she said, interrupting his thoughts.

"I know, but we're out of options. We have to draw him out."

"I want this whole thing finished and my baby safe, but we'll have to watch each other's backs carefully now," she said softly.

"Count on it." From now on, he'd be right beside her every step of the way—whether she wanted him there or not.

## Chapter Eighteen

As they rode in silence, Jake felt the warmth of her body wrap itself around him. It felt so right to have Annie beside him. Her strength and loyalty drew him to her gently, yet relentlessly. He wanted her, but in a way that went beyond the physical. He wanted to be the man she turned to when she was troubled, the man she chose to have beside her when she needed comfort. He wanted her to share the magic—that special feeling that told him without a doubt that they were meant to be.

He disciplined his thoughts. Right now she needed his protection, and that would take focus.

As they pulled up in front of a small stucco-and-frame house, Thomas came out from a side gate and walked over to meet them. "What brings you two over here? Have you found the diary?"

"Not the diary, no," Jake said. "But we did find something else."

"The evidence your father mentioned?"

Jake told him what they'd learned. "I'd like an explanation. It seems to me that my father would have been the last person around you would have turned to for a loan. And even after he helped you, it's obvious you continued to hate him. Why?"

Thomas hesitated before answering. "That money wasn't a loan. It was a payoff so I would stop pressuring him for Saya's diary. Though he couldn't prove it, he knew that I'd broken into his house a few times, searching for it. I think he was afraid that I wouldn't stop until I found it. He offered to pay me to back off. As he put it, it would be worth it to him if he didn't have to see me anywhere near his property or have me asking for the diary again."

"So you took the money," Jake observed coldly.

Thomas shrugged. "I knew Paul had more money than he deserved, and I needed the cash. But I kept my side of the bargain. I stopped breaking in, and quit asking for the diary. It wasn't getting me anywhere, anyway."

"Tell me who else was interested in the diary," Jake pressed, trying to narrow down the identity of the blackmailer.

"What makes you think that someone else was interested in it, or even knew it existed?"

"You're not known for discretion. I figured somewhere along the line you told someone else."

"Yeah, okay, maybe I did, but I never heard of anyone else wanting it."

"You mentioned to me before that you and my mother kept in contact. Did you know she had a private bank account?" Jake asked, watching his expression carefully.

Thomas raised his eyebrows, surprised by the question. At last, he nodded. "How did you find out? That was supposed to be a secret. Saya continued selling her sketches, though she did quit doing her oil paintings, and squirreled all the money away in a special account. She figured that if Paul ever pushed her too far, she'd have enough set aside to leave him. But I knew that was just talk. Saya would never have left your father. Love makes some people stupid."

"And my father never knew about the account?"

"Paul was never any good as a bookkeeper, according to Saya, so she got away with it. The account, eventually, grew into a modest sum. After she died, Paul's lawyer settled all of Saya's affairs and since she didn't leave a will, everything went to Paul. I found out later that nobody had bothered to check for bank accounts in her name, but I never said anything. To be honest, I wasn't in the mood to tell Paul, and I figured it could just keep collecting interest until you or Nick could claim it."

"Who else knew about the account, as far as you know?" Jake asked.

Thomas considered it carefully. "I'd bet Virgil Lowman did. But he never would have told your father."

"I thought Virgil and Dad got along."

"Virgil's a good businessman and he's always known his bank needed Paul Black Raven's money. But he was loyal to Saya. He would have continued to keep her secret even after her death."

"What happened to the money in that account, do you know?" Jake pressed.

"No, but I will tell you that one of the reasons I wanted Saya's diary was because I was hoping that she'd listed the account number in there. I figured that, with a bit of luck and some creative thinking, I could come up with a way to get some of that money."

"There's no legal way—" Jake stopped, seeing Thomas's grin.

"Your father didn't deserve that money," Thomas continued. "And you and Nick had been gone for years. Yet there I was and there it was—and I certainly could have used the cash." He waved to the small house behind him. "This isn't exactly the Black Raven Ranch."

"Taking the money—had you managed it—could have

cost you a jail sentence," Jake said, distaste evident in his tone.

"Only if I got caught. And, who knows, with the right connections I may have gotten the charges dropped."

"How well do you know Virgil?" Annie asked.

Thomas shrugged. "He wouldn't have helped me get the money, if that's what you're really asking. I'm not Virgil's friend. I don't know anyone who is, though plenty of people suck up to him because he has power. The only time I ever see Virgil outside the bank is if I run in to him at the Silver Slipper Casino."

"Are you and Virgil regulars there?" Annie smiled. "It's got to be an exciting place with all the high-stake games and chances to win big." Keeping her tone enthusiastic and nonconfrontational worked. Thomas seemed to relax and he answered her question without anger.

"I play the slot machines only," he said. "I don't have the money to gamble at roulette or the card tables. Virgil, on the other hand, has lost a bundle at blackjack, from what I hear."

Jake met his uncle's gaze. "Let me give you fair warning, Uncle. You're family, but if I ever catch you breaking in, or doing anything illegal that jeopardizes anyone at the Black Raven Ranch, there'll be hell to pay. Clear?"

Thomas gave him a cold, mirthless smile. "I always said that you had a lot in common with your father. Neither you nor your brother know or care about family."

"Apparently, Uncle, neither do you."

"For the record, I never harmed a hair on your father's head. And I had nothing to do with your poisoning, though you certainly gave me reason that night."

"That depends on your point of view. As I remember it, you threw the first punch."

Thomas didn't reply. "Just to show you that I'm not your

enemy, I'll tell you something else that may help you. But you'll have to take my word for it, because I have no proof.'' He smiled, his eyes never wavering from Jake's. ''Shortly after our disagreement that night at the ranch, a person called me and offered a thousand bucks to break in and steal all the business ledgers and stocks or bonds I could find in the house.''

''Who called—and did you take the job?'' Jake asked.

''I don't know who it was. His voice was disguised, and there was some really loud background noise, like an arcade or maybe a video game.'' He smiled. ''Now about the other part of your question—I'm not sure I should tell you if I took the job or not. Your 'fair warning' speech was very specific.''

''We'll consider this conversation part of a temporary amnesty,'' Jake snapped.

''I'll trust your word,'' Thomas said, obviously enjoying putting Jake in an awkward position. ''I was the one who broke into your house the day of the funeral. It wasn't for the money—that was just a bonus. I'd intended to break in all along. I wanted the diary and any record of the money Paul paid me—if such a record existed.''

''Didn't you meet the person who hired you when it was time to deliver my father's papers?''

Thomas shook his head. ''I was told to put everything in a storage locker at the bus station in Santa Fe. The key was taped where I could find it, and the money was waiting for me inside the locker. But, just so you know, I had nothing to do with the fires at the ranch.'' Thomas opened the door to his home. ''I still have some of the things I took from your house, like a pen-and-ink sketch Saya made of both you boys. Paul had hidden it in the special place in his bedroom.''

''How did you know the crevice was there?'' Jake asked.

"I'd seen Saya use it many years ago. In fact, I'd looked for the diary there a long time ago, but struck out. The sketch was there, and I didn't think of taking it at the time but, later, I decided that I wanted it because I knew the sketch had been special to her.

"I also took some pottery. Neither of those were part of what I was hired to take. You can have them back if you want."

Jake said nothing for a moment, then shook his head. "Keep them for now, though I may someday want the sketch back."

"I'll remember that. I only took it because I don't have any by Saya and it meant something to me. But the pottery was something else. I stole that because I wanted to confuse the tribal police by making it look like a burglary. I should have taken the guns in your hall cabinet. It would have been more convincing, but I don't like guns." When Jake refused his invitation to go inside, Thomas added, "If you're sure you don't want the pottery back, I'll keep the pieces. They add a nice touch to my house."

Disgusted with everything he'd learned, Jake turned and led Annie back to the car. "I can't look at him any more without wanting to take a swing at him."

"I can understand why," she conceded. "But he did tell us a great deal."

"*If* Thomas was telling the truth, I wonder why Lowman hasn't gotten back to me with information about my mother's account. He's had enough time," he said as they got under way.

"It's possible that the account remained inactive for so long it got placed in some old computer file and now they can't find it."

"I'm going to call and demand an answer."

"Sounds like a good idea. Well, at least we know one

thing for sure. Thomas doesn't have the diary, so he can't be the blackmailer. Or the killer,'' she added.

"If you can trust a single word he says."

"We have a curious situation here. Thomas says that the money he received from Paul was an unsolicited payoff. But I find it hard to believe that Paul would do that. I think what really happened was that Paul assumed Thomas had found the diary and was going to blackmail him. Having Thomas in possession of the diary must have really worried Paul, because Thomas could have easily given you or your brother a copy. So as soon as Paul saw the diary was missing, he sent Thomas the money before it was demanded, to let him know that he was willing to pay for his silence.''

"That sounds like my dad. Even if the odds were stacked against him, he would have done his best to maintain control over the situation. Giving the money to the blackmailer before being asked made my dad look like a benefactor, not a victim. He was undermining his enemy in the only way he could. But if *we're* right, Dad guessed wrong. Thomas wasn't the blackmailer."

Jake lapsed into a thoughtful silence, then continued. "My father was wrong about many things. The more I find out about how things were between him and Mom, the more I wonder why Mom stayed."

"Your parents had a rough time of it. But no matter how bad things got, they had you and Nick. Believe me when I tell you a child can give a woman the courage to face almost anything. She loved her husband and he was the father of her sons. She stayed willingly, not only for herself, but for you and your brother. In her eyes, no one could have replaced your father."

"What about you?" he asked, his voice quiet. "Your love for your husband was real and it resulted in the baby you're carrying. Could you ever accept another father for your child?"

He heard her breath catch in her throat. She hadn't expected the question, but her answer would mean the world to him.

"It's not the same thing," she said slowly. "My child's father died. Someday, I hope my baby will have another father. Fatherhood, to me, is not just something that happens at the time of conception. It's a matter of love and commitment."

As he looked at her he felt a powerful tug on his senses. He wanted Annie and the baby to be a part of his life forever. Three hearts—bound by love. Nothing else the world offered could compare to that. Yet by placing what he wanted ahead of her needs, he'd be proving that he was a lot like his father, as some had suggested. The last thing he wanted was to make a shambles out of their relationship and have the past replay itself. His mother and father had found only sorrow through their love. He never wanted that to be a part of what he had to offer Annie.

They returned to his home and, as they walked toward the living room, he paced his steps to match hers.

"We've made a lot of progress toward finding my father's killer in the last few hours," he said, "but there are still a lot of things that just don't add up."

"Based on what Thomas was hired to steal—business ledgers and stocks and bonds—I really think we should concentrate on Virgil Lowman as a suspect. He was Saya's friend, and from what we've seen, had feelings for your mother. If she confided in him, he might have known exactly where to find the diary. Blackmailing your father, a man he probably saw as his rival, makes sense if you look at it from the standpoint of revenge."

"But if he knew where it was all this time, why would he wait until just a few months ago to steal it?"

"Maybe he didn't steal it. He could have had it all along. Your father knew about the diary, but we have no clear proof he ever had it."

"Then why would Lowman wait until recently to blackmail Dad?"

"It could have something to do with his gambling. If he's been losing heavily lately, he may be in financial trouble." She paused, then added, "Remember the call Thomas said he received from the man who hired him? Thomas mentioned there was a lot of background noise. It could have been slot machines at the casino. Over the phone, they might have sounded like arcade games."

"And you're thinking Dad had evidence that proved Virgil was blackmailing him?"

"It's all conjecture, but it fits."

Jake's reply was cut off when the phone rang. "Virgil, it's good to hear from you," he said, identifying the caller for Annie's benefit.

"We finally have the paperwork we needed from state government and your attorney," Virgil said. "You can access your father's safe-deposit box any time you're ready. I've notified Mora."

Jake hung up and filled Annie in.

"We've been thinking of Virgil as a blackmailer, or worse, and here he is all of a sudden trying to help us," Annie said, cringing slightly.

"He was obliged to provide the paperwork. I'd scarcely categorize it as help."

Jake called Captain Mora and told him they'd be opening the box right away, something he knew the captain had been awaiting. He then filled him in on what they'd learned from Thomas, asking him not to press charges unless the evidence eventually led back to Thomas as the murderer.

As he hung up, Jake looked at Annie. "He'll meet us at the bank in twenty minutes. He's as eager as we are to see what's there."

They drove together to the bank and, by the time they arrived, Virgil Lowman and Captain Mora were waiting.

Lowman took them into an empty office. "According to law, I have to be present when you open the box. Tax purposes require that a representative of the state, or some other accredited individual, verify the contents. Captain Mora, of course, is here because of his ongoing investigation."

Jake opened the box as Annie stood beside him. "Interesting," he muttered.

Annie glanced down and saw three cash withdrawal slips that had been stapled to blackmail notes. "Those notes have photocopied sections that look to be from your mother's diary," she said softly.

"Handle them by the edges only," Mora cautioned. "We may be able to get usable prints."

"The withdrawals match the blackmail demands," Jake commented.

"What are those other papers?" Annie asked. "Anything important there?"

Jake studied them. "They're bearer bonds, and worth a small fortune, too. Since bearer bonds aren't made out to any particular individual, whoever has physical possession of them can cash the bond in. They're not very safe to leave lying around."

"That's probably why he kept them here. The bank did make those purchases for him," Lowman said.

"But why did he put them here, along with these notes?"

Jake asked, not really expecting an answer. "Was it just for convenience, or because they're somehow related?"

"I can't see any connection," Lowman said flatly.

Jake watched Lowman's expression carefully. "Are these all the bearer bonds the bank purchased on behalf of my father?"

Lowman shook his head. "There were more, I think, but I'd have to total up the amounts and check that against our records to be certain. That'll take some time. But I should tell you, it's also very possible your father sold or traded some of the bonds. That's what most people eventually do with them."

"I was hoping for more than this," Mora said, disappointed. "We already knew about the blackmail." He looked at Virgil. "Did he ever mention that to you?"

"Blackmail? No, not one word," Lowman said.

"Keep it to yourself for now, Virgil. What I'd like to do is take the contents of the box to my office," Mora said. "Do you have any objection, Jake?"

"Not as long as I get it all back eventually."

Mora looked at Virgil. "Would you give us a moment alone, please?"

Lowman nodded and walked out.

Annie watched him through the window as he walked away. Assured she could speak freely, she looked at Mora. "Captain, do you agree that Lowman's our best suspect?"

"Yes, but we have to move carefully. We don't have any solid proof against him and, if we tip our hand too soon, he could bolt or destroy evidence. Then we'll have nothing. Let him feel we trust him. That'll give me time to get some more information.

"I'd like to find out if he's the one who hired Thomas Ray. To do that, I have to access phone records to see if anyone called Ray's house from the Silver Slipper. If Lowman hired him to break in, the trail will start there. I also want to check if Lowman was in the casino or bank the day your father was killed. Casinos have video cameras everywhere, so it won't be hard to look into this. I'll also want to question the bank employees away from work.''

Mora placed one of the bonds in an evidence pouch, then the rest in a separate pouch along with the blackmail notes and the deposit slips. ''I'll keep these in our safe at the station.''

''What about the bond in the other pouch?'' Annie asked.

''I'd like to take this one to a bank in Santa Fe. I have a friend who'll be able to tell us more about bearer bonds like these.''

''I'd like to go, too, if you don't mind,'' Jake said.

''No problem.''

As they went out to the parking lot, Annie walked slowly, feeling even more tired than usual. Jake felt his gut wrench as he noticed her struggle. Annie was a strong woman, but she'd been pushing herself too hard.

''Why don't you let me drop you off at home?'' he suggested.

''At home.'' The words had a nice ring to them, but she wasn't going to be pushed aside now. She'd made a vow to catch Paul's killer and she'd see it through.

''I'm okay. I want to come along,'' she said firmly.

He knew better than to argue.

The Santa Fe bank was closed by the time they arrived, but Mora had made arrangements, and a tall Anglo man in his early sixties met them at the door.

Mora introduced them. ''This is Stephen Marcus. There's nothing about investment banking that he doesn't know.''

''He's right,'' Marcus said with an easy smile, ''even if

he is using flattery to divert from the fact that he's kept me here after closing.''

Marcus led them to his office, then seated himself behind his desk. He studied the bearer bond Mora handed him for a long time, brought two more out of a small document safe behind him, and set them down side-by-side. "Examine the differences in the paper quality and the fine detail work, and you'll see that what you brought today is only a very good counterfeit copy.''

After thanking Marcus, they went back outside, stunned by the news.

"I'll have Marcus come in to verify the others, but I'm sure the paper was identical on the other bonds, as well,'' Mora said, glancing at Jake. "And that raises all kinds of questions.''

"I know what you're thinking. We now have to find out if my dad knew they were only copies, and if this is part of the evidence he was collecting against the person blackmailing him.''

"And if all Paul had were copies of these bearer bonds, who has the originals? Lowman? Or is there another player we don't know about yet?'' Mora added.

Once they reached pueblo land, Jake drove Annie back to the ranch. He was worried about her. She hadn't said much and she appeared restless.

"What's on your mind? I can tell something's not right,'' he said at last.

"I've been expecting an important call. Staying away from the phone, even under these circumstances, was harder than I thought.''

"Is the call about the baby?''

She shook her head. "It's about my carvings. When I took them in, Sam Luna, the owner of the gallery, said there might be enough interest in the pieces to hold an auction. But I haven't heard from him since.''

"Did he give you any idea how much he expected them to go for?"

"No. Sam's a good businessman and I trust him, but the truth is, those carvings represent the best work I've ever done. I want to get a *very* good price for them. It's more than just pride, too. There are a lot of things I'd like to get for the baby.''

"If you need anything at all—"

She held up a hand. "You don't understand. I've bought everything the baby will *need,* but there are little things that I want to get for her."

As they entered the house, Jake watched Annie walk slowly to her room. He loved her and nothing would ever change that. He fought the desire to go to her room, to undress her and put her to bed, to hold her and whisper dark, erotic things to her. The man in him told him she wouldn't resist, that she wanted the same thing. But he wouldn't push her.

"Hey, Jake." Nick's voice interrupted his thoughts.

"We've got to talk, Nick," Jake said, leading the way to the study. "I need to fill you in on a few developments."

Jake told him everything they'd learned. "What do you think? *Is* Lowman the killer?" Jake pressed. "I could use your insight."

"At the end, Mom was bedridden from the cancer," Nick said, "but her mind was clear. She must have known that her diary had the potential to cause a lot of trouble, and that if Uncle Thomas got hold of it he'd probably use it to hurt Dad or us. She would have done her level best to see that the diary was destroyed, but she couldn't have accomplished that on her own. She may have turned the task over to someone else she thought she could trust—like

Lowman. I'm sure she must have known he had a thing for her.''

''That was Annie's theory, too. Poor Dad must have gone crazy looking for that diary until finally the black-mailer came forward. That is, of course, if we're right.''

''You know, even if we could prove Lowman is the blackmailer, that still wouldn't mean he killed Dad,'' Nick said. ''What we still lack is a clear motive and hard facts. The phony bearer bonds are important, but Mora will need more solid evidence before he can get a search warrant to go through Lowman's office and home.''

''I'm tempted to break into Lowman's house myself,'' Jake said. ''Even if all I found was Mom's diary, I'd take that as a win.''

''We have to get it back, but not if it compromises the case against a man who could turn out to be Dad's killer,'' Nick said.

The phone rang. Jake went to the desk and picked it up. It was the gallery calling for Annie. He hesitated, not want-ing to disturb her if she was resting but, as he looked up, he saw her standing at the door.

''It's the call you were waiting for,'' he said.

''I'll take it in the kitchen,'' she said, then hurried out.

Jake stayed in the study long after all the lights in the house were out, but Annie never returned. Once again, the woman who'd come to mean the world to him had shut him out of her life.

Jake walked upstairs to his room, a cold emptiness gnaw-ing at him. Annie had built a barrier between them, and as much as he wanted to make things happen, to force things to go his way, he wouldn't repeat the mistakes his father had made. A woman's heart was too strong to be won. Only love would compel her to surrender it and place it in the hands of another.

# *Chapter Nineteen*

Annie was restless the next morning as she and Jake set up the small piñon one of the hands had given them to replace the Christmas tree they'd lost in the fire. Once the tree stood securely in the *sala,* she went to her room and returned holding the glass ornament she'd been restoring during breaks from her carvings. The decoration had escaped the worst of the heat because it had been on a low outside branch and had fallen away from the flames. "It came along pretty smoothly after I got started, and I was able to restore the original artwork."

Jake took it from her hands and, for a moment, didn't speak.

"I actually retraced your mother's own design. There were parts that I couldn't restore, but I filled in the gaps."

Jake met her gaze. "I don't know how to thank you," he said, his voice thick with emotion.

Annie saw all she needed to in his eyes. "You already have."

Jake took her hand in his and pulled her to him, but suddenly the phone rang. Annie jumped then, walking quickly, went to answer it. It was a wrong number. Disappointment filled her, but she tried to hide it as she hung up the phone.

"What's the latest on the carvings?" Jake asked, accurately guessing what was going on. "Didn't you get the news you were hoping for last night? I waited for you to come back and tell me what was going on, but I guess you went to bed instead."

She realized then that she'd hurt Jake by not confiding in him, but how could she have done that? Her pride, her self-confidence, were all being tested to the max now. "Mr. Luna is auctioning the pieces today. Seven of his best customers were interested in the carvings and he thought this was the best way to make sure everyone got a fair shot at them."

"That's wonderful news," he said, his eyebrows furrowed. "So why do you look as if you're facing a firing squad?"

"What if they take a second look at the carvings, change their minds, and decide not to bid? Or what if we only get one offer—at a rock-bottom price?"

He smiled, placing one of the salvaged ornaments from the old tree so the charred side wasn't visible. He'd never seen Annie so unsure of herself. "It won't happen. I've seen your work, remember? Stop worrying."

"But it could happen. And if my carvings sell for peanuts, word will get around to all the galleries in the southwest."

"You're creating problems based on nothing but wild speculations. Relax."

"Easy for you to say," she muttered. "Your livelihood isn't on the line." The phone rang and Annie picked it up immediately, setting down the half-empty box of ornaments. The first bid had come in by phone, establishing a floor for the auction, but it was much lower than either Luna or she had hoped.

Her heart plummeted but she fought to keep her voice steady as she thanked Luna for calling.

"I gather the news isn't what you expected?" Jake asked, noting the crestfallen look on her face.

"At least we have a bid," Annie said, managing a smile. "Things could have been worse."

Hearing the doorbell, Jake went to answer it. Annie continued to decorate the tree, but her mind was on the auction.

Taking a break, Annie went into the kitchen to make herself a piece of toast. She was buttering the bread when Jake led Captain Mora into the room.

"I thought you'd like to hear this, Annie," Jake said, motioning for Mora to have a seat. "We're alone, so you don't have to worry about confidentiality, Captain. Martin isn't here, and my brother is out with some of the hands rounding up the horses before the predicted storm gets here."

Mora sat with them at the kitchen table. "I'm doing a complete background check on Virgil Lowman and, so far, I've discovered he has some pretty big problems that could give him a motive. It seems he owes three different casinos a great deal of money. They've refused to take his bets at their tables, and have had their collectors pay him a visit."

"This would certainly explain why he needed cash right now," Jake said.

"If he's been looking for sources of money, I think he's probably already cleaned out your mother's bank account," Annie said quietly. "That would have been too much of a temptation for him. He probably figured nobody would ever find out the money was there, and he'd never get caught."

Mora stood. "That's all I've got for you right now, so I better get back to work."

Jake walked him out but before he returned to the kitchen

the phone rang. Annie scooped up the receiver in record time.

"We've had a surprise," Luna said. "Another party, acting through a broker, just made a phenomenal offer."

He gave her the figure and her heart did a somersault. It was beyond anything she'd expected.

"The other bidders haven't countered, so it looks like this will be the final sale price."

She placed the receiver down, excited and happy. The moment Jake returned, she gave him the news. "It's really flattering to have someone pay that much for my work, but I can't help but wonder if there isn't something more going on here."

Jake laughed. "First you were worried about not getting enough money. Now you're worried because it's too much?"

"I'm happy but—" Annie suddenly sucked in a sharp breath. It felt as if her stomach had hardened into a rock. Then, slowly, the pressure and tightening eased, spreading downward before finally going away. She seated herself slowly in one of the kitchen chairs.

"What? Are you all right?" he asked quickly.

"Yes," she managed to answer in a shaky voice. "But I think I better call Elsie. I should have seen her yesterday, but I didn't get around to it."

"I'll call her right now," Jake said, picking up the phone.

AN HOUR LATER Annie sat with Elsie in her bedroom. Her blood pressure had been taken, the baby's heartbeat was strong, and everything was proceeding well. "You're having more of these Braxton-Hicks contractions because you're so close to term. Some can be very uncomfortable, but they're helping your body prepare for labor. Just remember, you're due anytime now, and if you get more than four per hour, it's time to call the troops. Tomorrow is Christmas Eve, too, so keep the number where I can be reached handy.''

''I will.''

''Is the baby quiet right now?''

Annie nodded.

''Then take advantage of it and get some sleep. You need to start being good to yourself.''

Annie fell asleep shortly after Elsie left. She'd meant to make it only a short nap, but it was ten-thirty at night when she finally woke up. As an idea for a new carving formed in her mind, she decided to go to her studio to sketch it out.

As Annie walked down the hall, she noticed the light was on in her studio. Peering inside, she saw Jake sitting on the easy chair by the window, going through some papers. A warm fire was burning in the horno-style fireplace in the corner.

''Is everything all right?'' she asked, moving to her carving desk.

''Yes, but I was worried about you,'' he said, standing and going to join her. ''I had a feeling you'd come here the moment you woke up, so I decided to stick around.''

''I woke up with an idea for my next carving,'' she said, and began sketching it out on paper. The figure of a mother breast-feeding her child materialized slowly on the paper as she gave it life.

''That's going to be beautiful,'' he said as she placed the pencil down on the pad.

She leaned back and tried to stretch, but her muscles protested. She forced herself to take a deep breath.

''Is it happening again?''

''It's not a contraction this time. My muscles are sore,

that's all. It would help to take a warm bath, but my weight makes me clumsy these days.''

"Let me help you, then." Seeing her hesitate, he added, "Annie, I'll just be there for you, nothing more.''

Temptation spiraled through her. His gentle hands on her, the warmth of the water. She could envision it all so clearly.

"Annie, let me do this for you," he insisted gently.

She wanted to stand firm, but the tenderness in his voice and her imagination made his offer irresistible. "All right," she whispered.

Jake led her gently to her bathroom. Then, while the tub was filling, he began to undress her. She didn't protest, allowing him to take over. Within a few minutes, she stood naked in front of him.

"Look at me," he said, tilting her chin upward until she met his gaze. "You have a beautiful, feminine body. Don't be embarrassed," he said, then helped her ease down into the tub.

Enveloped in the water, and bare to his gaze, she felt more vulnerable than she ever had. He knelt by the side of the tub, dipped his hands into the warm water, then moistened her shoulders, allowing the water to trickle down her body. He caressed her gently, asking nothing, and was rewarded by her soft sigh.

His touch was like magic, soothing her body and easing all her soreness away. Jake smoothed his wet palms over her breasts, then over the swell of her stomach, then moved lower, parting her legs. His touch was gentle, eliciting a slow fire that never pushed her over the edge, but led her gently toward it and kept her there.

"Don't stop," she whispered.

The water enveloped her in a gentle blanket; when he broached her body, she felt as though she were being rocked in a river of pleasure. Her body yielded to the exquisite sensations cascading through her until she came apart under his touch.

"I love the way you respond to me, sweetheart. When you sigh my name that way, you make me feel like one hell of a man."

She opened her eyes. "You are."

He kissed her then, long, slow, and deep. "What you need now is gentleness and love. I'm not asking you for promises, nor am I making you any that you aren't ready to accept. Just let me be what you need right now."

Her heart ached with love. "Then don't go. Just hold me," she murmured. As she stepped out of the tub, he dried her off, then took her back to bed. He placed the covers over her, then lay behind her, his arms securely around her until she fell asleep.

THE MORNING SUN was shining brightly when she woke up. She looked around but Jake was gone. Now, in the clear light of day, everything they'd shared last night seemed more like a wonderful dream than reality. Perhaps it was a little of the magic of the season. It was, after all, Christmas Eve.

Annie dressed and, as she entered the kitchen a while later, saw Jake. She was about to greet him when the phone began to ring. She picked it up and, after hearing the caller's name, handed the receiver to him. "It's Iris, for you."

Jake set his coffee cup down and took the phone. He listened for several moments, then spoke. "Where do you want to meet?" He hung up and looked over at Annie. "Iris wants to meet me alone by the crossroads at the north end of the pueblo," he said. "She sounds really frightened about something, but she wouldn't tell me what's going on." Jake grabbed his coat from the rack. "I better go. It shouldn't take me long but, in the meantime, make sure Martin or Nick can stay here with you."

"Nick is working," she said, looking out the window, "but Martin is just directing traffic and giving advice because of his burned hands. I'll ask him to come inside for a while."

"That should do it. I'll be back as soon as possible."

Intending to heat water for some chamomile tea first, she was pouring water into the teapot when she heard a knock at the front door. "I'm coming," she called.

As Annie opened the front door, she saw Virgil Lowman standing there, his pistol aimed directly at her stomach.

"Don't make a sound," he snapped. "I know you're alone in the house. Jake just left and everyone else is by the horse stalls. Nobody saw me driving up from the opposite side of the house. If you call for help, you'll die before anyone gets here."

"What do you want?" she asked, her voice trembling.

"Come with me." He shifted behind her, the gun pressed to the small of her back as he prodded her on.

"My coat," she said.

"Forget it. Just keep moving."

Quickly placing a letter in the mailbox, he pushed her toward his car as fast as she could walk. It was freezing outside, and she held her arms clutched to herself for warmth. He'd parked so the vehicle couldn't be seen from the corrals.

"Don't do this, Virgil. What can you possibly gain by kidnapping me?" she begged. "I'm about ready to have my baby, and the only thing I can do is slow you down."

"You've managed to ruin all my plans. I'd been led to believe that you were only staying at the ranch because you were broke. That's why I was hoping you'd be cashing in your check and getting ready to leave now that the art auction was over. But then, this morning I heard Martin's wife talking to her sister at the bank. I understand that you, Martin and the twins stand to inherit a chunk of money if you stick around for a year. So now it looks like you're not going anywhere, after all, and I wasted my money on those stupid carvings.''

''*You* bought my pieces?''

''Like I said, it would have been worth it, if you'd left. Jake would have been so distracted I wouldn't have had to worry about him. He and his brother would have gone back to their own lives, the ranch would have closed down, and I would have had a lot less to worry about.''

''Is that why you're kidnapping me? You want to distract Jake?''

''No, it's too late for that. Right now I just want Jake to do exactly what I tell him and the only way I can guarantee that, is by taking you away from him.''

''It's not Jake you have to worry about. Captain Mora knows about you, too. Were the bearer bonds the evidence Paul told me about after you stabbed him?'' she asked, trying to understand what was happening.

Lowman shook his head. ''They're just part of it. There's more, and Jake's going to find it for me—that is, if he wants to keep you alive.''

Her heart began to hammer against her ribs and she placed her hand over her stomach. She couldn't let this happen. She had to protect her baby.

''You blackmailed Paul, too, didn't you?'' she asked, stopping in front of his car, playing for time. ''Saya gave you the diary and trusted in your friendship, but you ended up betraying her.''

''Saya was a beautiful, gentle creature. If anyone betrayed her, it was Paul. All I did was make him pay for the hell he put her through.''

"Don't make it sound noble. You're not fooling anyone. You knew that the diary could hamper any attempt Paul made to reconcile with his sons, and that gave you an advantage you couldn't pass up. You were desperate for cash."

"Paul took the only woman I ever loved and treated her like dirt until the day she died. He owed me, and I saw to it that he paid. It's that simple," he said, pushing her inside the car.

"Are you trying to convince me or yourself? Let's not forget, you even stole from Saya. I bet her secret bank account is long gone."

"It wasn't doing anyone any good where it was. I drew from it for years. There wasn't much left when I closed it out. But it'll be hard to prove. I covered my trail well," he said, driving off pueblo land as fast as he dared.

"But now what? What else could Paul have hidden that you fear so much?"

"Paul found out I was the blackmailer, and then set me up. He took a couple of photos of me picking up the cash at the drop site. Then, once he knew it was me, he took a closer look at all his business dealings with the bank and discovered that his bearer bonds were just copies. He also knew my copier had a flaw he could trace. Once he had evidence that tracked it to my office, he came to me. He demanded that I pay back all the money I'd stolen and return Saya's diary to him immediately, or he'd have me arrested."

"But why kill him? He gave you a chance to make things right."

"I didn't have the money, don't you see? It was over a hundred thousand dollars when everything was added up.

He gave me a week to make restitution, but had he given me a year, it would still have not been enough. I couldn't borrow money, either. I have no collateral.''

They reached a solitary log cabin in the Santa Fe National Forest an hour later. Lowman grabbed a backpack, then forced Annie at gunpoint to walk through four inches of snow to the cabin.

"Get in," he ordered after unlocking the door. When she hesitated, he pushed her inside. Annie tripped forward, but caught herself before she hit the wooden floor.

"The lock doesn't look so sturdy," she said, looking back at the entrance. "What makes you think I'll stick around here?"

"The lock will hold you. It's brand new. The windows have bars on them, too, a little feature I added to keep teens who come up here in the summer from breaking in. And even if you manage to get out, how far can you walk in your condition? It's bitterly cold outside, there's snow on the ground, and there's nothing around for miles. You don't even have a coat. Now give me your shoes and socks, and I'll leave you some food and coffee from the backpack.''

"You can't leave me here, Virgil." She looked around the one-room cabin. There was no bed, just a few pieces of cheap wooden furniture. "Can't you see that if anything happens to me or my baby, you'll only make things worse for yourself?''

He slapped her hard enough to make bright spots of lights dance in front of her eyes. "Shoes and socks," he repeated.

She gave them to him, and he dumped the contents of the backpack, a thermos and a grocery bag, onto the small wooden table. Fear shot through her as another contraction began. Trying to ease the discomfort, she forced herself to walk in a circle, though the floor was like ice.

"Jake can't help you," she said. "He doesn't know where the photos you want are hidden, and neither do I. This is pointless."

Virgil kept between her and the door, even though they both knew she couldn't outrun him. "If he doesn't find them soon, you'll both be dead. You better hope that he's willing to put his neck on the line for you." Lowman slammed the door in her face, and she could hear him padlocking the door again from the outside.

"And if he does, will you keep your word and tell him where I am?" she shouted.

There was a moment of silence. "I could lie to you, but I won't. If I get what I want, there won't be any evidence against me. You and Jake will be the only witnesses, and I know you'll talk. I can't risk that. You'll both stay alive only as long as I need you. Meanwhile, enjoy your dinner."

As she heard his car pull away, fear gripped her. She didn't have a coat and already the temperature was dropping. She looked around, but there was no wood for the fireplace or fuel for the single kerosene lantern. In desperation, she began rolling some old newspapers up into tight balls for kindling. Then, using a small knife she found in the kitchen drawer, she dismantled one of the two cane chairs to use as fuel.

Several minutes later, she'd managed to build a small fire. The priority at the moment was staying warm. She then searched through the food he'd dumped on the table. There were cold cuts that tasted peculiar, but not necessarily rancid, and bread. That, and the fire would keep her alive for now. The hot coffee in the thermos was a blessing. The liquid warmed her, and she sipped it slowly.

Looking around for a blanket, she went to the old dresser opposite the fireplace and opened the top drawer. It was empty except for a small, leather-bound book. It looked old and worn but, despite that, had retained an elegance that spoke of days gone by. Curious, she opened it carefully and read a page at random. It was then Annie realized she'd found Saya's diary.

The words drew her as she saw into the soul of the woman who'd loved with all her heart, despite the odds.

No matter how difficult my life becomes, the love I have for my sons will keep me going and give me the strength I need. I could have given in to the cancer that consumes me, but it's for them that I fight and remain alive. The children need me. It's through their mother's love that they'll grow to see all the possibilities within themselves and learn to reach out for their dreams, whatever the cost. I will never give up, because to do so would be to fail them.

Annie's fear subsided as determination filled her. She understood Saya's fierce loyalty to her sons. As a mother-to-be, she would also do anything and everything she could for her baby. Lowman would not win.

She wasn't going to kid herself. Her situation was desperate. It would take a miracle for Lowman's plan to fail. But this was Christmas Eve, a time of miracles. Holding to that, she built up the fire, pushing the cold away again and buying herself a little more time.

## Chapter Twenty

Iris had parked within sight of several pueblo dwellings. The woman was genuinely scared, but Jake couldn't figure out what was going on. "You're saying that some anonymous caller told you that I was ready to pin my father's murder on you? Based on what evidence? Did the caller say?"

"All I know is that he said I better figure out a way to convince you I was innocent, because you were a man with powerful friends who could make a lot of trouble for me."

"If you know anything about the murder—"

"That's just it! I don't. All I can do is remind you that I cared about your father, and I would have never harmed a hair on his head."

"Tell me more about this caller," Jake prompted. "Did you recognize anything about his voice?"

She tried to remember. "He was speaking real softly and it sounded as if he was holding something over the mouthpiece. I could hear other voices close by, but I couldn't make out anything they were saying."

Jake felt an gnawing uneasiness. There was something about the situation that just didn't sit right with him. It was starting to look like a diversion, a ruse to get him away from the house. But why? The answer came swiftly, like claws tearing at his heart—Annie.

He ran back to the truck, not bothering to explain himself to Iris, and raced back to the ranch. Bursting through the front door, he called out to Annie, but got no reply.

His gut knotted with fear as he raced through the house, searching and trying to shut out the instinct that warned him that he was too late. Annie's coat still hung in the entryway, but she was nowhere to be found.

Getting Nick and Martin's help, they searched everywhere, including the outside buildings, without success.

"There are fresh vehicle tracks outside, but we had several workmen come through today," Martin said.

"Let's not jump to conclusions. We have no reason to believe she's in danger," Nick said.

"She is. I feel it in my gut, brother. We have to find her. Get the wranglers together and go talk to everyone in the pueblo. Find out if anyone saw or heard anything that could give us a lead."

"I'll call Captain Mora," Martin said. "We need to get him involved as soon as possible."

Jake knew with every shred of instinct he possessed that Lowman had taken Annie. But where? And why hadn't Lowman made his demands known by now?

As Nick reached for his coat, Martin came in, holding an envelope. "I checked the mailbox on a hunch and found this. It's addressed to you, Jake."

Jake opened it and found a typewritten note. He read it aloud.

"'Annie will be dead by midnight tomorrow unless you deliver all the copies of the bearer bonds taken from Paul's safe-deposit box. I also want the packet I know Paul hid in the house. It'll contain a photograph, among other things. You or Nick are the only ones capable of finding that evidence. Do it now and get ready to drop it off at a designated time and place, along with fifty-thousand dollars cash. I'll be in touch.'''

Martin looked at Jake and Nick. "Do you two know where Paul hid those things?"

Nick shook his head and looked at Jake, who shrugged.

"I haven't got a clue where that stuff is," Jake said, "but we can't let the kidnapper know that. Virgil Lowman has Annie. Though he didn't sign his name on the note, I know that as sure as I know my own name. But if I tip my hand and go after him, he may kill Annie. I have one chance—and that's to find her myself before he even knows what I'm up to."

"I can go to the bank passing myself off as you, and withdraw all the money I can," Nick said. "That'll give you a chance to track down where he hid her."

"Yes. Wear my clothes and jacket, and make sure Lowman sees you if he's there. But don't talk to him if possible. Martin, get Mora to help us. We'll need to make first-class duplicates of the copies Lowman made. We're not giving him the real evidence—at least not right off the bat."

"Where will you start looking for Annie?" Nick asked.

Before Jake could reply, Captain Mora came into the room. "I got Martin's call while I was on the road and came over right away. My men are looking for Lowman now. We won't make an arrest, we'll just tail him. Maybe he'll lead us to Annie."

"That's a good strategy, but we can't count on it working. We need another approach," Jake said, showing him the note and the instructions.

"If I'm right, Lowman knows we're on to him," Mora said. "That means he'll lay low until it's time for him to surface and pick up the evidence."

"Having Nick pose as me might misdirect him and buy me some time."

"It'll work," Mora agreed. "Most people can't tell you two apart anyway," Mora said. "But you'll still need to focus your search in the right direction."

"Can you run a fast check for me to see if he owns or is leasing any other property in this area?"

"I'll go back to my office, log into the main computer's data base, and let you know. I'll have an officer check his house, too, though I doubt he'd be stupid enough to keep her there."

As soon as Mora left, Jake went to the door. "There's another way of getting that information. Let's start by asking the wranglers. This pueblo has few secrets."

Working as a team, they spoke to the ranch hands. Finally Rick came through with the information they needed.

"He's got a cabin up in the Santa Fe forest," Rick told Jake. "My wife's family leased it to him in trade for a car." Rick gave him a hand-drawn map indicating the location of the cabin. "If you get caught in the storm that's coming, though, you'll have trouble getting in and out of there. Those roads, if you can call them that, are tough to navigate if there's more than a light dusting of snow on the ground."

Jake grabbed his jacket and Annie's, and had started toward the door when Nick called him back. "You'll need to wear my down coat. I'll take your leather jacket."

"You're right," Jake said quickly. "Remember to stay high profile. Let Lowman think we're doing exactly what he wants."

"Let me go with you," Martin said to Jake. "I can use my right hand now a little and my eyes are perfect."

"No. I expect Lowman will start watching the ranch house and following what's happening here. It's important that things look as normal as possible. While I'm gone, call Mora and apprise him of the situation. See if he can send me some backup. Then search as best as you can for the photo Lowman wants. Who knows, you might get lucky.''

Rick pulled a cell phone from out of his jacket. "Here. I got this when my wife started driving to Santa Fe every day to work. Take it with you now. It may come in handy.''

Martin managed to bring him extra blankets. "Just in case," he said. "And there's a rifle in the gun rack inside my truck.'' Martin handed him the keys with his good hand. "Take it. My truck's old, but big and reliable, and it has snow tires. I can't drive it one-handed, anyway. Nick will have to use your truck if the masquerade is going to work.''

Jake set out moments later. The weather was turning decidedly foul, with the temperature falling by the minute as the gray cloud layer continued to descend over the valley. After traveling for forty minutes, the predicted snowstorm hit with a vengeance. It would be a white Christmas. Hopefully Annie was inside, safe from the cold.

He entered the Santa Fe National Forest with snowflakes rushing at the windshield in their hypnotic spiral. By the time he made it to the old forest road, the snow was coming down hard, and he could barely make out the path. He tried calling home to check to see if Mora would be sending him backup, but the phones had gone down. He was on his own.

Cursing the storm, Jake continued along the narrow forest track for what seemed an eternity. Daylight soon turned to night, then, just as he was ready to turn back and assume he'd taken the wrong turn, he noticed an isolated cabin ahead. It looked deserted except for a tiny plume of smoke coming from the chimney. Jake parked the truck behind a mass of scrub oak, then approached on foot. Moving silently, he drew closer and peered through the bars that protected the windows.

In the dim glow within he saw Annie, alone, lying on her side on the floor beside the fireplace. The fire had almost gone out.

Fear slammed into him. "Annie!" He shouted her name.

She stirred. "Jake?" Her voice was weak.

"I'm going to get you out of there. Hang tight."

"I'm in labor," she managed. "I need to get to the clinic. I was so afraid you wouldn't find me," she added softly.

Her words wrenched his heart. "I'm here now, and I'll be inside in a moment."

The padlock was sturdy and refused his best efforts to pry it open. Trying to break down the door proved futile, as well, no matter how hard he kicked.

He looked around for tools, then remembered Martin kept a tool box behind the seat in the truck. Running back quickly, he found and took a large screwdriver and hammer, along with Annie's coat. He ran back to the cabin and hit the lock with everything he had. It snapped open and he burst in the door just as Annie screamed in pain.

She was deathly pale and drenched in sweat, though the cabin was barely above freezing. He knelt beside her and brushed her hair back. "Hang on, sweetheart. One way or another, I'll get you to the clinic."

Wrapping the coat around her like a blanket, Jake pulled the cell phone out of his pocket. "I'll see if I can get Elsie, and let her know we're on our way."

He dialed the number and, mercifully, got through. Elsie answered, though her voice was faint. "Elsie, talk to me. I'm bringing in Annie, but it'll take at least a half hour on these roads. Is there time?"

"How often are the contractions coming?"

Jake looked down at Annie, who had stopped shivering, and was sitting upright. But she looked so frightened. "How often have the contractions been coming? Do you have any idea?"

"Every two minutes, or so, I think. I haven't timed them."

Jake told Elsie, then got another question for Annie. "Elsie wants to know if your water has broken?"

"There hasn't been any big gush… All I had was a little trickle early this morning." Annie managed to get the words out between breaths.

"Listen carefully, Jake. The phone keeps going out so I'll make it fast," Elsie said after hearing Annie's reply. "We're going to have to come to you. The baby's due anytime. Give me your exact location."

"Oh, God!" Annie screamed as an unbearable pain pushed through her. "It's happening now. I can't…"

"Elsie, you better start talking—fast," Jake said, crouching by Annie. He quickly gave her the location of the cabin, then the line was silent.

"Elsie, are you still there?" Jake's voice rose slightly. The phone went dead. Jake tried the number again twice and got through the second time.

There was a long moment of silence, then Elsie's transmission came through again, faintly.

"I lost you, Jake. It's that way all over the pueblo. No one can get hold of anyone else so let me talk fast before the call breaks up completely. Annie's probably been in labor since her water broke. It doesn't have to be a big gush, but she didn't realize that. I'll get the EMTs if I have to walk over and notify them personally. They should be able to reach the cabin within a half hour."

*"What do I do now?"*

"Stay calm, and try to keep Annie calm. Remind her to

breathe through the contractions, she knows how. Things will get really intense as she completes the dilation stage, then she'll start to push the baby out. That's when you'll have to—'' The line went dead.

"Elsie? Elsie? Are you there?" Hitting the redial button, he looked down at Annie, who was going through another contraction, trying not to cry out in pain.

"Hang on, Annie, help is on the way. I'll run out to the truck and get some blankets to make you comfortable." Jake stood and hesitated, reluctant to be separated from the woman he loved for even a minute.

"Go now, while you can," she breathed. "But please come back right away. I need you, Jake."

"I'll always be here for you, Annie," Jake said, reaching down to touch her cheek. "And for your baby."

He ran out of the cabin, and returned with the blankets a few seconds later. He quickly prepared a warm spot for her on the floor, then tossed the remains of a chair into the smoldering fire, along with a newspaper he'd found in the truck. He had to bring the temperature up in the cabin, or they'd all freeze.

"We'll do this together, Annie. I'll be your coach." He took her hand.

Annie screamed, squeezing his hand tightly. The contraction seemed to last forever, but was immediately followed by another. Jake sat behind her, supporting Annie as she struggled to breathe through the pain.

"I need to push, Jake. It's time."

Jake placed his coat behind her, then moved around in front of her. Annie groaned as if she were being torn asunder, then, a few seconds later, Jake saw the baby's head. "The baby's almost here." Suddenly he saw that the cord had wrapped around the baby's neck. "Stop! Don't push, Annie. I have to move the cord."

Annie cried out, crazed with fear and pain.

With a gentleness he didn't even know he was capable of, he shifted the cord away from the baby's neck. "All right. Now, Annie, push!"

A few minutes later Jake held the tiny child in his hands. "Annie, we've got a girl. A beautiful, breathing, dark-eyed baby girl," he whispered, covering the infant immediately with a blanket, careful not to damage the umbilical cord.

Jake tried Elsie's number again and, this time, managed to get through, though the transmission was filled with static. Cradling the phone between his ear and shoulder, he gave Elsie the news.

"Jake, the EMTs are on the way. Don't worry about the umbilical cord. They'll take care of that. Just make sure the baby has a blanket over her, and give her to Annie," Elsie said. "Don't worry about anything now—just let nature take its course."

Jake handed the baby to Annie as the sun began streaming through the window. "Merry Christmas, my loves," he whispered.

As he looked at Annie and the baby, he knew that his heart and soul were theirs. Nothing would ever be more precious to him than Annie and the child he'd help bring into this world. Lowman was still free, but no matter what it took, he would find him and make sure nothing ever threatened Annie and her daughter again.

## Chapter Twenty-One

Jake held Annie's hand as the EMTs loaded her and the infant onto a stretcher. They'd already cut the cord and wrapped mother and baby in fresh blankets.

"The diary—your mother's diary," Annie said breathlessly, pointing toward the table.

"It doesn't matter now. What's important is that you two are okay."

"Please," Annie insisted. "Don't leave it behind. Finding it may be the only good thing that came from my being kept here. Your mother's courage kept me from giving up hope."

Jake walked over and picked up the diary, then joined the EMTs by the ambulance.

"I won't spend Christmas Day in the hospital," Annie told Jake as he sat beside her and the baby in the emergency vehicle. One of the EMTs, a friend of Jake's, had agreed to drive back in Martin's truck so Jake could be with them.

"Elsie will meet us at the house," Annie assured him. "This was arranged months ago."

"Then let's take the baby home," Jake said, touching the baby's face lightly. "Have you thought of a name for her?"

"I can't call her Jake. How about Jacqueline Noelle?"

"Perfect."

By the time the emergency vehicle delivered its precious cargo to the ranch, Elsie was waiting. Signing the release, she took charge.

At Jake's insistence, Annie and the baby were taken to his room. In the master bedroom, both mother and child settled down comfortably after Elsie and Doc had checked them out and pronounced them healthy.

At long last, Elsie stepped out into the hall and called Jake. "The ladies want you," she said with a smile, then retreated to give them privacy.

Jake sat on the edge of the bed, watching Annie nurse Jacquie. There was so much he wanted to say, but the words wouldn't come.

"I'll never forget today. You were just wonderful," she whispered. "We both needed you, and you were there for us. You risked your life to come and find us."

Jake knew he had to open his heart to her now. The time was so right. "Annie, I would have risked anything and everything for you. I love you and the baby. You've changed my whole life. I want us to get married and I want to adopt Jacqueline. I want to be her father in all the ways that matter, and raise her here at the ranch. This is our home now and I want us to be real family, Annie."

Holding the baby to her with one hand, she reached out for him. "That's what I want, too, Jake. I've never been happier or more in love."

Jake leaned over and took Annie's mouth in a searing kiss. "You and Jacquie are the center of my world. But I've got to go now so I can make sure you'll both remain safe."

"Lowman?" she whispered.

"He's still at large, but I intend to change that. Don't worry. He'll never threaten you again."

A knock at the door interrupted them. Nick entered the room. "Congratulations," he said, looking down at the baby who was now sleeping. "I hate to take you away now, Jake, but the call telling me where to make the drop should be coming in as soon as the phone lines are back up and we need to work out some details."

"Give me a moment here, and then I'll meet you downstairs," he said.

After Nick walked out, Jake reached into his jacket pocket and handed Annie the diary. "Keep this here with you for now. Later, we'll decide what to do about it. I need to tell Nick we have it and talk things out with him."

"What will you do? Will you read it?"

"I don't know. I've come to terms with the man my father was, but that process has taken me a long time. My father always seemed larger than life to me, but once I began seeing him as just a man, one capable of mistakes, I realized that I'd judged him too harshly. My father never knew how to love. And, until you came into my life, I was no different. But the diary is sure to contain some highly charged emotional passages and I'm not sure reading it will benefit any of us now. I'll need time to sort it out in my head, and Nick will, too.

"Before I go, I'll light a fire in the fireplace inside the nursery," he said, gesturing toward the adjoining room. "Did you know that room served as Nick's and my nursery years ago? Now it'll belong to my daughter—and all her brothers and sisters."

She smiled. "Ready to make new babies so soon?"

He grinned back. "As soon as you are." He checked out the kindling someone had brought up, and opened the glass fireplace doors.

"Be careful," she called, remembering a conversation she'd once had with Paul. "Some time ago, your father offered me the use of the master bedroom and the nursery when the baby arrived. He was planning to take one of the other empty rooms. But I remember him telling me *never* to try to light a fire in that fireplace until someone inspected and cleaned it out. Apparently, it hadn't been used for years, and he was afraid it wouldn't be safe.''

Jake checked out the masonry and opened the damper to look up the chimney. ''It seems sound enough.'' As he opened the door to the ash clean-out below the grate, he noticed a large envelope inside. ''Wait a minute. There's something in here instead of ashes.''

Wiping the ashes and soot from the envelope, he brought it out closer to the light and extracted the contents. There was a photograph showing Lowman picking up an envelope, then another showing the envelope was filled with money. There was also a sample note typed and written on Lowman's typewriter and, according to the letter his father had attached to it, a local private investigator had declared it to be a match for the type of print found on the blackmail notes. Last but not least, was a counterfeit bearer bond sealed in plastic and a nearly blank sample copy with a minuscule scratch in the corner circled in red ink. A note identified that the copy had been taken using Lowman's copier at the bank and proved that the bearer bonds had been copied on that machine.

''It's all here, the evidence Dad spoke about.'' Jake silently read the rest of his father's accompanying letter, then came to sit beside her. ''Dad gathered all this evidence, then gave Lowman a chance to make good. He also told Lowman that I was on my way and the information would be mine then. Lowman must have decided to kill him before I arrived, and take his chances with me.''

''That matches what Lowman told me. He never expected to let either one of us live.''

He nodded. "I figured that. I was just praying I could find you in time. Now we have more than enough to get Lowman sent to prison for a very long time. As soon as Mora gets in touch with us, I'll turn this over to him."

"Your father was a smart man but he took an enormous gamble putting the evidence in that fireplace clean-out."

Jake smiled. "I know why he did that. This room held special memories for him, and with your baby on its way, he saw it as a place where the past could finally yield to the future. A new cycle of events would begin here and mark a new era for the Black Ravens. He wanted us together, you know. I think, somehow, he knew that we'd both end up here one day. All in all, the nursery was a very appropriate place to hide the packet."

Assured that there were no more hidden surprises, Jake started a fire. Then, after giving Annie and the baby a kiss, he went downstairs to meet with his brother.

HOURS HAD PASSED, and it was already midmorning, yet they'd still heard nothing from Lowman. Nick was pacing by the phone when Jake entered the study with his third cup of coffee. "The phone's finally working again," Nick said. "I just tested it and got a dial tone. I called Mora and he said that the roads are closed. There's no way Lowman can go to check to see if Annie's still at the cabin or not."

"Good. That'll give us a big advantage." Jake's voice was filled with deadly intent. As he took a sip of coffee, the phone rang.

Jake picked it up, immediately going ahead with his plan to protest Annie's abduction, and insist that she be released. Lowman would expect this, and he didn't want the banker to even suspect that Annie and the baby had been rescued.

After a minute, pretending to calm down, Jake listened as Lowman tried unsuccessfully to disguise his voice while giving him instructions. When Jake finally placed the receiver down, he could barely contain the disgust he felt.

"He wants me to drop the evidence in the trash can beside the school near the west end of the plaza. He's given me thirty minutes to get there, to make allowances for the crowds."

"The sun's out and it's clearing up, so the Matachines Dance will be getting under way soon. Between the dancers, the pueblo residents, and whatever tourists have managed to brave the weather, it's going to be difficult to do anything," Nick said. "Everyone comes to the Christmas Day dance."

"I'm going to have Martin, Rick, and the other hands available guard the ranch," Jake said. "But I still need your help, brother. I'd like you to pose as me one more time and make the drop."

"Why?"

"I want to be the one who moves in on this man. I owe him for more than the death of our father."

"All right, but we better coordinate things with Mora so we don't all trip over each other."

After getting the tribal police captain on the phone again, Jake filled him in, bringing him up to date, and then explained his plan to catch Lowman.

"I like it. Let's go with it."

"Do you have what my brother needs to take to the drop site?" Jake asked.

"Yes, and I've had everything covered with a substance that will leave an ultraviolet stain on Lowman's hands. It'll be the icing on the cake when we bring him in."

"All right," Jake said. "Then we're all set. Nick will make the drop and leave the area. I'll monitor the drop site while you watch my brother's back."

"My men will have to be on duty elsewhere today.

There's only four of us to keep track of all the tourists and the villagers, so we'll be on our own with this. I wish there was time to call in for reinforcements, but there isn't.''

"Then we'll handle it," Jake said confidently. As long as Annie was here safe with the baby, he wasn't in the least bit worried about his ability to handle a weasel such as Lowman.

"Just make sure you don't move in on Lowman until I give you the word, Jake," Mora warned. "We want to wait until he's away from the plaza. I don't want any innocent bystanders to end up hurt because they were in the wrong place at the wrong time."

JAKE WATCHED NICK work his way through the crowd to make the drop. His brother kept his cool, even as the pueblo dancers came out. They moved in formation, the sounds of their rattles adding a rich vibrancy to the accompaniment of the drums and guitars.

By now, there were so many people in the way it was nearly impossible for Jake to follow his brother's progress to the drop site. Jake was circling slowly, his cowboy hat low on his face, when he saw a woman approach Nick. Listening carefully, he heard her ask him about Annie's new baby girl. A cold chill suddenly enveloped Jake. He should have known the secret would have been impossible to keep, particularly after the EMT rescue unit had been in. Even the weather couldn't stop gossip here on the pueblo. Worst of all, if the word was out, then Lowman would soon learn that Annie had been rescued—that is, if he didn't know already. Time was running out for all of them.

Nick made the drop, then moved back to join the crowd. He had almost reached the gathering when the dancers fired blanks from a rifle, symbolically killing the figure who represented evil. The crowd cheered and, as the dance came to an end, one of the masked dancers approached Nick.

Nick stiffened slightly and, sensing trouble, Jake edged closer. Nick was being prodded back toward the drop site. With people milling around, talking and greeting each other, no one paid any attention to the two men. Lowman had again resorted to a disguise to get close, and Jake cursed himself for not thinking one step ahead.

As Nick picked up the pouch containing the documents, Jake spotted the small handgun pressed into Nick's back. Jake edged even closer, wondering where Mora was, then saw him creeping up from the left.

"Just keep doing as I say, Jake," Lowman said to Nick, unaware that he'd taken the wrong captive. "I'm not using blanks, and plenty of innocent people could get hurt if you try something stupid."

Suddenly a loud explosion rocked the ground. People screamed and, in the distance, flames and flying debris blew out the windows of the bank at the north end of the plaza.

Some of the people rushed toward the bank, ready to help put out the fire before it could spread. The rest of the crowd went in the opposite direction, leaving the plaza as quickly as they could. Suspecting the explosion was only a diversion, Jake narrowed the gap between him and his brother, preparing to make his move against Lowman. Just then Captain Mora stepped out from behind a border wall and aimed a high kick at Lowman's ribs, knocking him away from Nick.

As the banker fell to the ground, he fired a shot at Mora. The officer grunted, taking the hit to his stomach and staggering back. Nick and Jake both tried to reach Lowman, but the banker whirled around with his pistol and the brothers were forced to dive for cover.

Lowman snatched Mora's keys from his belt and ran,

turning to fire a shot at Jake, who was just scrambling to his feet. As Jake hit the ground and rolled, the bullet struck the wall behind him. By the time Jake was able to resume the chase, Lowman was climbing into Mora's police utility vehicle, which was parked in the plaza.

Jake knew he'd never catch the banker on foot now. Seeing the direction Lowman was heading, Jake felt his blood turn to ice. "Get help for Mora," he shouted to Nick, who was examining the downed cop. "Lowman's going to the ranch, and I've got to stop him. I think he plans to use Annie and the baby as hostages because the road conditions won't let him make a quick getaway."

"Having a cop car will help him get close without rousing Martin's suspicions, too," Nick yelled, reaching for his cell phone, then muttering an oath. "I can't get through. The storm—"

"Keep trying. Use Mora's hand-held radio and call in help, but find a way to warn Martin."

Jake raced back to Martin's truck across the snow, his heart pounding against his sides. Fear, black and as cold as the winter wind, slammed into him as he thought of Annie and Jacqueline in mortal danger.

A minute later he reached the truck. Despite the icy conditions, he pressed down on the accelerator, determined to protect them at all costs. He took a shortcut down an old farm road, hoping to beat Lowman to the ranch, but Virgil Lowman knew the terrain as well as he did. And the man was desperate by now. Trying to burn down the bank to destroy evidence was ample proof of that.

Jake pushed the truck for all the speed it could muster, though the back fishtailed wildly in the wet snow. In the distance he could see the police vehicle Lowman had taken.

At long last, Jake skidded to a stop in the driveway beside the main house. Lowman had arrived just ahead of him. The lights of the police cruiser were still flashing and the engine was running. Grabbing Martin's rifle from the rack, Jake moved toward the house. He'd grown up with guns on the ranch, but he'd never thought of pointing one at a human—until now.

As he drew near, careful to remain behind cover, he saw Lowman smash the study window with his gloved fist. Jake brought his rifle up, but then he caught a glimpse of Annie inside. She didn't have the baby in her arms; she was holding something else, but he could hear Jacquie's wails clearly even from where he was.

Knowing that there was no way he could shoot in the direction of the house and not risk having the high-powered bullet penetrate the walls, he moved to his left for a safer field of fire. Leaves rustled faintly beneath his feet. Suddenly Lowman spun around, gun in hand, and Jake dove into the bushes.

"I know you're there, Jake," he said. "I can see the mist from your breath. Come out from behind cover so I can see you clearly."

"I'm armed, Lowman. Give it up. There's no reason for you to die."

He laughed. "Do as you're told, Jake. Drop the rifle and come out. I know there's no way you'll risk shooting me from where you are, not while I'm right next to the house."

Jake came out slowly. He couldn't shoot. Even if he hit Lowman, the bullet could pass through him and continue its trajectory through several walls until it finally lodged somewhere in the house. And bullets didn't discriminate. They could hit walls as easily as they could hit Annie or the baby. Lowman had the upper hand and there was nothing he could do—except, hopefully, divert him away from Annie and the baby.

Lowman allowed Jake to approach him. "Call Annie, Jake. Tell her to come out here."

Jake's smile was deadly. "Not a chance."

"Then say goodbye to your family," Lowman said, bracing his arm as he pointed the barrel directly at Jake's heart. "I'm taking out at least one more Black Raven before I leave, and it looks like it's going to be you."

"Drop it!" Annie appeared at the corner of the house, holding one of Paul's shotguns. "Put the gun down, and then step away from it."

Her voice was firm, and conveyed the strength of a woman prepared to do whatever was necessary to protect those she loved.

Jake looked at her with pride and admiration. Then, as he shifted his gaze to Lowman, Jake saw the fear in his eyes. Lowman had seen the shotgun and knew, as Jake did, that Annie wasn't bluffing.

Lowman put the gun down, following Annie's orders.

Jake picked up Lowman's pistol just as Nick came running around the side of the house, followed by Rick and Martin.

"What took you so long?" Jake asked with a crooked smile.

"Better late than never, I always say," Nick answered.

"I'm glad to see you're all okay," Martin said. Taking the rifle Jake had set down, he took charge of their prisoner.

Captain Mora pulled up in a police car and stepped out. Seeing the surprise on Jake's face, he grinned. "There's nothing like a bullet-resistant vest. But it still felt like being kicked by a mule. It knocked the wind clear out of me."

Mora strode up to Lowman and handcuffed him. "Your firebomb wasn't as efficient as you'd hoped. The sprinkler system you'd neutralized was turned back on, and it put out the fire within seconds. You're going away for a long time.''

Jake took the shotgun out of Annie's shaking hands. She hadn't moved. "It's okay, now, sweetheart. It's over.''

As the prisoner was taken away, Jake gathered Annie into his arms. A hush fell over the desert as he held her, then a gentle breeze rose from the west carrying the distant sound of many voices raised in Tewa song.

"It's the start of the new dance, a Tewa prayer for rain and fertility this coming season. But we already have our blessings.'' He kissed her for an eternity before easing his hold. "Let's go see our daughter.''

As they entered the house, Elsie came up, holding Jacquie who was crying, wanting to be fed.

Annie sat in the easy chair, and Jake brought the baby to her. With Annie guiding him, he placed the baby's mouth on Annie's breast and watched her begin nursing.

His family was together, and finally safe. This was one Christmas that would live in their memories forever.

# Author's Note

The Native American rites depicted in this novel have been abbreviated to avoid offending those whose religious beliefs depend on the secrecy of rituals. To protect the privacy of individual pueblos, the village depicted in this story is a fictional composite of the many Tewa pueblos.

\* \* \* \* \*

*Look for Nick Black Raven's story coming in 2000—only from Harlequin Intrigue.*

*Amnesia...an unknown danger...*
*a burning desire.*

**With**

HARLEQUIN®

# I N T R I G U E®
you're just

# A MEMORY AWAY

*from passion, danger...and love!*

Look for all the books in this
exciting miniseries:

**THE BABY SECRET (#546)**
**by Joyce Sullivan**
On sale December 1999

**A NIGHT WITHOUT END (#552)**
**by Susan Kearney**
On sale January 2000

**FORGOTTEN LULLABY (#556)**
**by Rita Herron**
On sale February 2000

A MEMORY AWAY...—where
remembering the truth becomes
a matter of life, death...and love!

*Available at your favorite retail outlet.*

HARLEQUIN®
*Makes any time special* ™

Visit us at www.romance.net

HIAMA3

**Get ready for heart-pounding romance
and white-knuckle suspense!**

HARLEQUIN®

# I N T R I G U E ®

## raises the stakes in a new miniseries

### The McCord family of Texas is in a desperate race against time!

With a killer on the loose and the clock ticking toward midnight, a daughter will indulge in her passion for her bodyguard; a son will come to terms with his past and help a woman with amnesia find hers; an outsider will do anything to save his unborn child and the woman he loves.

With time as the enemy, only love can save them!

### #533 STOLEN MOMENTS
**B.J. Daniels**
October 1999

### #537 MEMORIES AT MIDNIGHT
**Joanna Wayne**
November 1999

### #541 EACH PRECIOUS HOUR
**Gayle Wilson**
December 1999

*Available at your favorite retail outlet.*

HARLEQUIN®

*Makes any time special* ™

Visit us at www.romance.net

HICD

HARLEQUIN®

# I N T R I G U E ®

# Tough. Rugged. Sexy as sin.

*Seven brothers, Montana born and bred,
raised in the shadows of the Rocky Mountains
and a family secret. Ranchers at heart,
protectors by instinct—lovers for keeps.*

Look for all the books in Kelsey Roberts's
exciting new series:

## LANDRY'S LAW (#545)
### January 2000

## BEDSIDE MANNER (#565)
### June 2000

Watch for all seven *Landry Brothers* books—
only from Kelsey Roberts and Harlequin Intrigue!

*Available at your favorite retail outlet.*

HARLEQUIN®

*Makes any time special* ™